PRAISE FOR KELLY HASHWAY'S *THE MONSTER WITHIN...*

"Hashway does a great job creating characters that stir your emotions and a mystery you want to unravel."

– Cherie Colyer, author of the *Embrace* and *Hold Tight*

"Witches, lies, black magic, murder…and the ultimate act of selfless love. Kelly Hashway has a spellbinding hit with *The Monster Within*."

– Michelle Pickett, bestselling author of *PODs*

"Resurrection has a dark price. *The Monster Within* is a fast paced and twisted read that will keep you guessing to the end."

– Heather Reid, author of *Pretty Dark Nothing*

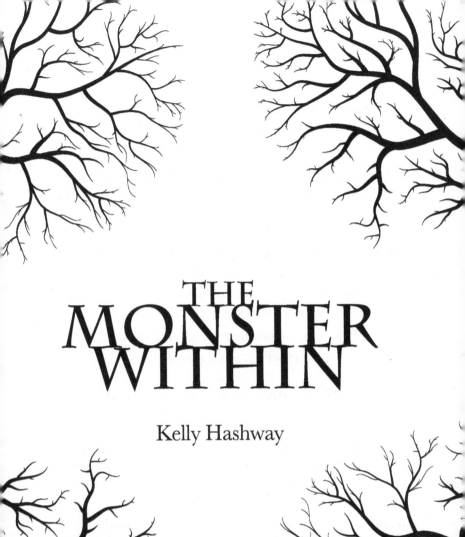

THE MONSTER WITHIN

Kelly Hashway

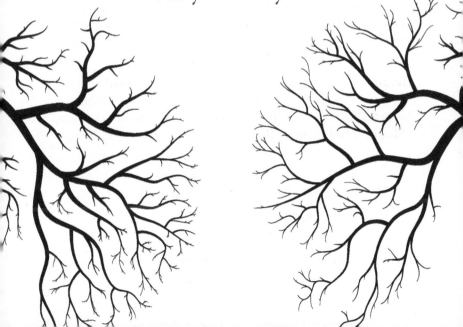

Spencer Hill Press

Contact: Spence City, an imprint of Spencer Hill Press, PO Box
247, Contoocook, NH 03229, USA

Please visit our website at www.spencecity.com

First Edition: June 2014.
Kelly Hashway
The Monster Within/by Kelly Hashway—1st ed.
p. cm.
Summary:

Description: Teenage girl resurrected from dead finds out she is a
monster, tangled between dueling factions of witches, and must
break the curse that brought her to life before she kills the people
she loves most.

The author acknowledges the copyrighted or trademarked status
and trademark owners of the following wordmarks mentioned in
this fiction: Band-Aid, Ford Focus, Goodwill, Kindle, Mack trucks,
Mazda 6, Post-it, Super Bowl, *The Blair Witch Project*, *The History
Channel*, Walmart

Cover design by Kate Kaynak
Interior layout by Errick A. Nunnally

9781937053857 (paperback)
9781937053826 (e-book)

Printed in the United States of America

Also by Kelly Hashway

Touch of Death (Spencer Hill Press)

Stalked by Death (Spencer Hill Press)

Face of Death (Spencer Hill Press)

Into the Fire (Month9Books/Swoon Romance, 9/14)
Writing as Ashelyn Drake

Perfect For You (Swoon Romance, 9/14)
Writing as Ashelyn Drake

Curse of the Granville Fortune (Tantrum Books, 10/14)

Out of the Ashes (Month9Books/Swoon Romance, 2/15)
Writing as Ashelyn Drake

The Darkness Within (Spencer Hill Press, 6/15)

Up in Flames (Month9Books/Swoon Romance, 11/15)
Writing as Ashelyn Drake

To Ayla with love.

CHAPTER ONE

MY life began again the second I pulled myself out of my grave and looked into his beautiful blue eyes. This was my second chance, and he was the one who had given it to me. I wasn't sure if I was a living being in the traditional sense. What did you call someone who came back from the dead? A zombie? Undead? I wasn't happy with either term. I certainly didn't feel like a zombie. I still had all of my own thoughts and memories. It was nothing like I imagined it would be.

"Sam." My name was barely a whisper on Ethan's lips. Even in the dim lights of the cemetery, I could see his eyes watering at the sight of me. "It worked. You're you again."

I looked down at my body, inspecting every limb. I was wearing a black dress. Mom's favorite, so I understood why she'd had me buried in it. I stared at my casket, unable to get over the fact that I'd been dead.

I raised my eyes to Ethan's. "How did you do it?"

"It doesn't matter. All that matters is you're here." He stepped forward and pulled me close to him, running his fingers through my long, dark hair.

I rested my cheek on his chest, wondering what lengths he had gone to in order to bring me back. Before I died, Ethan said he'd find a way for us to be together again. That he refused to lose me so soon. I had shrugged them off as the desperate words of a guy watching his seventeen-year-old girlfriend die of cancer. He'd been so amazing through all of it. He'd never left my bedside, and I remembered he'd been holding my hand when I took my last breath.

I tilted my head back to look at his tear-streaked face. "I have to know how you did it."

"Shh," he said softly. "I found someone who could help me, who knew what to do. Besides that, there's nothing you need to know."

He was keeping something from me, and that could only mean he'd done something big. Big enough that I would get upset if he told me. Still, being in his arms again was heaven. He'd given me the gift of life. How could I question that?

"How do you feel?" He held me by my shoulders and looked back and forth between my eyes. "You look like you. Everything seem okay?"

"Yeah. I feel like me. Not like a zombie or anything."

He squeezed my shoulders. "You're not. You're you. I promise. I made sure of it."

"But—"

He raised a finger to my lips. "We have to go. We can't stay here where someone might see you."

I hadn't thought about that. To everyone else, I was dead. My parents, my brother Jacob, my friends—they all thought I was dead. If I waltzed back into my old life, they'd think they were seeing a ghost. That, or they'd have me turned into a lab rat to figure out how I'd come back to life. Even I didn't have the answer to that. Only Ethan did. And what if they figured out he was responsible for me being alive again? What if they locked him up for messing with the laws of nature?

"Where are we going?" I was suddenly determined to leave as soon as possible.

"My cousin has a little cottage in the Poconos. He never uses it. It's not in the best shape, but we'll be okay there." Ethan let go of me long enough to close my casket and grab a shovel. "I have to get this back the way it was. No one can suspect your body isn't inside this grave."

"How long was I gone?" I had no sense of time, but the flowers on my grave were fresh, so I was guessing only a matter of days.

"Four days. The four longest days of my life." He dropped the shovel and wrapped his arms around me again.

I breathed in his scent, not even caring that he smelled mostly of dirt and sweat from digging up my casket. Besides, I couldn't smell much better. Nobody ever made a perfume in "Dirt-Covered Corpse" scent. "I'll help you cover the grave again."

"No." He let go of me and picked up the shovel. "You've been through enough. I'll do it. You go wait in the car. I can't risk anyone seeing you."

If Ethan got caught shoveling dirt back onto my grave, he'd be in serious trouble. But he was right. If he got caught and I was standing there with him, we'd both be totally screwed. I nodded and walked to his red Mazda 6. I had always loved his car. He used to take me for long drives down back roads, where we could pretend we were the only people in the world and there was no such thing as being terminally ill at seventeen.

I watched Ethan shovel the dirt back onto my grave, and it was surreal. I couldn't get past the feeling that I didn't belong here. I'd been dealt my hand, and yes, it sucked, but that should've been the end of it. I should've been in the ground or in the afterlife. Ethan walked back to the car, wiping his forehead with his sleeve. He threw the shovel in the trunk and got in the car in a hurry.

"Ready?" he asked, out of breath.

Was I? I wasn't sure, but I had to at least pretend for Ethan's sake. Whatever he'd done, it was huge. I owed him my life.

I forced a smile. "Ready."

He started the car, and as soon as we were out of the cemetery and on the road, he took my hand in his. Our fingers laced and rested on the middle console below the gearshift. Ethan's car operated as either an automatic or manual. When he was alone, he always drove it manually. But when I was with him, he kept it set to automatic so he could hold my hand while he steered.

I rested my head back on the seat and took a deep breath, wondering how long it would take for me to get used to being here again. I should've been happy, but something was nagging me. Pulling at my thoughts and screaming, "Look out!" Maybe it was just leftover anxiety from my illness, from knowing any moment could be my last. The final days had been awful. I hadn't been able to get out of bed. Mom and Dad had let me stay home because I hated being in the hospital. I'd spent too much time in a hospital for one lifetime. Ethan slept over every night. My parents had practically adopted him by that point. He loved me and refused to leave my side, except to use the bathroom.

Mom always said what Ethan and I had was more than high-school sweetheart stuff. Maybe she was right. Maybe the universe decided that, since I wasn't going live long enough to get married, have kids, and grow old, I should at least get to have the love of my life before I died. I was thankful for that much.

"What are you thinking?" Ethan asked, invading my thoughts.

"You were so amazing. Through everything. You were stronger than I was." I choked back the tears.

"Hey." He turned to face me, lifting our hands to his mouth and kissing my fingers. "Don't think about that. We have a second chance. This is our life now."

I didn't want to break his heart with all my questions about how we would survive on our own, how we would support ourselves when we hadn't even finished high school, but I couldn't say nothing, either.

"What's it going to be like? Our life? Will we be hiding out in the cottage?" Coming back to life to live in fear of being seen wasn't my ideal.

"No. We're going to get fake IDs. We'll enroll in school and do everything we would have if—"

"I hadn't died." I swallowed hard, remembering the pain the cancer had caused. "Will I have to change my name?" I never liked anyone calling me Samantha, but I'd grown fond of Sam, especially the way Ethan said it. It always sounded like a sigh. A happy, content sigh.

"You can keep Sam if you want. It's not like anyone is going to come looking for you."

That was true. As far as everyone knew, I was six feet under. "So you're not keeping Ethan?" I couldn't imagine calling him by any other name.

"Would that bother you?"

"A little." I knew I was being a baby, wanting him to keep his name, but he was my Ethan. He always would be.

"Okay, I'll keep Ethan then. We'll both just change our last names."

I nodded and gave him a weak smile. Somehow I knew a lot more than our last names was about to change. Samantha Thompson and Ethan Anderson would never be the same, and to the rest of the world, we wouldn't even exist.

It was about a five-hour drive to the cottage, not too bad. In the past, a long drive with Ethan had been heaven, but since I'd come back to life, things seemed different. Maybe Ethan thought I was the same old Sam—minus the cancer—but I wasn't. I couldn't shake this feeling that something was wrong. Wrong with me.

It was late, and a light rain dotted the top of the car, lulling me to sleep. You'd think after being dead, I'd feel refreshed. But I didn't. It seemed so hard to focus on things. The streetlights were bright. The air was damp, and even though it was early fall, I was chilled.

The car stopped, and Ethan's hand slipped from mine. I turned to him, blinking against the fluorescent lights of the gas station.

"Sorry," he said. "I didn't mean to wake you. I just need to get some gas and a few things from the convenience store. There's no food at the cottage. I thought I'd grab some crackers and soda. Stuff like that. I'll even see if they have black licorice for you. I know you love it."

I nodded and started for my seat belt.

"No. You stay." Ethan opened his door and stepped outside. I let my hair fall across my shoulders, trying to warm myself against the night air. "I'll be right back."

The trunk opened, and a moment later, Ethan opened my door, handing me one of his sweatshirts. "Here, you look cold."

I smiled. "Thanks." He knew me so well. I watched him walk inside the store and heard the soft *click* of the car locking again. He wasn't taking any chances with me. I knew he'd protect me from anything. He'd already protected me from death. He was my everything now. I would never see my family or friends again. I had to start over. The thought terrified me, but at least I had Ethan by my side.

I hugged the sweatshirt to my body. I was too tired to actually put it on, and this way I could breathe in Ethan's scent while I kept warm. I inhaled deeply at first, and then my breaths became shallow, which was weird considering how tired I felt. I yawned. Exhaustion overwhelmed me. Apparently it took a lot of energy to return from the dead.

I leaned my head on the window, hoping the cool glass would keep me awake, but my head spun, making me dizzy. My arms and legs tingled with the sensation of pins and needles. I felt like I had a million spiders crawling all over me. I threw the sweatshirt off me and onto the floor. My arms were bare. No spiders. But the feeling didn't go away. I panicked. The walls of the car were caving in on me. The air around me was tight, strangling me.

I searched the convenience store windows for Ethan, but all I saw was a guy in a cowboy hat and a woman taking her little boy to the bathroom. Where was Ethan? The lightheadedness was getting worse—more intense. My breathing was labored. In a panic, I reached for the door handle. It took me a moment to remember it was locked, but when I finally got it open, I stumbled out of the car into the fresh air. I gulped oxygen into my lungs, hoping it would make me feel better, but it didn't.

I was suffocating. Life was draining out of me. I collapsed to my knees, skinning them against the pavement. Wheezing, I crawled forward, trying to reach the convenience store door. Trying to reach Ethan. I needed help. I didn't know what was happening to me, but it felt like I was dying…again.

The gas station was almost empty at this hour. No one was pumping gas. No one was around to help me. I lifted my head, searching the windows of the store once more. The man with the cowboy hat was at the register. That meant he'd be leaving soon, and he'd have to walk past me. I pushed myself forward more, but my arms buckled under my weight, and I fell.

"Ethan," I choked out. This couldn't happen again. I'd just gotten my life back. How could I die again so soon?

I pushed my foot against the pavement in an effort to creep toward the door, but my black high-heeled shoe fell off, leaving me slumped on the ground with one bare foot. I inhaled, willing my lungs to fill with air, but I only coughed in response. At least the first time I'd died, I'd known it was coming. But now...this was a shock. I didn't know how to fight it, or if I even could.

The bell above the convenience store door jingled, and I raised my head slightly to see the man in the cowboy hat walking out. He was putting his change into his wallet and didn't even notice me in the dark parking lot.

"Please." My voice was barely audible.

He kept walking, removing his car keys from his pocket.

"Help," I tried again, but he unlocked his car with a high-pitched *beep* of the alarm disarming.

His foot was inches from me, yet he had no idea I was there. I reached my hand toward his leg and managed to grab hold of it. The second I made contact with him, I felt his blood coursing through the veins in his leg. It tingled beneath my fingers with a warmth that felt incredible on my freezing cold hand.

He jumped and looked down at me. "You scared the hell out of me! What are you doing down there?"

"Please." This time my voice was a little stronger. "I need help. I can't breathe." I released his leg, and my coughing started all over again.

"Whoa, easy there." He bent down and studied me for a moment before reaching for my shoulders and sitting me up. "Try to calm down. Are you here alone?" He fumbled for my missing shoe and put it back on my foot.

I tried to shake my head, but I wasn't sure if it moved at all. I felt like I was drowning. The life was draining out of me again.

"All right," he said. "Let's get you to the hospital. I'm going to bring you to my car."

Before I could protest or try to mention Ethan, the man scooped me into his arms and carried me to his car. I was too weak to fight him, and he was trying to help me, so I wrapped my arms around his neck as best I could. My fingertips grazed his neck, feeling the blood coursing through his veins once again. Instinctively, my other hand reached for his neck, but this time, I traced the line of his carotid artery, letting my fingers follow it down to his chest, where I felt his heart pumping beneath his clothes. Warmth washed over me.

"Don't panic. I'm going to get you help." He must have been

confused by what I was doing. Hell, *I* was confused by what I was doing, but somehow, I knew it was helping me. My breathing wasn't as labored. The dizziness was subsiding.

He opened the rear door and started to lower me onto the back seat, head first. I slipped my fingers through the opening in his button-down flannel shirt and felt the heat of his skin.

"It's okay," he reassured me.

My hand was above his heart now, and I flattened my palm against his chest. My right hand remained on his neck, resting on his carotid artery. Suddenly, an intense surge of energy flowed from the man to me. His blood was pumping life into me. My lungs filled, and my chest heaved. I felt more alive than I had when Ethan brought me back. My eyes closed in response to the relief I felt. I wasn't going to die. Whatever it was that had threatened my life was gone. I was alive again.

A wheezing sound forced my eyes open. But this time, *I* wasn't the one wheezing. I stared at the man leaning into the car, hovering above me. He was no longer holding me. My back was resting on the seat. His hands gripped the seats. His face was red, and he gasped for air. He looked down at my hands, and my eyes followed his.

I could see the color returning to my limbs, but at the same time, the color was leaving the man's face. He turned from red to purple to white. Ghostly white. Deadly white. *Corpse* white.

The cowboy hat fell from his head, revealing gray hair. I was sure he'd had dark hair. Why was it completely gray now? His skin felt softer under my fingers. His neck was wrinkled and aged. I was about to pull away and ask him if he was okay, when, with one final gasp, he slumped forward onto me. I let go of him and stifled a scream. What had just happened?

"Sir?" My voice was strong again but filled with fear. "Sir?"

I tried to move him, but his face was buried in the fabric of my black dress. I pushed myself up onto my elbows, and the man shifted slightly to my right, falling into the small space between the front and back seats.

His eyes stared up at me, completely devoid of life.

He was dead.

I had killed him.

CHAPTER TWO

I STARED at his wrinkled form for a moment, unable to believe what had happened. My hands shook. I turned them over, examining both sides, horrified that I had somehow ended this man's life with my bare hands. I wasn't sure how it had happened, what I'd done. All I knew was I was to blame. I was a killer. The sound of the bell above the convenience store door brought reality slamming back to me. I raised myself up in the back seat to look out the window. Ethan was walking back to the car with a bag in one hand and a tray with two cups of coffee in the other.

I couldn't stay here. I couldn't let Ethan know what I'd done. I scrambled across the seat and out of the car, keeping low so Ethan wouldn't see me. As he fumbled with his keys, I ran around to the side of the store. I took a deep breath and patted the front of my dress, trying to regain my composure. Stepping out from the shadows, I called Ethan's name. He looked up at me in surprise.

"Where were you?"

"I had to use the bathroom." My voice shook as I motioned over my shoulder, hoping he hadn't noticed the bathrooms were inside the store, not around the side of it.

He narrowed his eyes at me. "You left your door open."

"Yeah, sorry. It was an emergency." I got back in the car and helped him with the bag and coffees, trying to push the image of the dead man out of my mind. "I guess my body is functioning properly." I forced a little laugh, but inside, I was crying, crying for the man I'd killed.

9

Ethan smiled and leaned over to kiss me softly on the lips. "I told you. You're just fine. Completely you again. Everything is functioning exactly as it should be."

Then why had my body given out on me? Why had I felt like the life was draining out of me until… I wondered how long it would take someone to find the man slumped in the back seat of his car. If I was normal again, alive, then how had I killed him? Drained the life out of him?

Ethan tapped my forehead. "Where did you go?"

I shook my head. "Sorry. Being back takes a little getting used to, I guess."

A woman screamed, and Ethan and I turned to see what was going on. The woman was standing by her car. The same car I'd gotten out of only moments ago. The car where the man was dead in the back seat. I looked around the parking lot, noticing there were no other cars. Of course the woman and the little boy were with the man who'd tried to help me. My heart tore to pieces as I watched the woman try to shield the little boy's eyes from the sight of his dead father.

"Stay here," Ethan said. "I'm going to see what's wrong."

I grabbed his arm, squeezing his wrist as if my life depended on keeping him in this car. Maybe it did. "Don't. We can't draw attention to ourselves. We don't even have our fake IDs yet. Please, Ethan."

He looked at me with such love in his eyes. "I won't let anything happen to you."

Too late. Something already had. Something I didn't understand.

Ethan started the car and pulled out of the parking lot without another thought about the woman or why she was screaming. I felt awful. I'd played the helpless damsel in distress card. That wasn't me at all. I was a killer, a monster. And I hated that Ethan was willing to forget about the poor woman and little boy just because I'd asked him to.

"Hey, what happened to your knees?" Ethan reached over and pushed up the hem of my dress, exposing my skinned knees.

"Oh, it's nothing." I gently pushed his hands away. "I fell when I got out of the car. It's these high heels. I'm not sure why Mom had me buried in them. I've never worn high heels a day in my life." I was babbling to cover up how much I was freaking out on the inside.

Ethan rubbed my cheek with his thumb. "Aw, sweetie, why didn't you rinse the cuts in the bathroom? They could get infected."

Damn it. I didn't even think about my little lie leading to more questions. I wasn't used to lying, not to Ethan.

"I guess I wasn't thinking clearly. I wanted to get back to the car as quickly as possible. I don't like being away from you." I hoped that sounded believable and not too needy. Ethan and I had always been together, but we weren't exactly codependent. We were fine on our own, too. Only that wasn't true for me anymore. The first time Ethan left me alone, I'd done something horrible, unforgiveable.

"Give yourself time. You'll see there's nothing to be afraid of. Everything is like it was before, only without the—"

"Cancer," I finished for him. No, I didn't have cancer anymore, but I did have some sort of disease. One that kept me on the verge of death. One that made me feed off another human being's life. I was like some zombie-vampire hybrid. This was so much worse than having cancer.

Ethan kept stealing sideways glances while he drove. Finally he said, "New rule. No one uses the C-word anymore. It doesn't exist. It's all in the past."

I nodded. There wasn't really a word to accurately describe what I'd become now.

We drove the rest of the way in silence. Ethan seemed to know I needed time to process things. He was always good at reading me. Only this time, I hoped he couldn't read too much. What would it do to him to know he'd brought back a monster? I had to protect him from that. He was all I had.

I nodded off again, most likely because my brain couldn't handle what I'd become, and when I woke up we were parked in a gravel driveway. A rundown old shack stood in front of us. The roof looked like it was about to cave in, and the front door was hanging crookedly. I could tell the cottage—at least that's what Ethan had called it—had once been white, but the paint was almost completely peeled off. The only way to describe the color now was rotten wood tone.

Ethan shut the car off and turned toward me. "Well, this is it. I know it isn't much, but I can fix it up a little. My dad always made me help him when he did stuff around the house. I'm sure there are some tools in the shed around back, and we have a little money if we need to buy paint or wood."

"We have money?" Where did he get money from?

"I emptied my bank account before—" Before he'd brought me back from the dead. "It's enough to get us going. I'll find a job once we get settled. Something to pay the electric and water bills."

"I can get a job, too."

He opened his mouth to protest, but I shot him a look. I was not going to sit holed up in this cottage while he worked. I'd never been that kind of girl, and I wasn't about to start now. Besides, sitting would give me too much time to think about that poor man and what I'd done to him.

"Maybe we can find something at the same place. We only have one car, so it would be easier if we could drive to and from work together."

That seemed like a lot to ask—a place looking for two new employees to work the exact same shift. But I didn't want to be negative, so I just nodded.

"Well, should we go inside?"

I swallowed hard, wondering how much worse the inside could be. I forced a smile and opened my car door. Ethan met me at the hood of the car and took my hand. I didn't say anything, but I had a feeling he was afraid one or both of us would end up going through the front steps. They definitely needed to be replaced. I walked up the edge by the railing, hoping it would have the most support.

Keys weren't going to be an issue. The door was open. Who would lock a place as decrepit as this? Ethan held the door for me as I slipped inside. I stepped just far enough for him to reach behind me and fumble for a light switch. A single bulb went on in the center of the living room. The fixture had four bulbs, but only one was working. And for that, I was thankful. Seeing this place in better lighting would've been even more depressing.

The living room consisted of a worn-out couch and a wooden table with a broken leg. To the left of the living room was a tiny kitchen with a sink, stove, refrigerator, and table for two. Beyond that was a bathroom too dark to see into, but I could imagine the horrors waiting for us in there. Beyond the living room was a door, which I could only assume led to a bedroom.

That sent shivers down my spine. Ethan and I had the best relationship I could imagine. We couldn't have been closer. But…we hadn't exactly slept together. We almost did once. When I stopped my treatments, and we knew the end was near. It was one of the things I wanted to do before I died, but I was too weak. Now Ethan and I would be living in this tiny cottage with one bedroom. One bed. I loved him. I didn't doubt that. But I was scared. I didn't know what was going on with me. What was wrong with me? I'd already lied to Ethan. I couldn't be that intimate with him when I couldn't even tell him the truth about what happened at the gas station. Tears welled up in my eyes. I couldn't stop picturing that man's wrinkled face.

"Hey." Ethan rubbed my arm. "I know it's pretty bad, but I promise I'll fix it up. The sun is already coming up, so I'll check the shed and see what I can get started on right away."

"You haven't slept. You must be exhausted."

He smiled. "Are you kidding me? I got you back. I'm so energized I could repaint the whole place and fix that table without taking a break." He kissed my forehead. "How about you? Are you tired?"

I wasn't. Ever since the incident at the gas station, I'd felt full of life. I hated that I felt so good, knowing I'd been responsible for that man's death. I pushed the thought away. I couldn't deal with it right now. "I'm fine. I'll see what I can do in here. You know, start cleaning." I looked around, not a clue where to start.

"Good luck." Ethan squeezed my elbow gently before heading back outside.

The entire place was covered in about five inches of dust, so I figured I should open some windows and start wiping everything down. The sun poured into the kitchen window, and I blinked against it. My eyes weren't used to the brightness anymore. I turned away, my eyelids fluttering with a flurry of black spots. My legs wobbled, and I staggered back, bumping my hip against the cabinet under the kitchen sink.

"Ow." I was reaching for my hip when my vision went black. I couldn't see a thing. Only darkness. "Ethan!" I called out. Before I could say another word, my vision returned. But it wasn't the cottage I saw. It was a garden with flowers and a long, red carpet. A couple stood under a beautiful wooden archway with roses woven around it. I turned my head, searching for something familiar, something that would tell me what this place was and why I was seeing it. My eyes scanned the crowd sitting in the white seats. Rows of dresses and suits. Finally I saw a man with gray hair. He was dressed in a nice black suit, but he wore a black cowboy hat on his head.

Oh, God. It was *him*. The man I'd killed. I knew it was.

He took his wife's hand and squeezed it. "Can you believe our son is twenty-seven years old and getting married?"

His wife turned and smiled at him. "Yeah, twenty-seven. That makes us pretty old."

He patted her hand. "No, it makes us lucky."

Everything went black again. I blinked my eyes, begging my sight to return. Even seeing the dilapidated cottage would've been better than this. The darkness reminded me of death. Forms started to take shape as my vision slowly returned.

What was that? How had I seen that man? And on his son's wedding day? Maybe I hadn't killed him. Maybe he'd just fainted in the car, and I was too scared to notice. Maybe the universe was trying to let me know I wasn't a monster after all.

"Hey, babe." Ethan opened the door, letting the sunlight filter into the room. "Do you want—" I must have looked awful, because the second he saw me, he rushed to my side. "What's wrong?"

How did I answer that? I didn't want to lie to him, not after all he'd done for me. I put my hand to my hip. "I hurt myself. It was stupid. My eyes are still a little sensitive to the sun. You know, from—"

"Sure." He didn't let me finish my sentence. "Let me see. Did you cut yourself?"

"I don't know. I didn't look at it yet."

He started lifting the hem of my skirt, trying to see how bad my hip was, but I stepped back.

"What?" He looked hurt.

"I—I'm sorry. Everything is making me jumpy."

"Including me?"

That had been the wrong thing to say. Now I'd insulted him. "No." I reached for his hand. "You know I love you."

"But you don't want me to see you...naked." He nodded, but I could tell he didn't really understand.

"I know we almost...once, but things are different now. *I'm* different."

He cupped the side of my face in his hand. "No, you're not. What do I have to do to make you believe that?" He searched my eyes for an answer, but I didn't have one to give. "You're the same, and so are we."

"I just don't know if I can pick up where we left off. I need a little time to adjust. This is a lot for me to take in all at once." That was only half of it, but I couldn't bear to tell him the rest.

"Do you want me to sleep on the couch or something?"

"No." I took his hand again. "We can sleep in the same bed, but let's take things slow, okay?"

"Is that all that's bothering you?"

No, but I didn't say that. Instead I leaned forward and kissed him softly on the lips. "What did you want to ask me when you came in?"

I could tell he didn't want to drop this, but he wasn't going to fight with me over it. "I found some paint in the shed. It's off-white. Do you want me to paint anything?"

"Everything. This place needs a major face-lift."

"Okay. I'll get started on the outside first while you finish cleaning up a bit in here."

"Thanks." He started to walk away, but I held on to his hand, making him turn back to me. "I promise I'll be okay, and we'll get back to where we were. I just need time."

"You have a lifetime."

Yes, I did. Thanks to him. But after the incident at the gas station, I wasn't sure that was what I wanted.

I went back to the cabinet below the kitchen sink. It had come open when I bumped into it. I figured it was as good a place as any to store cleaning supplies, so I started digging through it. I found some old sponges, an almost-empty bottle of dish detergent, a few pans, and a wooden box. I shimmied forward, trying to reach the wooden box. My scraped knees rubbed against the edge of the cabinet, making me wince. I really needed to clean out those cuts and bandage them. This place was dirty enough to infect any open wound.

I was about to stand up and take care of the cuts, but then I thought that maybe the wooden box was some kind of medical kit. It might have some Band-Aids or at least some gauze. I ducked my head and reached farther into the cabinet. My fingers wrapped around the box, and I pulled it out from its hiding place. I sat on the floor, ready to fix my knees. The box had no latch at all, but there were brass hinges on one side, which meant the top opened sideways instead of lifting off. I raised the front edge and tilted it back.

It wasn't a medical kit. The box was filled with weird stuff. Red berries, leaves, and herbs I couldn't identify. I dug deeper, feeling something smooth and cool in my fingers. I pulled it out and gasped. It was a small animal bone. At least I assumed it was an animal bone. Dropping it back into the box, I wiped my hands on my dress. I didn't want to risk touching any more bones, but I couldn't help wondering what else was in there. I picked up the box with both hands and gently tilted it so the contents shifted to one side. More bones. Something shiny peeked through the leaves and herbs, so I tilted the box again to get a better look.

A red stone in a platinum setting rested in the leaves. I knew the stone. It was a ruby. My birthstone. But more than that, I knew the ring. Ethan had given it to me for my birthday just a few months ago. I picked it up and placed it on my finger. A perfect fit.

Now the question remained. Why was my ring in this box with a bunch of bones? I'd given it back to Ethan two weeks before I died. I wanted him to have it to remember me. He told me he didn't need a silly ring to remind him of me, but I'd insisted. I couldn't believe he'd stash it in a box with the rest of this stuff.

What was he keeping from me?

CHAPTER THREE

I WAS still staring at the ring when Ethan came back into the cottage.

"Everything okay in here?" He cocked his head at me. I probably did look a little strange staring at my own hand.

I held my hand up, facing the ring toward him. "What was this doing in a box under the sink?"

"What?" He narrowed his eyes and met me in the kitchen, taking my hand in his. "Where did you find this?"

I pointed to the wooden box on the floor. "Why would you put my ring in a box with animal bones and leaves? What's going on, Ethan?"

He bent down and inspected the box. "Sam, I've never seen this stuff before. None of it. I couldn't even tell you what these things are." He stood up and looked at the ring again. "That can't be the same ring."

If he were anyone else, I wouldn't have believed him, but I knew Ethan wouldn't lie to me. We were always honest with each other, which was why I hated keeping the incident at the gas station a secret.

"Where's my ring? What did you do with it after I died?"

"I put it away. I couldn't look at it. It just reminded me you were gone." He lowered his head like he was ashamed of seeming weak.

"That makes sense." I rubbed his arm, trying to let him know I understood. "But now that I'm back, could you get the ring for me? I'd like to wear it again."

He nodded. "Yeah. I left it at a storage place my cousin uses. It's not too far from here. I could get it in a few days, after we get settled."

"Thanks." I forced a smile and took off the ring, placing it on the counter. If it wasn't the one Ethan had given me, I didn't want it. Especially after it had shared a box with animal bones.

"I'll get rid of this." Ethan picked up the wooden box. "I'm not sure what it was doing here anyway. Rick isn't a hunter or anything. I don't know why he'd have animal bones lying around."

They weren't lying around. They were being kept in a box. There was a big difference, but I didn't think insulting Ethan's cousin was a good idea. If it weren't for his cottage, we'd be homeless. But more than that, I wasn't in a position to insult anyone after what I'd done.

We spent the rest of the day cleaning and painting. By nighttime, the place looked…bad. But that was a step up from uninhabitable, so we were making progress. Ethan had even thought to bring a dead-bolt for the front door. There wasn't much he hadn't thought of.

"Hungry?" Ethan asked, bringing in a bag from the car. I recognized it from the gas station and shuddered. "We should close some of the windows now. It's getting a little chilly outside." He put the bag on the table and started shutting the windows. If only that were the reason I was shivering.

I opened the bag and saw dinner consisted of crackers and bottled water.

"Sorry, they didn't have black licorice." Ethan put his hands on my shoulders. "I'll check the general store in the morning. They usually have that kind of stuff."

"You've been here before?" I took a seat and opened the box of crackers.

"A few times, when I was a kid. My aunt and uncle used to come here in the summer. My mom and dad let me come with them some-times." He looked around. "Obviously that was a long time ago."

"Obviously." The décor wasn't from this century. I laughed but immediately felt guilty. I couldn't be happy, not after…

"You can decorate it any way you want. Doesn't matter to me." He shoved a whole cracker into his mouth and took a swig from his water bottle.

I smacked his arm. "You're going to choke."

"What, you don't know mouth-to-mouth?" He grinned, and bits of cracker spilled onto the table.

"Very attractive."

"Just trying to make you smile."

There wasn't much to smile about, but I didn't want Ethan to think I wasn't grateful to be alive, to be here with him.

I reached for his hand and squeezed it. "You don't have to try to make me smile. I'm happy just being with you."

"Oh yeah?" He raised an eyebrow, and I knew he was up to something. "Then let's try a round of 'Where would you rather be?'"

I laughed. It was a game we used to play when the cancer treatments made me too sick to get out of bed. "You sure you want to do that?" I mocked him, gesturing at the dilapidated cottage.

"I think I can handle it. Lay it on me."

"Okay." I took a deep breath and closed my eyes. Part of the game was picturing yourself in the place you wanted to be. I was usually so good at it that I could smell the ocean and taste the salt in the air. My dream place was the beach. I hadn't been there since I was diagnosed with cancer. My parents went all out and got us a week at the best resort in Myrtle Beach. We drove twelve hours there and back, but it was worth every leg cramp and crappy oldies song Dad had made me suffer through. I loved the beach. And they'd let Ethan come along.

"Earth to Sam," Ethan said. "Did I lose you to this dream location?"

"I'm walking out on the pier at Myrtle Beach. The warm breeze is blowing through my hair. The waves are gently crashing against the shore, and I'm holding hands with this smokin' hot guy."

"Anyone I know?"

I shrugged and opened my eyes. "Maybe."

"Oh, I see how it is." Ethan nodded. "All right, what's fair is fair. My turn." He closed his eyes. A devilish grin formed on his lips, but then he reached across the table and took my hand. "I'm having dinner with the most beautiful girl in the world, and we are about to start our new life together. Just the two of us. And there's nowhere I'd rather be."

A single tear escaped my eyes, and I smiled. Because that was

Ethan. Absolutely perfect. For a moment, I forgot that I was a monster who didn't deserve him.

There were no dishes to clean up, so after we put the box of crackers in the cabinet over the stove, we were finished with dinner. We looked around the place, trying to figure out what to do next.

"Want to watch some TV?" Ethan walked over and fiddled with the ancient TV in the living room. I watched as he pressed every button on the set and the remote, but all he got was static and more static. He gave the screen a good whack with the palm of his hand before giving up completely. "Or we could talk."

The couch cushions were airing out in the yard so it wasn't like we could sit comfortably, even if the TV was working. We were slumming it.

"Actually, I'm kind of beat. I think I'd like to go to sleep." I motioned toward the bedroom, and my cheeks got hot.

"Okay." He studied my face for a moment. "Do you want me to take the floor tonight?"

"No. Don't be silly." I took his hand and led him into the bedroom. I was trying to act normal, but it was more difficult than I thought it would be. I was nervous. Here we were, alone in our place. I felt like a kid playing house. Only I wasn't a kid, and neither was Ethan.

He'd brought clean sheets, so at least there was a thin layer of protection between us and the mattress that might very well have been older than the both of us combined. I folded back the top sheet, patting down the wrinkles. I felt like a damn hotel maid doing turndown service, not like a seventeen-year-old girl going to bed with her long-term boyfriend. It was pathetic. *I* was pathetic.

"Hospital corners, impressive," Ethan mocked me.

"I'm sorry. Why is this so hard? Why don't I feel like me?"

"Come here." He sat down on his side of the bed and reached for me. I took his hand and sat next to him. "How don't you feel like yourself?"

How did I answer that? I was dead—or undead. I'd killed a man. I was hiding out in a tiny broken-down shack in the middle of the Poconos, and I was keeping things from the one person I trusted most in the world. I didn't feel like me, because this wasn't me.

But I couldn't say that.

"I guess it's just hard to know how to act. The last time I was alive, I had cancer. There's a big part of me that doesn't remember not being sick."

"You know what I think?"

I shook my head.

"You need to stop thinking." He cupped the side of my face in his hand and brought his face closer to mine. "Want me to help?" He stared into my eyes, making sure I was okay with this. Thankfully, I was. Being with Ethan was normal, and I wanted normal. I leaned forward, brushing my lips against his. He welcomed the kiss and pulled me closer to him.

Ethan was right. I needed to stop thinking. So, that's what I did. I let myself get lost in him. In us. I kissed him the way I had before the cancer got so bad I could barely function. I kissed him like a normal teenage girl kisses her boyfriend. He returned each kiss with more hunger and passion than I'd ever felt. My head spun, and I loved every second of it.

We didn't do anything we hadn't done before. He didn't want to push me, and I loved him for that. By the time my eyes closed, I was out of breath and completely content. No bad thoughts. The world only consisted of Ethan and me.

I slept soundly until around three-thirty. I heard a wheezing and opened my eyes, expecting to see Ethan snoring next to me. He was quiet. The noise wasn't coming from him. It was coming from me. My hands shook with cold, and my lungs struggled for air.

Oh, God! It was happening again. Just like at the gas station. The image of the man with the cowboy hat rushed into my mind. I remembered how warm he'd felt. How I'd wanted to take that warmth from him. And I had. I'd stolen his life.

Ethan rolled onto his side, and without realizing I was doing it, my hand crept toward him. My fingers brushed against his shirt. Heat radiated from his body. My breathing started to calm down, like when I'd touched the man's leg. No! I pulled my hand away and scrambled out of the bed. I wouldn't do that to Ethan. I couldn't hurt him. Not him.

I ran from the room and struggled with the dead bolt Ethan had installed on the front door before hurling myself into the night. My body was giving up on me, betraying me with every step, but I forced myself to move forward. To get away from the cottage. To get away from Ethan.

I tripped over the paint can Ethan had left on the front steps and fell forward onto the grass. My chin hit the ground, and I winced in pain. Why did the universe want me dead? I got to my feet and headed for the car. I didn't know where I was going, but I knew I wouldn't get there on foot. I was too weak. I reached for the hidden key in the hideaway box in the front wheel well. If I hadn't already been having trouble breathing, I would've held my breath as I got in the car and started the engine. I prayed Ethan wouldn't wake up at the sound. *Please, let me get far enough away that I won't hurt him.*

I threw the car into reverse and backed out of the driveway. I could barely control the car. My limbs were weak, and steering was nearly impossible. I pulled onto the road, and tires screeched to a halt. I focused my energy on hitting the brakes before I totaled Ethan's car. The headlights of the other car stopped right alongside me. I didn't crash. I was okay.

The driver threw his door open, yelling curse after curse at me. He stormed up to me and flung my door open.

"What the hell are you doing? You could've killed me, you stupid bitch!" He reached inside the car and grabbed my arm. His touch was so warm. I felt his blood in his veins. Instinctively, I reached for his chest.

"Hey!" He smacked my hand away, but I persisted. "Listen, honey, I'm not gonna lie. You are pretty easy on the eyes." I ignored him and slipped my hand under his shirt. "Well, okay." He pulled his shirt over his head. "Maybe this almost accident wasn't so bad after all." He leaned toward me, and I reached for his neck. I felt the life coursing through his body and into mine. He bent his head toward me, thinking I wanted to kiss him, but before he met my lips, he choked.

"What?" He coughed, but I held on to him. I knew what was happening, yet I couldn't stop. I watched in horror as the skin around his eyes wrinkled with age. His hair turned gray and started falling out of his head in clumps. Still I clung to him, drinking in every last bit of life as it left his body. His knees buckled, and he slumped onto the road right outside my door.

No longer connected to him, I was flooded with emotion. I'd killed again. My hands shook, but this time, it was out of fear. Fear of myself. I couldn't keep doing this. I couldn't become this hideous creature that killed to survive. Yet that was exactly what I was.

I could hear a car's engine coming toward us. I had to do something. Fast. Fueled by adrenaline, I dragged the man to the passenger door of his car and got him inside. Then I got back into Ethan's car and pulled it back up the driveway, just enough that it wouldn't be in the road anymore. I raced back to the guy's car and got in the driver's seat. I put the car in drive and peeled out. I cringed, hoping I hadn't left tire marks on the road. Too late to worry about it now. I drove about a half-mile to a big decline. One thing about the Poconos, there were plenty of hills. I put the car in park and dragged the guy across the seat so it looked like he was driving. I slumped him forward onto the steering wheel and buckled his seat belt around him. I closed his door and ran around to the passenger side. I put the car in drive, lunged back out, and slammed the door as the car started down the hill.

I hoped the car wouldn't hit anything too bad. The guy was already dead. I didn't want the car to explode and the police not to be able to identify his body. Although even his family might not recognize him now, all balding and wrinkled. Tears streamed down my face. I couldn't handle this, any of it. I sprinted for Ethan's car, not caring that my bare feet were being torn up by the gravel on the road. I stuck close to the edge of the trees, in case any more cars came down the road, but the night was quiet. I was sweaty by the time I reached Ethan's car and drove it back up to the cottage. I returned the key to the hideaway box in the wheel well and slipped into the house.

After bolting the door I took a moment to catch my breath. I was a mess in more ways than one. My chest heaved and tears streamed silently down my cheeks. I couldn't go back to bed like this. I needed to get cleaned up first.

I tiptoed to the bathroom and closed the door behind me. Ethan was a pretty sound sleeper, but I had no idea how loud the water would be coming through the old pipes in the cottage. I locked the door and worked out an excuse before I turned on the faucet. If Ethan heard me, I'd simply say I couldn't sleep.

The pipes clanged as the water made its way to the shower. I slipped out of my pajamas and got into the stall. The water wasn't hot by any means. Lukewarm at best. But it washed the tears from my face as I let the emotions of the past twenty-four hours consume me. I'd come back from the dead and killed two people. Sure, the guy from tonight had been a total creep, screaming at a young girl and then trying to make out with her. I was less than half his age. But that didn't make what I'd done okay.

Nothing made that okay.

CHAPTER FOUR

BY some stroke of luck, Ethan slept through my shower, and I managed to slip back into bed. I didn't sleep at all. There was too much going on in my head to even drift off for a minute or two. But when I felt Ethan stir next to me, I closed my eyes and pretended I was off in dreamland. He rolled over and kissed my forehead before heading to the shower.

I got dressed and prepared myself for day two of my new life. For Ethan's sake, I pretended to be the happy girl, thankful to get a second chance at life. I ignored the nagging thoughts tugging at me as I took the box of crackers from the cabinet and placed it on the table. I tried not to think about what I'd done and how long this would go on, because if I had to keep killing people to stay alive…

"Hey, babe. Did I wake you?" Ethan came into the kitchen wearing nothing but a towel. I nearly fell over at the sight of him. Maybe it was all the manual labor he'd done the day before or maybe it was just good genes, but Ethan looked incredible. His dark hair was wet and tousled in a sexy, messy way. His abs were as chiseled as I remembered, and I refused to let myself think about the rest of him.

"No, you didn't wake me." I looked down at the table, needing to take my eyes off him. "I couldn't sleep anymore."

He walked over and kissed my cheek. "You were out when I got up. I guess you slept well."

At least until three-thirty. I nodded and managed a weak smile. "Crackers?" I motioned to the box on the table.

"Actually, I want to go to the diner down the street. I saw a sign in the window yesterday when we drove by. They're hiring."

We *did* need jobs, and I really needed a strong cup of coffee. "Sounds good."

Ethan got dressed, and we headed out to the car. As soon as I saw it, I shivered, remembering the events of the night. I wondered if everyone at the diner would be talking about the accident. I was sure someone had found the car by now.

I buckled up, and Ethan's face twisted in a weird expression.

"What?" I asked.

"My seat is really far up. I feel like I'm driving a clown car or something."

The seat! I'd forgotten to move the seat back after I used the car last night. I couldn't help thinking that maybe part of me wanted to be caught. Caught and stopped, no matter what that meant for me.

"Uh, you must've moved it when you were unpacking the car." I hated myself for coming up with an excuse, for not confessing.

"It's weird, but I don't remember moving the seat. I don't see why I would've needed to."

"Well, yesterday was kind of a long day. You were probably so tired you moved on autopilot." I shrugged, trying to act casual.

"I guess you're right." He adjusted his seat, started the car, and backed out of the driveway.

I stared out my window, looking for tire marks from the almost accident or from when I'd peeled out in the guy's car. I only noticed a small skid, nothing big. As we approached the hill, my chest squeezed tight. I closed my eyes, unable to look at the damage I'd caused.

"Whoa," Ethan said.

I winced. How bad was it?

"Check that out. That car is wrapped around that tree. The guy must've been drunk or something."

I forced my eyes open. Nothing more than tiny slits. The black car was on the side of the road, and like Ethan had said, the front end was crumpled around a huge tree trunk.

"No way did he survive that. Don't you think?"

I swallowed the acidic taste in my mouth, and my bottom lip quivered.

Ethan squeezed my hand. "Oh, man. Sam, I'm sorry. I shouldn't be saying things like that. Not so soon after…"

Great. He thought I was upset because he was talking about death. In a way I was, but not at all how he thought.

"I'm okay. You didn't do anything wrong."

"Yes, I did. I shouldn't have been so insensitive."

"Really, I'm fine. Can we please drop it?"

He didn't say another word. He dropped it just like that.

We pulled into the diner. One of those old-time red and silver ones you see in movies. I liked it. It was small, but it seemed welcoming, and for some reason, my mood lifted a little as we walked inside and sat in a booth by the door.

"Good morning," an older woman with bleached-blonde hair and lipstick redder than a fire truck welcomed us.

"Morning," Ethan said.

I forced a smile.

"I'm Gloria." She placed two menus on the table. "Now what can I get you two to drink while you look these over?"

"Coffee," we both said.

"Coming right up." Gloria turned and headed to a coffee station behind the counter.

"So, what do you think?" Ethan asked.

I picked up a menu and opened it. "I'm torn between a Belgian waffle and scrambled eggs."

"No, I mean about working here." He nodded toward the Help Wanted sign in the window.

"Oh. Um, sure. This seems as good a place as any."

"What will it be?" Gloria set our coffee down.

"I'll have a Belgian waffle, please." I handed her my menu.

"I'll have the steak and eggs," Ethan said. "And we'll each take a job application, too."

Gloria looked back and forth between us. "You two aren't here on vacation?"

Ethan shook his head, but Gloria looked to me for confirmation.

"Our families moved here yesterday." The little white lie slipped off my tongue. "We could really use the work."

"Well, then. You've got yourselves some work."

"Really?" Ethan almost fell out of his seat he was so happy. "Just like that? No application? No interview?"

"Honey, have you seen these legs?" Gloria took a step back and hiked up her pant leg. Big varicose veins ran down her shin. "They've been working too long and too hard. I need help. This is my place, and I'll be damned if I go out of business because all the fancy resorts have their own restaurants. Nobody's gonna come to my diner—no matter how good the coffee and pie are—if the service is poor."

At the mention of coffee, I took a sip. It was delicious. "This is amazing. Secret recipe?"

Gloria winked. "One I'll teach you right after breakfast. You can be my new waitress."

"What about me?" Ethan asked.

"I'm thinking you'd fill the busboy position just fine. Sound good to you?"

"Sounds great." Ethan's smile lit up the diner. "Thank you."

"I'll be right back with your orders," she said.

Ethan reached for my hand. "See, things are working out great already."

Before I could answer, I saw spots. Black spots that filled my vision. Not again. "Um, I need to use the restroom."

"It's straight back there." I could barely make out Ethan's face as he motioned behind me.

"Be right back." I used the booth to find my way out of the seat. Everything was black now. I ran my fingers across the other booths and tables as I made my way to the bathroom. I hoped I didn't look too suspicious.

"Hey!" a girl yelled as my hand grazed her shoulder.

"Sorry."

"You need help, honey?" I recognized Gloria's voice.

"Yeah, I got something in my eye. I need to wash it out. I can't see much of anything right now."

She took my arm and led me into the bathroom, placing me in front of the sink.

"Thank you. I'll be fine now." I reached for the faucet, hoping Gloria would leave. I didn't know how I was going to react when my vision came back. What would I see this time?

"Sure thing. I'll be right outside if you need a hand."

I pretended to fiddle with the water until I heard the door close. Then I gripped the sink to steady myself. A scene began to take shape. A house. A man walked through the front door. It was the guy from last night. He loosened his tie and kicked his shoes off, getting dirt on the carpet.

"I don't smell dinner!" he yelled.

A woman came out of the kitchen carrying a tray of drinks and appetizers. "I thought we'd start with some bruschetta while the roast finishes cooking."

Without warning, he knocked the tray from her hand, and the wine and bruschetta splattered all over the cream-colored carpet.

"I work all day, and you think some tomato on bread is enough to fill me? Why isn't the roast ready? Did you go out with your friends again today? How many times do I have to tell you to make sure you're home in plenty of time to get dinner on the table?"

The woman cowered as he pulled his hand back. I shook my head, trying to break free from this scene. I didn't want to see any more. The woman's scream rang in my ears as my vision went black. It was over.

I was breathing heavily, and I slumped forward onto the counter. The guy I'd killed had been awful, unbearable. He was sexist and vile. He hit his wife. A small part of me was glad he'd never get to hit her again. Glad that she'd be free.

"You okay?"

I looked up to see the reflection of a girl with jet-black hair. I jumped and turned around to face her.

"Sorry. Didn't mean to scare you."

I stared at her, happy that my sight was my own again. Her eyes bored into me. They were almost cat-like. They looked really eerie, probably because she had bleached-blonde eyebrows. I doubted a single hair on this girl's face or head was her natural color.

"I thought I was alone."

"Yeah, you were pretty zoned out. I thought you were having a fit or something."

"I'm fine. Thanks." I turned back to the mirror and fussed with my hair. I had to look together so Ethan didn't think something was wrong.

The girl eyed me for a minute before leaving. I sighed. I had to get a hold of myself. Whatever was happening to me, I had to find a way to deal with it. If Ethan knew what was going on, it would crush him—it was already destroying me. I took a few deep breaths to calm my nerves and walked back to the table.

The food was already there, and Ethan was shoveling it in. I smiled when I saw a triangular piece missing from my waffle.

"Sorry," Ethan said, looking all innocent. "It looked really good. I gave you some eggs though. You said you couldn't decide between a waffle or eggs, so now you have both."

"Thanks." I smiled at him. No. No way could I tell him any of this. I'd figure it out on my own.

The bell above the door jingled, and a police officer walked in. He went right to the counter, where Gloria met him with a cup of coffee. "Late night, huh?" she asked him.

"You said it." He sat down on a stool, and he and Gloria talked for a few minutes. I couldn't hear a word, but I didn't need to. This was about the guy I'd killed. This was probably the officer who'd found the car and reported the "accident." I sipped my coffee, not that the caffeine was going to ease the sinking feeling in my stomach. Even after the cop said goodbye to Gloria and walked out of the diner, I was still on edge.

Gloria approached with the coffee pot and *tsk*ed as she refilled our cups.

"Was that about the car we saw on the way here?" Ethan asked.

She nodded. "Bad one, too. Officer Crawford said the guy must have had a massive stroke while he was driving. They identified him by his license, but when they called his wife at the resort where they were staying, she said he looked years older. More wrinkles, balding, and what was left of his hair was completely gray. The paramedics said strokes can age a person quite a bit, but even this was beyond anything they'd ever seen."

The few bites of waffle I'd manage to get down were on their way back up. I couldn't listen to this. I was the only one who knew the truth. The ugly, horrible truth.

"Was he from around here?" Ethan asked.

"No. He was a tourist. I think his name was Herman Owlander," Gloria said.

Ethan cringed. "Awful name."

"Awful man, too, if you ask me." Gloria put the coffee pot down on the table and leaned toward us. She looked around before whispering, "He and his wife came in here earlier in the week. He was ordering her around like she was a servant. I'm telling you, I was tempted to pour a pot of scalding hot coffee all over his unmentionable parts. Not that I'm saying I'm glad he's dead, but there's something to be said for getting what you deserve. If you treat people like that and show no regard for other living beings, well, sooner or later, karma is gonna come around to bite you in the ass."

Ethan laughed, but I couldn't. Gloria was right. Herman obviously didn't care how he treated other people, even his own wife. The universe had given him what he deserved.

I wondered what the universe had in store for me.

CHAPTER FIVE

WHEN we finished breakfast, Gloria took me up to the counter to give me a tutorial on how to be a waitress. She said there was nothing to being a busboy, so Ethan said he'd go food shopping and get a few other things we needed for the cottage.

"I'll pick you up in about an hour." He looked at Gloria. "Will that be long enough?"

"Depends. Do you want to start making money today? Because I could sure use some help with the lunch crowd."

I shrugged. "Why not?" I had to keep my mind busy, or I'd go insane.

"Should I come back for lunch to start my shift?" Ethan asked.

"The crowd usually starts in around eleven-thirty. See you then." Gloria practically pushed Ethan out the door. "Don't you worry about our girl. I'll take care of her."

I gave Ethan a smile. "See you soon."

He nodded and left.

"So, I guess you should tell me your name," Gloria said. "Got to know who to make the checks out to."

My name? I hadn't gotten my fake ID yet. I hadn't even thought about a new last name. I must've looked terrified because Gloria gave me a stern look.

"You aren't in any trouble, are you?"

"No. It's just that I don't have a bank account to cash checks."

"Oh, well those are easy enough to open up, but I'll tell you what.

Until you get settled and open that account, I'll pay you in cash. How does that sound?"

"Great. Thanks."

"But I do need to know what to call you."

"Sam. My name's Sam."

"Wouldn't have pegged you for a Samantha."

"Well, actually, I don't go by my full name. I prefer Sam."

She narrowed her eyes at me. "How does your mother feel about you using a boy's name instead of the one she gave you?"

I tried to keep my composure at the mention of Mom. I missed her so much. Not that I'd ever consider trying to contact her. She needed to move on, get over my death. And me showing up now—an undead killer—would destroy her.

"You *do* have a mother, don't you? Or did I just put my big, over-worked foot in my mouth?"

"Not anymore," I said. "But it's okay. She never minded me going by Sam."

"Well all the same, I think I'll call you Samantha."

I figured there was no use arguing with her. She'd given me a job and was willing to pay me in cash. How could I complain?

I followed Gloria around all morning, learning the ins and outs of the ancient coffee pot, carrying plates of food to all the tables, and refilling the sugar dispensers. By eleven, I was exhausted. But it was a good exhausted. Keeping busy meant I didn't have time to think.

The door to the diner opened, and the girl from the bathroom walked in. What was she doing back again? She took a seat at the counter right in front of me as I put out a new tray of mammoth muffins.

"Twice in one day?" I asked.

"Excuse me?" She looked at me like she didn't recognize me.

"You were here earlier. In the bathroom." Did she really not remember me? I would've thought my display in the ladies' room would be burned into her memory.

"Oh, right." She sounded completely disinterested.

"What can I get for you?"

"Coffee. Black."

I grabbed a mug and poured the freshly brewed coffee. I breathed in the heavenly scent. Gloria had shown me the secret ingredient. A tablespoon of cinnamon. It smelled divine, yet the taste was so subtle you couldn't quite pinpoint what it was.

"Here you go." I placed the coffee in front of her. "Would you like a muffin? They're fresh."

"No. Just the coffee."

No big tip here. I wiped the counter even though it was already clean. I needed something to do while I waited for the lunch crowd.

"You live here?" the girl asked.

"Um, yeah. You?"

"Unfortunately." Her tone was as bitter as her black coffee.

"I take it you don't want to be here?"

"Look around. This is a resort town. Though I can't understand why. Ooh, mountains. Ooh, a river. Big deal." She took another sip.

"It's pretty, especially with all the leaves changing colors."

"Leaves. Yeah, very exciting."

I wasn't sure why she was even talking to me. She was obviously a miserable person. I moved away, pretending to check on the sugar dispensers I'd already filled.

"You going to school?" she asked.

"I will. I moved here yesterday, so I haven't gotten around to enrolling yet." I still wasn't sure how Ethan and I were even going to pull off getting into school. We couldn't exactly ask our old school for our records. We'd be using fake names.

"I guess I'll see you around." She got up and walked out of the diner. I reached for her cup, noticing she didn't even leave me a tip. No big loss. I would manage without the quarter.

Ethan walked up to the counter. "Hey, how's it going?"

"Good." I kissed him hello. "Gloria's got me working the counter until the lunch crowd hits. She said it's good practice at a slower pace."

"I'm glad she's not pushing you too much on your first day."

I took his arm and pulled him toward the coffee pot. "Did you figure out how we're going to enroll in school? We won't have any transfer records."

"Don't worry about it." He reached in his back pocket and took out an ID. It had my license photo but the name was different.

"Samantha Smith?" I met his eyes. "You couldn't come up with anything more original than Smith?"

"The good thing about a common name is there are plenty of records to choose from." He wagged his eyebrows at me.

"You stole some girl's records?" I said in a loud whisper.

"I didn't steal them. I simply duplicated them. Totally different."

I sighed. It wasn't a bad plan, but Ethan had never done anything this sneaky before. He was changing—because of me.

"Oh, you moved here from Phoenix."

"Phoenix? I've never even been to Arizona."

"You've got to take what you can get."

I rolled my eyes and pocketed my fake ID. Sam Smith it was. "What name did you get?"

"Ethan Jones. Floridian."

"Well, look at that, we both came from the south."

"Yup. Oh and I had to get you a P.O. box. If we have the same mailing address, people will get suspicious. I don't want to pretend to be brother and sister because I'm not about to stop acting like your boyfriend."

I laughed, thinking of how grossed out people would get if they thought we were related and stole kisses by our lockers. Ethan had thought of pretty much everything. I was thankful for these moments of normalcy, but it didn't take long before Herman's face popped into my head.

Gloria came out of the kitchen. "You're early."

I jumped, hoping she hadn't heard any of our conversation.

Ethan smiled. "What can I say? I'm happy to have found a job so quickly."

"I like that." Gloria handed him an apron and a dishcloth. "There are empty tubs on the cart over there. Fill one up and leave it in the kitchen for the dishwasher. Oh, and wipe down the tables in between customers. That's about all the instruction you need."

The lunch crowd was pretty intense. Ethan and I were running back and forth for a good two and a half hours. Other than spilling one cup of coffee down the front of my shirt, I did pretty well. No messed up orders, no unpaid checks, and the tips were good. I was starting to feel like a normal, working teenager until the black spots started to appear. At first, I thought I'd spilled coffee on the counter, but when I wiped at them, they didn't go away.

"How are you holding up, Samantha?" Gloria asked.

"Um, actually, I could use a bathroom break. Would you mind covering the counter for me?" I didn't wait for a response. I left the dishcloth on the counter and headed for the bathroom before I lost my sight completely. Or worse, had another vision in front of a diner full of people.

I didn't want to see Herman again. The last glimpse of his future—I guessed that was what I was seeing, the life the person would have lived if I hadn't killed them—was unbearable to watch. I remembered what Gloria had said about the universe coming back to get you. Maybe this was my punishment. Having to see what I'd taken from the people I killed.

I splashed cold water on my face as everything faded from my view. I braced myself for whatever horrors Herman was about to commit. But it wasn't his face I saw. It was an older man, probably in his seventies. He was holding his wife's hand and smiling at the young children playing a game on the floor.

The children were adorable, but I kept my focus on the old man. Something about him was familiar. His eyes. They had a warmth to them. A warmth I knew.

"They're not being too loud, are they, Dad?" asked a younger woman coming into view.

"No, no. Let them be. They're children. They're supposed to be loud. Besides, there's no better sound than the laughter of your great-grandchildren. You'll understand that someday."

The woman walked over and kissed the old man's cheek. "They adore you, Dad."

"The feeling is mutual."

My vision blurred and went black. I was sad to see it go. They all seemed so happy. But then I remembered I was seeing things that would never happen. Things that couldn't happen because I'd ended the person's life. But who was that old man? He didn't look like the guy with the cowboy hat. They had different-colored eyes. Was I seeing my next victim? Was that possible?

Next victim? What was I thinking? I couldn't let myself take another life. I *wouldn't* let myself. I had to find a way to keep from dying without taking life from another living being. This had to stop.

"Samantha!" Gloria called.

My sight was slowly returning, and I could see that the door was open a crack.

"We're backing up. Hurry it along in there!" Gloria was sweet, but from the way she'd screamed at the dishwasher when he took too long on his break, I knew she didn't tolerate her employees wasting time.

I rushed back into the dining room. "Sorry!" I grabbed the coffee pot from Gloria's hands and made my way from table to table.

The rest of the day was a blur. A flurry of activity. But no more visions and no loss of breath. Ethan and I stayed through dinner, too. Finally at eight, Gloria waved us out.

"That's enough for today. I'll see you both after school tomorrow."

School. The next big thing I had to tackle in my new life.

"Dismissal is at two-thirty, so I'll expect you here no later than three."

"You got it," Ethan said.

I waved goodbye and followed Ethan to the car. I slumped into the seat, practically melting into the leather.

"I'm beat, too," Ethan said.

"At least I made some good money in tips." I pulled a wad of bills from my pocket.

"Not bad." Ethan smiled as we pulled out of the parking lot. "So, I got us all registered for school."

"How did you do that?"

"I filled out all the paperwork online and paid a homeless couple to go to the school and pretend to be my dad and your mom. All we have to do is report to the guidance office in the morning to pick up our schedules."

"I don't suppose you were able to work your magic and get us into all the same classes, were you?" I leaned my head back on the seat. Even my hair was tired.

"Honestly, I have no idea what our schedules will be like. Only that the school has block scheduling, so we have four periods a day along with lunch. But we were placed in classes based on Samantha Smith's and Ethan Jones's records, remember?"

I turned my head just enough to look at him. "Please tell me Samantha Smith wasn't an honors student." I'd missed a ton of school thanks to all my cancer treatments. If I was put in honors classes, I'd fail for sure, and the school might look deeper into "my" record.

"Actually, she was a solid C student. I'm sure you'll make it look like she had a sudden change in appreciation for a good education."

"I don't want any sudden changes. I have to perform to her ability, or people might get suspicious."

"Relax." Ethan squeezed my hand. "Everything's going to be fine." He let go of me, which was odd because he always held my hand when he drove. "Um, there's one more thing. Samantha Smith was the star cross-country runner at her old school in Phoenix, so you might want to dust off your running shoes and do a few laps around the cottage this evening to warm up."

"What?" I nearly jumped out of my seat.

Ethan burst out laughing. "I'm kidding!"

I smacked his arm. "That's so not funny." But I couldn't help laughing. "Okay, tell me more about Ethan Jones from Florida. What's he like?"

"Oh well, he's exceptionally attractive, has a 4.0 average, and is a total chick magnet. I don't need to change a thing."

"No, not a thing." My tone was full of sarcasm. Though truth be told, Ethan was all those things.

"Nah, really he's an A/B student. No extracurricular activities, which is good since I'll be working at the diner after school."

Things seemed to be working out. Everything except my problem. The problem I couldn't mention to Ethan. I tried to tell myself I'd adjust to being alive again. My body would get used to it, and I wouldn't need to steal life from others after a while. I knew I was fooling myself, but I repeated it over and over in my mind. I was so lost in my thoughts I almost didn't hear Ethan say, "What the hell?"

The car stopped in the driveway. I looked at the cottage. It was surrounded by rocks. A circle of rocks. All strategically placed.

Someone had made a big circle around our house. It was something straight out of *The Blair Witch Project*.

CHAPTER SIX

"**D**ID you do that?" I asked, knowing there was no way Ethan had anything to do with the rocks. He was as surprised as I was.

"No, and no one knows we're here—other than the water and electric companies. I mean, my family hasn't been here in years. None of them would think I'd come here when I left home. I'm sure it's the last place they'd think to look."

Ethan's family had had sort of a falling-out about a year ago. Something about his uncle gambling away all his savings. The family had even staged an intervention, but when that didn't work, his aunt and uncle had moved away, leaving the cottage in their son Rick's name. The cottage had been abandoned long before all that, and since Rick didn't like the Poconos he up and left.

"I don't get it." I shook my head. "Why would someone take all that time to arrange a bunch of rocks like this?"

"Maybe it's a prank." Ethan opened his door. "It could be some local kids messing around. This place does look eerie all by itself in the woods."

I nodded. He was probably right. Some kids were bored and decided to scare some younger boy or girl by convincing them this was a gathering place for witches. That had to be it.

"You stay here. I'll go inside and look around, make sure no one broke in while we were gone."

"Okay." I locked the car doors behind Ethan. For a moment, I thought how ironic it was that I'd be scared of some kids. I was a killer. They should've been afraid of me. Then again, I felt fine right now, and I touched Ethan all the time without hurting him. It was only when I felt the life draining out of me that I was a danger to other people. Not that that made it any better.

I scanned the woods. It was hard to see with the sun setting, so I couldn't be sure if the people who did this were still lurking around, trying to scare each other. I didn't see anyone. Not even an animal in sight. We were all alone. Secluded on our little hill.

Ethan came back out of the cottage, shrugging his shoulders. I opened my door and met him in the driveway.

"Everything looks fine." He kissed my cheek. "See, just a prank."

I eyed the rocks. "Real funny."

Ethan moved one of the rocks out of the way, and we went inside. It was starting to get dark, and I was wiped from my first day as a working stiff. Pun completely intended. All I wanted was a hot shower. Of course, we didn't have hot water. We had lukewarm water. It would have to do.

"You can shower first," Ethan said, reading my mind. "Who knows how cold the water will be the second time around? I don't want you turning into an icicle."

"You sure?"

"Yeah, go ahead. I'm going to play around with the TV some more. See if I can't get us a station that works."

I grabbed my pajamas and headed to the bathroom. I set the faucet all the way to hot, hoping for a miracle. When I stepped inside, I was shocked by the chill in the water. It reminded me of the coldness I felt before I needed to... What exactly *was* I doing? Feeding off humans? I shook away the thought as I washed off as quickly as possible. As I shut off the water and grabbed my towel, I realized I hadn't felt that coldness of death creeping up on me since last night. Maybe I was getting better. Maybe I wouldn't need to kill anymore. I hugged my towel to me and prayed that was true.

"Woo hoo!" Ethan yelled from the living room. "Babe, we have a channel!"

I laughed as I pulled on my pajamas—thankfully, Ethan had volunteered to take my clothes to Goodwill after I died, but instead he'd kept them for me. I stepped into the kitchen and made my way to Ethan, who wrapped me up in his arms.

I caught a glimpse of some crime show on channel two. Ethan hated those shows, but he was so happy to have anything to watch. He always could find the good in any situation. I let my towel drop to the floor and took his face in both my hands. "I love you."

He smiled and kissed me so hard my head spun. I struggled for air, but this time, it was by choice. Ethan picked me up, wrapping my legs around him. The next thing I knew, we were in the bedroom. *Our* bedroom. My heart raced. Was this it? Was this the way it was going to happen?

Ethan gently placed me on the bed and stepped back for a second, studying my face to judge my reaction to the change of location. My mind was a flurry of thoughts, but the one at the forefront was that Ethan was too far away. I reached for him, and he joined me on the bed.

"Are you—?"

"Don't ask me." I returned my lips to his.

He pulled away. "But I want to make sure—"

I smothered his mouth again. I didn't want to ruin the moment with the "Are you sure you want to do this?" talk. I was sure. For the first time since I'd come back, I felt like myself again. I wasn't letting this feeling go.

Ethan's kisses got softer, and I knew it was his way of giving me a chance to change my mind. That wasn't going to happen. I pulled him closer, noticing he smelled faintly of sweat and brown gravy. A customer had spilled his gravy all over the booth, and Ethan had had to mop it up. I didn't think I'd made a face or anything, but Ethan leaned back and sniffed his shirt.

"Wow, I need a shower. Maybe we should…" He was afraid to suggest we stop or even wait, so he was leaving the decision up to me.

"You know what? It's not late. Go shower. I'll be here when you're finished."

He kissed me one more time. "Five minutes tops." I've never seen him run so fast.

I laughed to myself as I lay on the bed, staring up at the ceiling. I thought I'd be more nervous, but this didn't seem so nerve-wracking after all the other stuff that had happened to me. I was happy, and Ethan was perfect. Still, the air in the bedroom felt heavy. I got up and opened the window to let some fresh air in. The windows had locks on them, so they only opened about five inches, but that was plenty. There was a slight breeze, and I bent down, sticking my nose in the opening and breathing in the night air.

I closed my eyes and smiled. Tonight was going to be amazing. Unforgettable. A whiff of smoke made me open my eyes. Smelling smoke in the middle of the woods was never a good thing. Someone stepped in front of the window, and I jumped back. A yelp escaped my lips, and I stumbled into the bed. A guy was standing outside the window, looking into my bedroom.

"Ethan!"

"Wait," the guy said. "Don't scream."

Don't scream? Yeah, right. "Ethan!" I yelled even louder.

"Let me in," the guy said. "I need to talk to you."

I knew he couldn't get in through the locked window, and I couldn't remember if we'd bolted the front door, so I ran from the bedroom.

"No!" he called after me.

Ethan met me in the living room, soaking wet with shampoo still in his hair.

"There was someone outside our bedroom window!" I pointed toward the bedroom as if Ethan didn't know where it was. I was freaked.

Ethan clutched his towel to his hips and ran to the bedroom. "They're gone." He came back out a second later with a pair of jeans and a T-shirt on. "I'm going to check outside. Lock the door behind me."

I barely processed the words. I was having trouble figuring out why anyone would be spying on us. Why anyone would even come to an abandoned cottage at night. It made me wonder about the wooden box with the strange things inside. Maybe this place hadn't been totally abandoned after all. Maybe someone had been using it. For what, I didn't know.

Ethan grabbed my arms, holding me by my elbows. "Sam, are

you listening to me? I want you to stay here." He put his cell phone in my hand. "Call 911 if anything goes wrong."

If anything went wrong? Like that guy hurting Ethan? "Don't go out there." I gripped his arms. "You don't have to. We can call the police. Tell them about coming home to find the rocks and then the guy peeking in our window. Let them handle it."

"Calling the police has to be a last resort. My parents probably have my picture posted everywhere by now, trying to find me, and that includes in the police database. I doubt anyone here would recognize me, but I'm not taking that chance unless I absolutely have to."

He was right. I couldn't put him in that situation. He'd run away for me. He'd done all this for me. I had to let him handle the peeping Tom his way. I nodded.

"Lock the door behind me." He grabbed a flashlight and a hammer and went outside. I closed the door, but before I could reach for the lock, Ethan's cell phone buzzed in my hand. The display showed his mom's number. She must have been worried sick. My illness had hit her hard. She knew her son would be devastated when I died, but I was sure she didn't think he'd run away. I hated that my being alive was causing her pain.

I let the call go to voicemail, and when it beeped with a new message, I played it. It wasn't the only message. There were fourteen according to the mechanical voice. I couldn't listen to them all, but I played the most recent one.

Ethan, please, let me know you're okay. I just need to make sure you aren't hurt. I know losing Sam was hard on you, but you need your family right now. We need you, too.

Her sobs tore my insides to shreds.

Something slammed into the side of the cottage. By the sound of it, it was close to the bedroom. I ran for the bedroom and peered out the window. Ethan was leaning against the house, slumped forward in pain.

"Ethan!" I had to help him, but the front door swung open. The guy saw me instantly. I backed farther into the bedroom, pushing the door closed, but a foot blocked me.

"I need to talk to you." The guy rammed the door open.

I screamed and backed away as he stepped into the bedroom and closed the door behind him. He had platinum-blond hair and alarming blue eyes. He was skinny but strong, judging by how he forced his way into the room.

"Who are you?" I yelled, hoping it was loud enough to alert Ethan—if he'd recovered.

"I'm trying to help you."

He moved toward me, and I backed into the corner between the bed and the closet. I looked around for a weapon, something to use to keep this guy back. I reached for the lamp by the bed and picked it up.

"Stay back!"

"I'm not going to hurt you. Put that down. We don't have much time, and there's so much I need to tell you."

"I'm not putting this down, and I'm not having a discussion with some random guy who broke into my house."

He reached for the lamp. "Come on. Give me the lamp."

"Give you the lamp? Oh, yeah, sure. You've trapped me in a room with you. Let me give you a weapon to bash my head in." I scoffed. "Not happening."

"You have to listen to me." He stopped moving toward me and dropped his arm like something had snapped inside him. "Besides, why would you use the lamp on me when you can kill me with your bare hands?"

My bare hands? Oh, my God! What did he know? Had he seen me last night? He could've been in the car that was driving by. He could've been the one who put the rocks in a circle around the cottage. He knew what I was, and he was trying to scare me.

"Sam, you need to hear what I have to say."

A lump formed in my throat. "How do you know my name? Who are you?"

"Sam!" Ethan shouted.

"Ethan!" I gripped the lamp tighter in my hands in case the mystery guy tried to attack me out of desperation.

The bedroom door flew open, and Ethan's eyes rushed from me to the guy. He lunged for him. "Get the hell away from her!" Ethan grabbed the guy by the front of his shirt and threw him into the living room. I heard a crash and knew our TV had gone down with him. So much for our one channel.

I held onto the lamp, yanking the cord from the wall, just in case Ethan lost the upper hand before we got rid of the intruder. I rushed to the doorway and stayed there as Ethan grabbed the guy and hauled him to his feet. He pulled back his arm and slugged the guy right in the nose. The sickening crunch of bones breaking made me cringe so much my shoulders practically went through the roof. The turkey and cheese sandwich I'd inhaled between refilling drinks threatened to make an appearance.

Blood poured from the guy's nose, and there was a small part of me that felt sorry for him. Ethan backed off a little and watched the guy stagger backward. His eyes were glued to me. "You have no idea what you're doing," he said, reaching for the door.

"If I ever see you near this place or Sam again, I'll break a lot more than your nose." Ethan gave the guy a final shove in the chest. He slammed the front door behind him and bolted it. The back of his head looked sticky with dark red blood from where he'd slammed into the side of the cottage. I had no idea where the flashlight or hammer was or how the guy had gotten the upper hand on Ethan. All I knew was Ethan was hurt.

I dropped the lamp, not even caring that the bulb shattered on the floor. I ran to Ethan and buried my head in his chest. My whole body heaved as I sobbed.

"Shh. It's okay. He's gone." Ethan rubbed my back, trying to calm me.

But in that moment, nothing could calm me. I'd died, come back a killer, and now someone knew my secret. Knew it and might want to hurt me because of it.

CHAPTER SEVEN

I SPENT the night in Ethan's arms. I barely slept, afraid I'd start gasping for air. I wouldn't kill Ethan in my sleep. I'd never let that happen. So I lay awake, listening to his rhythmic breathing. I hoped he didn't have a concussion, but he assured me it was only a scratch, nothing bad. Still, when the first rays of sun peeked through the window, and Ethan rolled over, I checked his head for gashes. Not a one. His pillow didn't have so much as a drop of blood on it. He'd be okay.

I turned over to check the alarm clock. Ten after six. I had to get up and face my first day of school as Samantha Smith. Since Ethan had gone shopping during my training at the diner yesterday, we finally had more than crackers to eat. The good part about working at the diner every day after school was we'd never have to cook dinner for ourselves. Gloria said dinner was part of our wages. I think she just liked being motherly. She was sweet like that.

"Morning." Ethan finally emerged from the bedroom, sleepy-eyed with his hair sticking up in every direction. He was the only person I knew who could make disheveled look sexy.

"Good morning." My eyes drifted to the bit of bare stomach that was exposed as he stretched his arms over his head.

"What? Do I have something on me?" He looked down, trying to figure out what I was staring at.

"No, it's just you. I'm admiring you." I smiled and took another spoonful of cereal.

His face lit up. "Admire all you want." He kissed the top of my head before heading into the bathroom. Ethan got ready quicker than anyone I knew. I had about two minutes before he'd be rushing me out the door. I cleared my dishes and grabbed a protein bar for Ethan. He ate one every morning.

Someone had moved the rock back in place during the night. That, or the peeping Tom had tripped over it and knocked it back in place. Either way, we had to step over the rocks to get to the car. The drive to school wasn't long at all. There were about ten schools in the area. Who knew a resort town would have so many local residents? The high school was huge. I had no doubt I'd get lost. We pulled into the parking spot Ethan had secured for us.

He squeezed my hand. "So we have to find the guidance office first. They'll have our schedules. And then—"

"We're split up and thrown to the wolves?"

"It won't be that bad. So, we might not be in the same classes. It's only school. We'll be together at work and at home."

"I know." I was acting clingy again, and I didn't like it. It wasn't me. But I was nervous. It had been more than twenty-four hours since I'd killed Herman. What if that feeling came over me again at school? I didn't want to kill anyone.

The guidance office was nestled in the middle of the school. The security or hall monitor, whatever he was called, brought us there. A little old lady who reminded me of my grandmother was sitting at the desk when we walked in.

"Can I help you?" She smiled at us, which threw me. Most people who worked in the school offices back home hated when they had to interact with the students, but this woman seemed happy to have someone to talk to.

"Hi, I'm Ethan Jones, and this is Samantha Smith. We're transfer students."

The woman—Mrs. Melrose, according to the nameplate on her desk—nodded and began flipping through some files. "Yes, I have your schedules right here. What a coincidence that you arrived together."

Ethan and I forced smiles on our faces. How did we explain how we knew each other? I was supposed to be from Phoenix, and Ethan was supposed to be from Florida. It didn't really make sense.

"We sort of bumped into each other in the parking lot. He looked as lost as I did," I said, thinking on my feet.

Ethan nudged me with his foot, and the slightest smile crossed his lips. "I wasn't going to turn down the chance to meet a pretty girl on my first day." He winked at Mrs. Melrose. I think she misunderstood what he was saying, because I swear she started blushing. Yuck! She was well past the "cougar" label.

"Well, if you need anything, feel free to stop in the guidance office anytime." She handed us our schedules.

We muttered "thank you" as we studied our schedules. It was worse than I'd thought. I was in all middle-level classes, which wasn't bad, but Ethan's schedule was packed with honors courses. He'd always done well in school, but he'd only taken honors history. The guy watched way too much of The History Channel. I wondered how he'd manage with such a tough schedule.

"At least we have lunch together," he said, trying to make the best of the situation.

We managed to find our lockers. Ethan's was at the opposite end of the hall from mine, which meant I probably wouldn't even be able to catch a glimpse of him between classes with the crowded hallways.

He walked me to my locker and kissed me goodbye. "Good luck. I'll see you in a few hours."

Hours. Lunch was hours away. I gave him my best fake smile and opened my locker. I realized I didn't have any books yet, and I hadn't worn a coat to school, so there was really nothing to put in my locker. I slammed it shut and looked for room 213, English literature with Mr. Ryan. I hoped we wouldn't be studying Middle English. It was a different language and way too difficult to read.

When I got to the door, I wasn't sure if I should walk in or knock. I could see Mr. Ryan sitting on the edge of his desk and reading from a book. I didn't want to interrupt him, so I opened the door and quietly crept inside. I recognized the book, *The Strange Case of Dr. Jekyll and Mr. Hyde*. I'd read it sophomore year. At least I knew I'd do well on my first exam. Mr. Ryan's reading was full of emotion, nothing like the way Mrs. Belfry read aloud to us back home.

No one even noticed me standing in the doorway. They were all into Mr. Ryan's reading. I saw a few girls practically drooling and realized it might not just be Mr. Ryan's voice that had them so mesmerized. He was young with dark, almost black hair, like mine. Even though he was sitting I could tell he was tall and in great shape. Yes, I might like English lit this year. Not that I had a crush on Mr. Ryan or anything. He was a teacher and that made him old in a completely different way. But he was easy to look at and listen to.

Finally, he shut the book and smiled. "Writing like this captures your heart and doesn't let go. It's like—" He turned and saw me for the first time. "Well, hello. Let me guess, Samantha Smith. New transfer student from…" He held his hand up. "Don't tell me. I know this. Phoenix, right?"

I nodded. "You got it."

"Any seat is fine. I don't assign them. I want my students to feel comfortable. You can't absorb great literature if you aren't comfortable."

I looked around, spotting an empty seat by the window.

"Grab a book on the back shelf." He pointed to a bookshelf filled with not only school-approved books, but novels I'd buy if I saw them in a store. When I got really sick, Mom bought me a Kindle, and she let me load it with books. I wished I still had it. It would make staying awake at night a lot less boring.

"Have you read *Dr. Jekyll and Mr. Hyde* before?" Mr. Ryan asked, breaking me out of my thoughts.

"Yeah, back at my old school." I sat down with my novel.

"Would you care to pick up where I left off in the reading?"

Why did teachers always like to make the new kid read aloud? Did they think it would make the other students accept us? Because, really, it just made everyone look at you like the new school freak you were.

"Um, I don't know where you were." Lamest excuse ever.

"No problem," Mr. Ryan said. "We are in chapter nine. Um, Mr. Milton, will you please show Ms. Smith the correct page and passage?"

The redhead sitting next to me leaned over and took my book, opening it to the page. He pointed to a paragraph. "There."

"Thanks." I wanted to sink into my seat and die of humiliation.

Not only was I the new girl who had interrupted class, but now I had to read out loud. The girls in the front row glared at me. Thanks to me, they wouldn't get to listen to Mr. Ryan's hypnotic voice anymore. I cleared my throat and began reading, eager to get this over with.

"*He put the glass to his lips, and drank at one gulp. A cry followed; he reeled, staggered, clutched at the table and held on, staring with injected eyes, gasping with open mouth; and as I looked there came, I thought, a change—he seemed to swell—his face became suddenly black and the features seemed to melt and alter—and at the next moment, I had sprung to my feet and leaped back against the wall, my arm raised to shield me from that prodigy, my mind submerged in terror.*

"'*O God!' I screamed, and 'O God!' again and again; for there before my eyes—pale and shaken, and half fainting, and groping before him with his hands, like a man restored from death—there stood Henry Jekyll!*"

I stopped, unable to read any more. It was too familiar, and not because I'd read it before. It was too familiar, because it was *me*. Or at least it could've described what was happening to me. Restored from death, pale and shaken, gasping with open mouth. It was what happened to me before…I stole the life from someone.

"Ms. Smith, is everything okay?" Mr. Ryan looked sympathetically at me.

"I-I'm sorry." I let the book fall from my hands and ran from the room. I tried to ignore the whispers of the other students. I had no idea where the girls' bathroom was, so I kept running. I found a stairwell first and decided that was a good enough place to hide. I flung open the door and ran down to the landing in the middle of the stairs. I sat down and buried my face in my knees. Life wasn't supposed to be this hard, was it? I'd thought after having cancer, nothing would be difficult. Didn't the universe owe me something? Or was this my punishment for giving in to what I'd become? For taking human life instead of letting my own drain out of me?

The bell rang, forcing me to wipe my tears and get up before I was trampled by hundreds of students rushing to their next class. I checked my schedule. French? How had I not noticed that before? I'd never taken French. I contemplated going to the guidance office and telling them there was a mistake. But they'd check my records—well, Samantha Smith's records—and see there wasn't any mistake. I wasn't going to figure this out in the three minutes between classes, so I headed in the direction I thought French was in.

I turned the corner and bumped into a girl with a stud in her nose. "Watch it!" she yelled, giving me the evil eye.

"Sorry." I found my classroom at the same time the late bell rang. Just great. I was going to have to enter the second room of the day with all eyes on me. I was reaching for the doorknob when I felt the first tightness in my lungs.

No! Not again! Not here! I turned and scanned the hallway. It was empty. Through the window in the door, I saw the teacher notice me and walk toward me. I took off, running back down the hall the way I'd come. I had to get away from everyone before I could take another life. It registered what that would mean. I'd die. Again.

Still, I pushed my legs forward, feeling the wobbliness creeping up them. I was losing control of my body. I managed to make it to the stairwell again, slumping forward as I pushed the door open. I fell to the floor. I was trapped. Too weak to pull the door back open or climb up the stairs. This was how it would end. My lungs tightened, making me sputter and cough. I watched my fingernails turn blue as my body went cold. "Ethan." I wished I could see his face one last time, but at least this was the end. I would rather die than kill again.

The door opened behind me, and a guy nearly tripped over me. "Whoa!" He caught himself before he fell on top of me. I tried to back away, to keep him from touching me, but I couldn't move.

"Hey, do you need the nurse?"

I couldn't speak or even shake my head, and I cringed as he stepped closer. I had to warn him to stay back. Not to touch me.

"Come on. I'll take you to her." He bent down next to me. "Do you think you can walk if I help you?"

I felt the warmth radiating from his body. His leg was right next to my side, and I could feel it warming my hip. He reached for my hand.

"No," I choked out.

He must have thought I was answering his question, because he said, "Okay, I think I can carry you."

Before I could even attempt to protest, his arm wormed its way under my shoulders. My chest didn't feel so tight anymore, and I tried to resist the urge to touch him as he scooped me into his arms. I stared at the artery in his neck. With every pulse, it called out to me. My fingers had a mind of their own and were working their way, crawling up the guy's shirt. They found his neck and rested on his artery.

"Wow, you're freezing cold," he said.

I begged my brain to fight against my movements, to regain control, but my other hand was tugging at the guy's shirt.

"Am I hurting you?" He repositioned me in his arms.

My hand found his skin and worked its way to his chest. The guy started to say something, but a pained look came over his face. I closed my eyes as his life flowed into me. He wobbled and fell to his knees, but I held on. *I* was holding *him* up now. Slowly I was returning to normal, and he was dying. Desire to live compelled me to hold on. Only one of us would survive. The monster within said it would be me.

After a minute, I felt the heat leave his body. He was dead. I opened my eyes, horrified at the disfigured face inches from mine. He was wrinkled and withered. No one would mistake him for a high-school student. He looked about ninety years old. I'd done it again, and this time it was a kid my own age. I was so disgusted with myself I wanted to vomit. But the hideous creature I'd become forced me to move him before someone found us. Between teachers on hall duty and the cop who patrolled the halls, this place had security all over it. It wouldn't be long before someone came. Suddenly being the new kid who freaked and ran out of English lit seemed pretty good. I'd never be able to explain what had happened here.

I reached my arms around the guy and lifted him by his armpits. Immediately I could tell I wasn't strong enough to carry him out of here. Stealing a person's life didn't make you superhuman. A monster, yes, but not superhuman. I decided to slide him across the floor. There was an emergency exit behind us. It would set off an alarm, though, and I'd never be able to drag the body away before someone saw us.

I leaned him against the door while I thought about my options. This exit wasn't going to work, and no way could I drag the guy up the stairs. I went to the stairwell door, leading back to the hallway, and looked out it to see if the coast was clear. It wasn't.

The school cop was walking down the hall, and he was heading my way.

CHAPTER EIGHT

I LUNGED to the side to get out of view of the window in the door. I had to do something. Now! I rushed to the exit door, a plan already forming in my mind. No one would recognize this guy as a student. I searched his pockets for a wallet, identification of some sort. His school ID was in his back pocket. I took it, shoving it into my jeans. I looked around for something to break the glass on the door. I had to make it look like this guy was breaking into the school.

I remembered seeing a fire extinguisher on the landing. I sprinted up to it and used the little metal bar meant to break the glass in case of an emergency. This definitely was an emergency. I grabbed the fire extinguisher, careful not to cut myself on the glass, and rushed back down the stairs. I peeked out the window. The cop was only a few doors down the hall. I ran at the emergency exit and rammed the end of the fire extinguisher into the glass. It took a few tries, but I managed to break it. And with the help of the handle, I was able to pull some glass shards so they fell on my side of the door. Maybe that would make it look like the window was smashed from the outside. I used my shoulder to open the exit door. The alarm blared in my ear. Definitely loud enough to give an old man a heart attack.

I took off back up the stairs, pausing only long enough to put the fire extinguisher back in the case. I ran the rest of the way up the stairs and waited behind the door. I was sure there would be an announcement the second the cop found the guy.

The alarm stopped, and the PA system crackled on. "Attention all students, faculty, and staff. The school is going into lock down. Any students in the halls should report to the nearest classroom."

The announcement repeated, and I walked to the nearest room. Oh crap! Mr. Ryan's class. I knocked on the door.

"Ms. Smith?" Mr. Ryan looked at me like he'd seen a girl who'd committed social suicide. Even he knew I was off to a bad start here. "Come in, come in. I was about to lock the door."

"Sorry. I was in the bathroom when I heard the announcement."

"No problem. I guess this is turning out to be some first day for you, huh?"

The girl sitting in the desk by the door stuck her foot out and tripped me as I walked by. "Walk much?" she said with a laugh so nasty I wanted to smack her. If only she knew who she was dealing with. If only she saw my Mr. Hyde.

"You okay?" Mr. Ryan asked me after he told the class to push the desks to the back of the room and away from the door.

"Yeah." Only I wasn't okay. My victim count was up to three. I'd never be okay again.

I took an empty seat. Mr. Ryan looked around the room and smiled at us, probably trying to keep the class calm. Everyone was on edge since the announcement, and they didn't have a clue that the real danger was in the room with them.

We were stranded in the room for another forty minutes. Mr. Ryan finally gave up and let us talk or do homework. Since I didn't have a friend in the class or any homework to speak of, I sat there trying not to think about what was going on downstairs—what the police would find. I'd tried to keep my fingerprints off the emergency exit. But there was the broken glass on the fire-extinguisher case, and my fingerprints were all over that. Someone was bound to notice the broken glass case sooner or later.

The PA system crackled to life. "All students are to report to lunch. Sophomores report to the multipurpose room. Juniors and seniors report to the cafeteria. Lunch will be served in both locations. All teachers and staff not assigned to cafeteria duty, please report to the auditorium for a mandatory meeting."

After the announcement repeated—because apparently they liked to say everything twice around here—Mr. Ryan unlocked the door. "Everyone to the cafeteria please. I don't know what happened, but I suggest none of you cause any trouble. Do as you were instructed."

Nods went around the room. People listened to Mr. Ryan. I was the last one to leave.

"Oh, Ms. Smith." Mr. Ryan followed me out of the room. "I hope tomorrow's a better day. Don't judge us just yet, okay?"

I nodded. So far the school hadn't done anything wrong. I had. The freak-out in class over the book we were reading, the fire alarm—they were my doing. And neither of those compared to the corpse in the stairwell.

I went to my locker, thinking maybe Ethan would meet me there before lunch. I'd grabbed a copy of *Dr. Jekyll and Mr. Hyde* from Mr. Ryan's class on my way out, so I actually had something to put in my locker this time. It took me a minute to remember the combination. My hands shook, and my mind was spinning. I kept trying my old combination, from my old life. Who would've thought I'd miss my old life? But I did. Sure, the cancer had made things rough, awful even, but right now, I would've taken that over whatever this was. I'd rather be the one hurting than hurting other people.

I finally got my locker open, and the first thing I saw was a silver necklace hanging from the hook. I reached for it, surprised by its weight. It looked heavy, but it wasn't. It was a spiderweb pattern, and in the center was a ruby, just like my ring. I'd forgotten about my ring. I had to ask Ethan when he thought we could drive out to his storage box and get it. I really missed wearing it.

I looked around for Ethan, expecting him to jump out and surprise me…again. The necklace was the first surprise. But since Ethan didn't seem to be around, I put the necklace on myself. It felt oddly warm against my skin. After all, it had been hanging in a cold, empty locker. Ethan must have had it in his pocket before he snuck it in here. He amazed me sometimes. I didn't even think he'd seen my locker combination on my schedule. He was sneaky, and I loved him for it.

I was so happy about my gift that I almost forgot about what was going on in the school. A teacher carrying a walkie-talkie started ushering kids out of the hall. "Get to where you're supposed to be."

His voice was stern. "Seniors report to the cafeteria. If you're not a senior, you have no business in this wing as it is, so move!"

I couldn't wait for Ethan any longer. Maybe he'd already been sent to the cafeteria. That would explain why he hadn't met me. I closed my locker and followed the crowd. I hadn't seen the cafeteria yet, so I didn't know how to get there on my own. For once, it felt nice to feel like I was part of the crowd, blending in, even if just on the outside.

We headed to a stairwell on the back side of the school—nowhere near the stairwell where… The hall monitors had those stairs blocked off. We were like cattle being herded. I stepped down the last stair when someone shoved me from behind. I fell forward, grabbing on to the backpack of the guy in front of me to avoid falling on my face.

"Hey." He whirled around.

"Sorry." I regained my composure, and a girl stepped in front of me, blocking my path. I recognized her as the one who'd tripped me in Mr. Ryan's class. Not what I needed right now.

She looked me up and down and scoffed. "You know, Mr. Ryan was only being nice to you because he felt sorry for you. He can tell a loser when he sees one."

"I bet he's glad you sit by the door then, so he can get rid of you sooner at the end of class." I'd had enough. I wasn't letting this girl walk all over me.

She let out a guttural grunt and lunged at me, shoving me hard in the chest. I fell backward, hitting my tailbone on the bottom stair. Chants of "Fight, fight, fight!" rang out. I'd thought we were among the last people in the stairwell, but apparently news of a chick fight spreads quickly. Suddenly it seemed like half the school was there.

"Hey!" someone yelled, and most of the kids scattered. I figured it was the principal or something. A trip to the office would make my horrific day pretty much complete. "Ms. Tilby, report to Mr. Snyder's office. Now."

I looked up to see Mr. Ryan standing two stairs behind me. Oh, this wasn't going to ease things between me and the ultimate fighter chick over here.

"But, Mr. Ryan, she—"

"I saw the whole thing, Ms. Tilby, and I'll be having a discussion with Mr. Snyder as well. You better make sure our stories match, or you'll find yourself suspended for a week instead of three days."

Suspended? I closed my eyes and sighed. This girl was going to kill me the next time she saw me.

"Ugh!"

"Shannon," Mr. Ryan said. She calmed down at the sound of her name, and I wondered if Mr. Ryan had called her by her first name on purpose. From what I'd seen, he always addressed people by last name.

Shannon glared at me one last time before heading for the office. I used the railing to lift myself up. I never knew you could have a pulse in your tailbone, but mine was throbbing.

"Are you okay?" Mr. Ryan reached out a hand, like he was getting ready to catch me if I stumbled.

"Seems like you've had to ask me that a lot today. You must think I'm the weakest girl on the planet."

"Not at all. Like I told Ms. Tilby. I saw what happened between the two of you. I also heard what you both said."

Ugh, he'd heard me talking smack. I wondered how many days suspension that would get me. Maybe Gloria would let me work an extra shift on those days. We could use the money.

"Normally I don't encourage students to talk to each other in that manner, but seeing as you're having a rough first day, I think you handled yourself rather well. Most girls your age would've pushed her back after she shoved you, but you kept your cool."

That was me. Cool as a corpse.

"I think you should get to the cafeteria now. I have a meeting to get to. Actually, now I have two meetings to get to." He shook his head.

"Sorry about that."

"It wasn't your fault."

I nodded and walked through the doors. "Um, do you think you could tell the principal it was just a misunderstanding? If Shannon hates me, she'll make my life miserable."

"I can't lie." Mr. Ryan sighed. "But I'll let the principal know you would rather handle this yourself. He might go easier on her."

"Thanks. Could you tell me where the cafeteria is?"

"Turn right and go about halfway down the hall. It'll be on your right. You can't miss it. You'll hear it well before you get there. It gets pretty noisy, and with the extra crowd in there at once today, I'm sure it will be eardrum-shattering."

"Thanks again." I headed the rest of the way to the cafeteria on my own.

Mr. Ryan was right. The noise coming from the cafeteria was intense. And without even stepping inside, I knew what everyone was talking about. The alarm, what could have caused it, who was to blame. Who knew I'd become so popular on the first day of school?

I pulled the door open and was met by the stern stare of a teacher. "What took you so long?" she asked.

"Um, I'm new." I hoped that would work. "I didn't know where the cafeteria was and then there was—"

"Was what?" she prodded.

"A problem in the hallway, but Mr. Ryan took care of it for me."

"Mr. Ryan? And what's your name, so I can verify this with him later?"

"Sam. I mean, Samantha Smith."

She took a pen out of her pocket and jotted my name down on a small slip of paper on the table next to her. "Very well. Go find a seat."

I moved away from her, not wanting to be within sight of her glaring eyes. I didn't see Ethan anywhere, and the longer I roamed around, the more attention I drew. Finally, I decided to get on the lunch line. I had a little money on me from my tips yesterday. Most of it was in a shoebox in my closet, but I brought some in case lunch wasn't too disgusting. The line was winding down at this point. That was one perk to being late. I grabbed a red plastic tray and some plastic ware. I saw they had salad, so at least something was edible. I took a big serving in case the hot food item was meatloaf or something equally rubbery and inedible.

When I got to the hot food station, I was glad I'd taken the extra salad. The woman behind the counter stood there with her ladle in one hand and a glove on the other. "Meatloaf and hot biscuits?"

"No, thank you. I'm fine with a salad." I grabbed an apple sitting in a fruit bowl by the register, but that didn't appease her either. "I guess I'll take a biscuit, too."

"$2.50," the cashier said.

I gave her the money and followed the line back into the cafeteria. Now I had to find Ethan because I wasn't sitting alone to eat my pathetic lunch.

I decided to walk around the edge of the cafeteria, thinking Ethan would be at the end of a table, since he didn't know anyone either. I passed six rows of tables and still no Ethan. I turned the corner and walked up the side rows. Finally, I heard my name. I turned around and saw Ethan walking toward me.

"Hey, where have you been? I tried to stop by your locker, but they wouldn't let us go down the hall. They sent us straight here. I've been looking for you everywhere." He took me by the arm and led me to a table in the middle of the cafeteria.

I wasn't sure if I should tell him about the incident with Shannon and Mr. Ryan, but I didn't get the chance to because I was assaulted with a chorus of "hello" from a bunch of kids sitting at Ethan's table.

"This is Sam," Ethan said.

How had he made this many friends already? And wasn't he in honors classes? These kids didn't look like your typical brainy honor student types.

"I met these guys in Sculpture & Design."

I had a hard time not choking on my salad. Ethan was the least artistic person I knew. He'd never pass a sculpture class.

I smiled at everyone and leaned toward Ethan. "How do you plan on pulling that off?" I whispered.

He took a sip of bottled water. "No problem. I told them I was big into abstract art at my old school. I made a bunch of weird-looking stuff, and they all thought it was genius. Even the teacher."

Ethan was fitting into his new life with no problems, and really, he should've had the more difficult time trying to live up to the real Ethan Jones's standards. My life should have been the easy one. Average student with no extracurricular talents. Piece of cake. But my day had sucked. Sucked the life right out of... No. I'd lose it if I thought about that guy.

I sighed, and the necklace wobbled a little, warming my skin where it touched. Okay, one part of my day hadn't sucked. I had a beautiful new necklace from the best boyfriend I could ask for.

I leaned over and kissed Ethan's cheek. "Thank you for my necklace. It's beautiful. It's going to match my ring perfectly when we get it from the storage place."

Ethan pulled back. "What necklace?"

I elbowed him. "The one you left in my locker." I smiled and held it up for him to see how much I loved it.

He narrowed his eyes. "Sam, I didn't leave that in your locker."

"Yes, you did. I found it before I came here. You must have put it there between classes to surprise me." As I said it, I realized it couldn't have been Ethan, or I wouldn't have to explain this to him.

"It wasn't me, Sam."

"Then who?" I looked down at the necklace, the perfect match for the ring Ethan had given me.

"That's what I'd like to know."

CHAPTER NINE

I RAN through all the possibilities in my head. The office had assigned me to the wrong locker. Some guy left the necklace for his girlfriend, but he mixed up the locker number. No, he wouldn't have known the combination if the locker number was wrong.

"There must be a mistake. That locker must belong to someone else." But it had been empty. That seemed odd, but it was possible whoever owned the locker wasn't big on studying. No, the locker would be filled with books if that were the case. Nothing was adding up.

"Maybe you have a secret admirer." Ethan looked around as if he was going to spot some guy staring at me.

"I doubt it. So far, I've only made enemies." And a corpse. I shook the thought from my mind. "The only guy who's been nice to me is a teacher, and I'm sure the necklace isn't from Mr. Ryan."

"Did I hear you say Mr. Ryan?" the girl across from me asked. "Hi, I'm Beth. I have Mr. Ryan for English lit last period. He's a major hottie." Her cheeks flushed, which didn't really help my case.

Ethan eyed me.

"It's not from him," I assured him. "I just met him, and he has no idea where my locker is."

Ethan went back to eating, but I could almost see his mind working, trying to make sense of the situation. "Are you going to keep it on?"

I hadn't thought about it. I really did love the necklace, but if it was meant for someone else, I had to return it. Only how did I return something if I had no idea where it came from?

"I'll ask around, you know, with the girls who have lockers near mine, and see if any of them know who it belongs to or who it was meant for."

"But in the meantime, you're going to wear it?" He hated the idea. That was clear.

Still, I didn't want to take the necklace off. It felt so warm against my skin, and it was my birthstone. "I think I should keep it on. That way, people will see it, and if the person who left it in my locker sees it, they'll let me know it's theirs and that leaving it in my locker was a mistake."

Ethan gave me a look that said he didn't quite believe me, but he didn't push the subject. Instead, he passed me his water bottle. "You forgot to get yourself a drink."

"Thanks." I ate my lunch, trying to avoid Ethan's gaze, which was fixated on my necklace. I didn't see how he could be jealous. So someone messed up and left it in the wrong locker. It obviously wasn't meant for me.

At the end of lunch, the PA system came on again. "All students are dismissed for the day. Please proceed to your assigned buses. Students who drive to school should leave campus immediately."

"What's that about?" Ethan asked.

"Didn't you hear?" Beth leaned across the table. "Someone tried to break into the school. That's what the lock down was about. The only reason they didn't dismiss us sooner was because they had to wait for the buses. There was a big accident that closed the road to the school. I guess the police checked the building and deemed it safe, so they sent us to lunch in the meantime."

"How do you know all this?" Everyone had been in the class-rooms. How could she know about the break-in—or what I'd tried to make look like a break-in?

Beth shrugged. "The alarm. Only the emergency exits make that sound. So, either someone tried to break out or someone tried to break in. If a student was running out of the building, the principal wouldn't have ordered a lock down. That has to mean someone tried to get into the school today."

It had been a while since I'd been in an actual school, so my knowledge of lock down drills was rusty at best. But to everyone else, it was probably obvious. That was what I wanted, but I wasn't ready to face all of this yet. Not that I ever would be ready.

Ethan put his arm around my shoulder as we walked out to his car. "Bad first day?"

"You could say that."

"Want to tell me about it?"

I got in the car and leaned my head back on the seat. "Not really. Let's just go to work. I'm sure Gloria will let us pick up the extra hours."

I was right. Gloria was happy to see us. The lunch crowd hadn't died down yet, so I threw on an apron and got right to work.

"You're a peach." Gloria slumped down on a stool at the counter. "I need a minute to rest my legs."

"No problem. I've got it covered." Work was the distraction I needed. I could forget about school. Forget about the mystery necklace. Forget about…my Hyde side and what it was capable of.

I placed orders as fast as Gloria's husband Jackson could cook. Actually faster.

"Samantha, if you don't slow down out there, Gloria's going to have a fit. The customers will expect the service to always be this speedy, and her legs can't handle it. Not to mention I can't cook this quickly."

Gloria and Jackson seemed like the cutest couple ever. They bickered, but everyone knew it was all in good fun. Yesterday, the customers had loved it. I swore Gloria and Jackson staged arguments just to get the customers to stay longer and spend more money. I could picture them at home each night scripting the arguments for the next day.

"I'll slow down, Jackson. I'm just working off some pent-up energy from today."

"Come sling some burgers for me then. That'll work off the energy."

I laughed and grabbed the order for table seven. "I could, but that would mean Gloria would be back to serving tables by herself.

Do you want me to tell her you're recruiting me?" I smiled at him, already knowing the answer.

Jackson rolled his eyes. "The last thing I need right now is that woman's wrath. Off with you." He shooed me out of the kitchen, and for a brief moment, I felt normal. This place had that effect on me. Or rather, Jackson and Gloria did.

"Did that man have you doing work for him in there?" Gloria asked the second I came out of the kitchen.

I shook my head. "He told me I was working too fast. The orders are piling up on him."

Gloria sighed. "Ethan, honey."

Ethan put the tub of dirty dishes down on the cart by the kitchen door. "Yeah?"

"Why don't you go see if you can help Jackson in the kitchen?" It wasn't a question, more like an order. "Samantha and I can bus our own tables for a while."

"Sure." He gave my elbow a quick squeeze before he left.

I headed back to the counter, which was filled with new customers. Most of them were younger, and I realized that school closing early had a lot to do with the sudden rush. I guess no one else ate the school's meatloaf either.

Most of the students didn't even look at me. To them, I was just another employee to wait on them. I filled soda after soda and put in six more burger orders. I wiped a spot clean at the end of the counter and pocketed my one-dollar tip. Immediately, the seat filled up again.

"Seriously?" I mumbled.

"Is this seat taken?"

I looked up to see the girl from yesterday. The one who'd caught me freaking out in the bathroom after I'd seen a glimpse of what Herman's future would've been if…

"Huh? Oh, no. Have a seat."

She raised an eyebrow at me. She was already sitting.

"What can I get you to drink?" I placed a menu in front of her.

"Coffee."

"Black, right?"

"Only way to drink it."

I poured her some coffee and set it in front of her. "I'll be back to take your order in a minute. I have to go check on another table."

"I'm not eating."

"Oh, okay." Great. She was taking up counter space and not ordering a meal. More tips down the drain.

I rushed around and, in another hour, things calmed down. Ethan stayed in the kitchen. Last time I got an order, he said he was having a blast with Jackson. Gloria said he could continue working in the kitchen and just help with cleanup at the end of the night. You would've thought she was offering him a two-week paid vacation. He was overjoyed.

I refilled the coffee girl's cup seven times. Seven! She was a bottomless caffeine junkie.

"Can I get you anything else?" I asked, trying to drop the hint that she was abusing the free-refill policy.

"Nope."

"Fine." I noticed the saltshaker was empty, so I unscrewed the cap and got the big container of salt to refill it.

"What are you doing?" The girl sounded horrified, as if I was maiming a puppy right in front of her.

"My job." I couldn't keep the annoyance out of my voice.

"Do you have to do that where I'm sitting? You might get salt in my coffee. I paid for this, you know."

I slammed the salt shaker down and glared at her. "No, you didn't. You haven't gotten your bill yet. And that cup is free, just like the six other free refills you've gotten."

Gloria came out of the kitchen and gave me a look. I waved her off, letting her know I was fine. I knew this girl was a customer, and I was supposed to treat her nicely, but I was wiped, and she was getting on my nerves.

"Listen, it's been a long day, and I'm tired. If it bothers you that much, I'll go refill the salt at the other end of the counter."

She glared at me for a second, and then her eyes fell on my necklace. "Where did you get that?"

I touched the necklace, feeling its warmth on my hand. I'd forgotten I was still wearing it. I'd tucked it under my shirt to keep it safe while I worked, but it must have slipped out at some point.

"I found it in my locker at school today. I don't think it was meant for me, though." I shrugged. "The funny thing is, it's my birthstone, and it matches a ring my boyfriend gave me."

"A ring?"

Why was I telling her all this? I didn't even like her. "Never mind." I took the salt and moved to the other end of the counter.

She got up and followed me, sitting down in the seat in front of me.

"What gives? I thought you didn't want me refilling the salt and getting it in your coffee? I moved away from you, so why did you follow me?"

"Forget the salt." She moved back a little. Apparently she really disliked salt. "Tell me about the necklace and the ring."

"Why?"

"Because I like jewelry."

I looked her over. She wasn't wearing any jewelry. None. She was in a simple green dress, like the other day. How many green dresses did she own?

"Why aren't you wearing any then?"

"Huh?"

"Jewelry. If you love it so much, why aren't you wearing any?"

She looked down, avoiding my eyes. "None of it goes with green."

That was the lamest excuse I'd ever heard. "Whatever." I finished refilling the salt and went to check on the coffee pot.

"I'll take another cup," the girl said.

"Really?" I whipped my head around to look at her. "How do you not have to pee by now?"

She laughed. "I drink this much coffee all the time. I'm used to it."

It was odd to hear her laugh, but at the same time, it was nice.

"What's your name?" I asked.

"Why do you want to know?"

"I served you eight cups of coffee—no, make that nine." I poured her another. "I think that deserves a name."

"What's yours?"

Was she always this much of a control freak? "Sam."

"Nora."

"Is that a family name? You don't hear of many Noras these days."

"Says the with girl with a guy's name, *Sam*." She emphasized my name, making it sound more masculine than I could've imagined.

"I was never a big fan of Samantha."

"My grandmother's name was Lenora Prudence." She rolled her eyes, and I didn't need to ask what her full name was.

I nodded, wishing she'd finish her coffee and leave. I'd had my fill of her for the day. Maybe two days.

"So, about that necklace." She pointed to it.

"I already told you. I found it in my locker. I thought my boyfriend put it there, but he didn't. Can I get you your check?"

"Who gave it to you then?"

"I don't know. I don't think it was meant for me. It was a mistake or something. Was that a yes for the check?"

"But you said it's your birthstone, so why would you think it was a mistake?" She ignored my question again.

"Because I don't know anyone else at school. I just moved here." I tore her bill from my pad and slammed it on the counter.

"I'd like another cup," Nora said.

"Don't you think you're taking advantage now?"

"What do you mean?"

"The people who run this place are really nice, and you're drinking all their coffee for a measly $1.75. That's pretty crappy."

"Okay, I'll tell you what. I'll pay my bill if you take off that necklace."

I wrinkled my brow. What a weird thing to say. "Why do you care if I'm wearing this necklace?"

"What's the big deal? You said it wasn't meant for you, so take it off."

"No." I suddenly felt very defensive.

"Fine," she said. "I need to use the restroom."

"Fine." I matched her tone. "Then you can settle your bill," I called after her.

I took her cup of coffee and dumped it into the tub of dirty dishes. I was cutting her off. I wanted her gone. I started cleaning the counter, trying to wipe away any trace of Nora and her strangeness.

After a while, she still hadn't come out of the bathroom. I stormed in there, ready to demand she pay up and leave.

"That's enough, Nora. You owe me money." I flung the bathroom door open.

The bathroom was empty.

CHAPTER TEN

AFTER Nora's little disappearing act, I was really pissed off. She hadn't paid her bill *or* left me a tip. I couldn't get her off my mind all evening. And her wanting me to take the necklace off only made me want to keep it on more. I tucked it under my pajama top and slept with it on. And for the first time since I'd come back to life, I slept soundly. No visions. No bad thoughts. Nothing. The warmth of the ruby on my skin lulled me to sleep, and I didn't wake up until my alarm went off.

I thought Ethan was still sleeping when I got dressed, but as I pulled my shirt over my head he said, "You slept with that on?"

I jumped and tugged my shirt into place. Ethan sat up in bed, staring at me, waiting for an answer. "I guess I forgot to take it off last night."

"You didn't shower with it on, did you?"

I shrugged. "Kind of. Why?"

"It's weird. You have no idea where it came from, yet you're hanging on to it, keeping it close to you at all times."

I knew it was weird, but I felt different with the necklace on. I felt more alive. More like Jekyll and less like Hyde. "Look." I sat down on the bed and took his hands in mind. "I don't have the ring you gave me, and ever since I found the duplicate in that wooden box under the sink, I can't stop thinking about it. This necklace," I reached up and touched it, "reminds me of that ring. It reminds me of *you*."

As I said it, I realized how true it was. I felt stronger with the necklace on because I felt like I had Ethan with me at all times. It was crazy because the necklace wasn't even from Ethan, but that was how I felt—rational or not. Right now, I needed strength to fight whatever it was that was wrong with me.

Ethan touched my cheek. "Why do you need a necklace to remind you of me when you have me? In the flesh." He kissed me softly.

I stared into his eyes, wishing I could tell him everything. Spill my guts and let him know why I was acting so strange. But I couldn't break his heart like that.

"Yesterday was…tough. Nothing's the same. I don't have any friends here. I'm pretending to be someone I'm not." I stopped when I saw the hurt expression on his face. "I'm glad I'm back. I'm glad I have a second chance with you, and I can't thank you enough for everything you've done to make sure we can have this life together. Things are great when we're together." I looked down, watching the sunlight reflect off the ruby. "But you can't always be with me."

Ethan sighed and nodded. "Okay. If it means that much to you, then wear it." He lifted my chin so I was staring him in the eyes. "But we're going to that storage facility tomorrow morning. We'll get your ring, and then you can find the real owner of that necklace and give it back."

I smiled. "Deal."

"And as for making friends, we haven't even had one full day of school yet. Give yourself time. Besides, I think you and Beth kind of hit it off yesterday at lunch."

Beth. She was the one who'd figured out what happened with the alarm and the lockdown. She seemed nice enough, but if she could piece together yesterday's incident that quickly, she wasn't someone I wanted to get too close to.

Day two of school was almost as bad as day one. I didn't kill anyone, so I considered that a vast improvement, but no one seemed to want to talk to me. I found out why pretty quickly. Shannon Tilby. Looking at her, I never would've thought she'd be the popular type. She was a bitch with a capital B, but that's where her source of power came from. Everyone was afraid of her. So whatever she said, went.

Thanks to Mr. Ryan and me, the principal reduced Shannon's punishment to a week's worth of detention, but she was still out to get me. She started a rumor that I was after Mr. Ryan. Yuck. He was cute for a teacher, but that was just it. He was a teacher, and he was like thirty-two or something. Ancient. He was the kind of teacher you liked because he wasn't all wrinkly and didn't smell like old cheese. But of course all the girls believed Shannon, and that meant lots of angry looks and mumbled insults in class and the hallways.

Even Mr. Ryan seemed strange around me, and I couldn't help wondering if the rumor had gotten back to him. If that were the case, he'd probably avoid me out of fear of losing his job. There went my one ally. And worse yet, Shannon was in my class. Apparently she really had been in the girls' bathroom—the excuse *I'd* used—when the announcement was made. That was the only reason why she'd been in Mr. Ryan's second period. How I hadn't noticed her in my class yesterday, I didn't know.

After English, I went straight to the guidance office to beg Mrs. Melrose to change my schedule. She refused to switch my English lit class, so I focused on French.

"Please, I can't take French this year. I was doing terribly in it at my old school, and if I fail, my parents will kill me." That sounded normal enough.

"I'm sorry, Ms. Smith, but according to your records, you were maintaining a C average in French. That's hardly failing. I see no immediate reason to change your schedule."

"I cheated," I blurted out in a fit of desperation. "At my old school. I copied off the girl who sat in front of me. I thought she was a straight A student, but it turned out she didn't do as well in French. See, I didn't even cheat well. I'll flunk on my own."

Mrs. Melrose shook her head. "Do you realize you just admitted to cheating?"

I nodded and lowered my head. "I feel awful about it, which is why I'm telling you. Please." I leaned forward, placing both hands on her desk and putting my sad, pleading eyes right in her face. "Isn't there an opening in any other class that period? Sculpture maybe?" Ethan's class.

Mrs. Melrose sighed and shook her head again, but she typed something into her computer. "There's one spot open."

"Oh, thank you!" I practically jumped up and down I was so relieved.

"But Sculpture is an honors art elective. According to your records, you've never taken an honors course. You may be worse off than if you stayed in French."

"I'll work really hard. I'm interested in art, and I know a few students who take it. I'm sure I could get one of them to tutor me if I need it." I wasn't sure why Mrs. Melrose was so worried. How tough could Sculpture be, even if it was honors? Ethan was pulling it off.

"You'll need both the teacher's signature and a parent signature on this form to okay the schedule change." She handed me a form.

"Done." I smiled back at her. Forging a signature would be no problem.

"You may report to Sculpture & Design for the remainder of the period, but I need this form signed and returned to me on Monday, or you'll be back in French. Understood?"

"Understood. Thank you." I took my permission form and ran out of the office before Mrs. Melrose could change her mind. Sculpture & Design was on the first floor, around the corner from the cafeteria. I had planned to meet Ethan at lunch since French was on the other side of the building from the cafeteria, and I wanted to go to my locker in between periods. I decided to go to my locker now. After yesterday's glimpse at the food selection in this place, I'd bagged my lunch—a turkey and cheese sandwich Ethan had made me at the diner last night.

I took the back staircase. I still couldn't go near the other one. Everyone was talking about the break-in. The guy hadn't been identified yet. I wasn't surprised. His ID was at the cottage in my jeans, not that he looked anything like his school picture anymore.

I tried to force the thought from my mind. I had to focus on being normal. Instinctively, my hand went to the necklace. I held it as I opened my locker. I slipped my copy of *The Strange Case of Dr. Jekyll and Mr. Hyde* inside and grabbed my lunch. When I pulled it out, I saw there was a yellow Post-it note stuck to it.

The necklace suits you. Wear it always.

I looked around the hall as if I expected to find someone watching me, waiting for me to get the note. But I was alone. The necklace wasn't left in my locker by mistake. Someone had given it to me.

Someone who had seen me wearing it today. Was it a student from English class? Or was it someone who had a locker near mine? Either way, Ethan wasn't going to like this. At all.

I crumpled the note as I shut my locker. I found the nearest trash can and got rid of the note. Ethan didn't need to know. It would only upset him, and that was the last thing I wanted to do. No, *the* last thing I wanted to do was kill someone else, and the necklace was making me strong enough to avoid doing that. I knew it was.

I hurried to Sculpture, eager to get there before the class ended, but as it turned out, the bell rang as I stepped into the room with my permission slip. Ethan came to meet me at the teacher's desk.

"What are you doing here?"

"Transferring out of French. There's an opening."

"And you are?" asked the extremely artsy-looking woman teaching the class. Her hair was jet black with a blue streak down the back, and her dress was the deepest emerald green. It stopped at the knee, which was where her black lace-up leather boots came to. And her nails! They were black with silver stars painted on each one. This woman definitely wasn't your typical high-school teacher.

"I'm Samantha Smith." I still wasn't used to the sound of my new name. "Mrs. Melrose said I could transfer into this class. I just need your signature on this form before I have my parents sign it."

"Are you an art major?"

Major? This was high school. Who had a major? "Um, I'm very interested in the class, and I think I'd like to pursue a degree in art in college," I lied.

"She's my girlfriend," Ethan said. "I've seen her artwork. It's amazing."

The lies were piling up, and I hoped no one was keeping track of the stories we were telling because they didn't line up. We'd need to work on that before someone figured out the truth.

"I see. Well, if you are half as talented as Ethan, then I look forward to seeing your work this semester." She reached for my form and signed her name.

I glanced at it, wanting to thank her by name to pretend like I already knew who she was. "Thank you, Ms. Matthews."

"See you Monday."

Ethan draped his arm around my shoulder as we walked to the cafeteria. "This is great. Now we'll have two periods in a row together."

"My thoughts exactly."

We sat down at the same table, and I dug into my sandwich. Ethan had packed two sandwiches for himself, an Italian sub and a meatball sub. The guy was a bottomless pit, and he never gained an ounce. The thought made me picture his perfect abs again. I shoved my sandwich in my mouth to cover up the drool.

"So, did you hear?" Beth asked, taking a seat with her tray of unidentifiable food.

"Hear what?" Ethan said. "That Sam is going to be in our art class? It's awesome, right?"

"Cool." She smiled at me. "But that's not what I was talking about."

I tensed up, expecting Beth to say something about the guy from the stairwell. About the supposed break-in.

"Trevor is missing. He never went home after school yesterday."

"Who's Trevor?" Ethan asked with a mouthful of meatball sub.

"Trevor Davis. He's the star pitcher of the baseball team and one of the best running backs our football team has."

Ethan shrugged. "I don't know him."

I did. I'd been too chicken to look at his student ID, but as soon as Beth said Trevor's name, I knew who he was. My stomach lurched, and I put my sandwich down.

"You okay?" Ethan asked. "You look a little green." His eyes dropped to my sandwich. "Is the food making you feel sick? Jackson said the cold cuts were fresh." He picked up my sandwich and sniffed it.

"The sandwich is fine, but I don't feel so hot." More like cold. Stone cold. Deathly cold. Cold-blooded killer cold. I clutched my necklace like it would give me support.

"You want me to walk you to the nurse?"

"No. I'll be fine." I sipped my water, and Beth took that as her cue to continue.

"Anyway, Trevor never went home, and Shannon is, like, freaking out."

"Shannon?" I choked on my water. "Shannon who?"

"Tilby. According to her, she's *the* Shannon of the school. I heard from Angela that there was a sophomore named Shannon, but Shannon made her use her middle name instead."

"No way," Ethan said. "That can't be true."

He hadn't met Shannon Tilby. I didn't doubt she'd bully a sophomore like that.

"They had a date," Beth said. "Trevor was supposed to take her to this fancy restaurant. She told everyone about it. He never showed up. She called his cell, but he didn't answer. So, she drove to his house to ream him out in person, and his parents said he never came home from school. Turns out he left his cell at home, too, which is why he never answered."

"Did they call the cops?"

"Not yet. He's taken off like this before, so his parents are waiting a bit before they declare him missing," Beth said.

Ethan crumpled up the wrapper from his meatball sub. "Maybe he didn't want to go out with that Shannon chick, so he took off for a little while."

"Are you kidding me?" Beth's eyes bugged out. "No one bails on Shannon. It's social suicide."

"Maybe that's why he's not in school today. He knows he screwed up." Ethan dug into his Italian sub, not giving it much more thought. It was strange how he'd seemed to stop caring about other people. Not like him at all.

But I couldn't dismiss the Trevor issue. Sooner or later, the police would figure out the old man they'd found dead in the doorway was Trevor Davis. And when word got around school, Shannon would be devastated. She'd be angry. And even though she might not know I was to blame for Trevor's death, I had a feeling I'd be on the receiving end of her wrath anyway.

CHAPTER ELEVEN

THE rest of the school day was a blur. I went through the motions of attending class. Kids whispered thoughts about where Trevor could be. There was even a rumor that he ran off with Mrs. Wentworth, the school nurse, who happened to be absent both yesterday and today. I hadn't met her yet, but I heard she was fifty. If I wasn't dying inside knowing the truth, I would've found that one funny.

The end of the day couldn't come soon enough, and when the dismissal bell rang, I bolted out of history and ran to my locker. I still hadn't told Ethan about the note I found earlier, and I wasn't planning on telling him. I put my books in my locker and slammed it shut. I turned around, and Ethan was standing inches from my face.

"Whoa!" I jumped. "You scared me."

"Sorry." He kissed me before wrapping his arm around my shoulders and walking me out of the building to his car. "Was today any better?"

"A little. Getting out of French and into your art class was a definite plus."

"Yeah, and you seemed to be settling in with the guys at lunch. Beth really likes you. She told me in Spanish."

"That's nice." I tried to keep the worry out of my voice, but Beth was a threat to me. She knew too much about what went on at this school. I'd have to be extra careful around her.

We drove to the diner, and first thing, Jackson asked Ethan to work in the kitchen again. Ethan was delighted to get away from busing tables, and he was becoming quite the chef. Okay, not really. I mean, flipping burgers and making club sandwiches wasn't exactly a science, but it was good to see him happy. One of us needed to be.

I put my purse behind the counter and tied my apron around my waist.

"How was school?" Gloria asked, slipping me a piece of peach pie.

"Fine. What's this for?"

"I made it this morning. Thought you might like some since there's a lull in the crowd right now. I remember what those school lunches were like back in my day. I have a feeling they probably haven't gotten much better." Her face scrunched up in disgust.

"Um, actually, Ethan made me a sandwich last night. I hope that's okay. I didn't even think, but I should've paid for it. I'll pay for it now." I reached for my purse.

"You'll do no such thing." Gloria took my purse and put it back behind the counter. "I insist you pack your lunch from here every day. You got that? I'm not going to have you get sick eating the mush they pass off as food in that place. I need you here to help me. If that costs me lunch five days a week, then so be it. You can make up for it by taking a few of my tables."

I smiled. Having Gloria around was like working for my grandmother. She kept me well fed in exchange for doing work around the house—or, in this case, the diner. In a way she made it a little easier to be away from my family.

"You're the best, Gloria."

"I know. It's a curse." She playfully waved a dishcloth at me. "Now eat. I'm expecting the after-school crowd in about fifteen minutes."

I ate my pie and brewed a fresh pot of coffee. No sooner had I wiped the counter when a crowd of kids came in.

They sat in a big booth in the back corner, and they were loud. I recognized a few faces, but luckily I didn't see Shannon. I took a deep breath, grabbed a handful of menus, and walked over to their table.

"Hi, can I start you off with some drinks while you look over the menu?"

"Yeah, I'll have a root beer," the big guy in the varsity football jacket said.

The girl next to him smacked his arm. "Don't you dare order yet. Shannon's not here. She'll kill you if you get your drink before she does."

I rolled my eyes. Why did people hang out with Shannon if she was such a royal bitch?

"I'll come back." I turned and started walking away.

"No you won't."

I stopped and sighed. Shannon was here.

"I want a diet birch beer, and don't water it down with a bunch of ice. I only want six cubes. I said cubes, not crushed ice. Got it?"

I turned around to face her. "Sorry, we don't have diet birch beer. We have regular birch beer or diet cola. Take your pick. And as for the ice, it comes out of a machine. You get what you get."

She glared at me, and the vein in her forehead twitched. "I want to speak to your manager."

"Sure." I smiled and walked back to the counter, leaving Shannon standing there with her arms crossed.

"What are you smiling about?" Gloria asked. "That girl looks like she just gave you a mouthful."

"Oh, she did. She's a fun one, and she asked to speak with you. She wants to know why there's no diet birch beer and why I can't give her exactly six cubes of ice in her drink. I'm sure she'll have some choice words about my attitude, too."

"Snotty little high-school brat," Gloria mumbled before pasting a fake smile on her face and walking over to Shannon.

I pretended not to watch as I refilled coffee for a couple near the door, but it was hard not to stare. Gloria started off nice—for about a whole two seconds, because that was all Shannon gave her before she went off on a tirade about rude employees and not meeting the customer's needs.

Gloria let her rant for a minute before she put her hand up. "You can stop right there."

Shannon stepped back in shock. "Excuse me?"

"That's enough. I'm not going to have you come into my

establishment, making impossible demands, and insulting my best waitress—"

"If she's your best waitress, then this place has more problems than I thought."

"I'm not finished, so you shut your mouth, or I'll throw your size-zero behind right out that door. I have the right to refuse service to anyone, and right now, I'm refusing to serve you."

My smile was so wide I could've fit an entire slice of peach pie in my mouth. Ethan was peeking through the window on the kitchen door. The kids with Shannon stared in horror, waiting for Shannon's comeback.

"How dare you, you old hag!" Shannon was bright red, and she stepped toward Gloria.

Without thinking, I stormed over to her, grabbed her arm, and yanked her back. "Don't talk to Gloria that way. She told you to leave, so leave before I call the cops."

Shannon laughed in my face. "What, you think you're going to make me leave? I'll have you on the ground crying before you lay another finger on me. You have no idea who you're messing with."

Something inside me burst. Maybe it was pent-up anger, maybe it was petty girl-fight instincts, but I lost it. I wasn't about to throw down with Shannon and mess up the diner, so I hit her where it hurt most.

"I guess when the guy you like dumps you and the entire school finds out about it, the way you get over the humiliation is picking on someone who's old enough to be your mother." Really it was more like grandmother, but I didn't want to insult Gloria. It was Shannon I was trying to hurt.

"You bitch!" Shannon lunged for me, but Ethan was already out of the kitchen and pinning her arms behind her.

"That's it. You're out of here." He pushed her out the door and let it slam behind her. She turned around to face him, but he yelled through the glass. "Take one step toward this place, and I'll have the cops here before you can take a swing." He held up his cell to show he was serious.

Shannon screamed and stormed over to the window where her friends were sitting. She smacked the glass with her open palm to get their attention. "Let's go!"

"We haven't eaten yet," the big football player complained.

"Come on," the girl next to him said, obviously not happy about having to leave either.

They filed out, giving Ethan and me dirty looks in the process. Yup, I was officially going to have a crappy school year.

"Sorry," I said to Gloria. Now that it was over, what I'd said to Shannon registered. I couldn't believe I'd brought up Trevor. I really was a monster.

"You have nothing to be sorry about. That one there is a bad seed. There's nothing else to be said about it." Gloria turned to the customers who'd witnessed the outburst. "Free peach pie all around."

Smiles and nods let me know all was forgotten. Ethan kissed my forehead and headed back to the kitchen while I sliced up the pie. When everyone had a piece, I wiped down the booth where the kids had been, trying to erase all memory of them and Shannon.

The bell above the door jingled, and I looked up to see Nora. I followed her to the counter.

"You didn't pay your bill last time. I'm not serving you anything until you give me the $1.75 you owe Gloria for the coffee."

Nora reached in her purse and picked through her loose change until she had $1.75 exactly. No tip. Again. I grabbed the money and put it in the register. Then I purposely started refilling the saltshaker right in front of her.

Nora got up and moved two stools away from me. "Coffee. Black."

"In a minute. I'm busy." I continued to slowly pour the salt into the shaker.

"Do I need to throw her out, too?" Gloria asked. "This is bad for business, you know." By the look on her face, I could tell she wasn't going to put up with me not getting along with any more customers today.

"No. It's fine. She tried to stiff you on the bill last time. I made her pay up. I'll get her some coffee."

Gloria nodded and went into the kitchen.

I poured the coffee, not even caring that I was spilling it onto the saucer under the cup. Let Nora drip coffee on her green dress. Wow, another green dress. Did she own any other clothes?

"Here." I shoved the cup in front of her. "Let me guess, that's all you want."

"No, I want that necklace you're wearing." She sipped her coffee.

"What?" I stepped back. "Are you really going to start that again?"

"How much do you want for it?" She pulled a pile of bills out of her purse.

"You've got to be kidding me. You've cheated me out of a tip twice *and* skipped out on your bill, and you carry around a wad of cash like that?" I liked her less and less every time I saw her.

"I don't believe in banks. Now, how much for the necklace?"

"It's not for sale, but feel free to leave the tips you owe me."

"Everything is for sale. Name your price."

"If you're so eager to spend your money, why don't you go buy yourself another dress? Try a color other than green for a change."

"Fine." She stood up and walked out.

Gloria came out of the kitchen. "Did she leave without paying her bill again?"

Damn it! "I'm sorry."

"Samantha, I can't have customers skipping out on their checks. We'll all be out of jobs then."

"I know. I'll take the money out of my tips."

Gloria shook her head, looking disappointed, and walked over to the couple by the door.

The rest of the night was better. No more drama. Just a lot of drink refills, cleaning tables, and trying to get back on Gloria's good side. By the end of the night, she finally broke down and smiled at me.

"Go home. Get some sleep. Tomorrow's a new day." She sounded like a generic greeting card.

"I'm really sorry about earlier. It won't happen again." And if it did, I'd pay Nora's bill before Gloria noticed.

Ethan held my hand on the drive home, but he didn't turn up our driveway. He drove past it.

"Where are we going?"

"It's a surprise. You look like you could use a change of pace."

Actually, it was the change of pace in this new life that was throwing me. I needed the old Sam back. The one who didn't have a monster lurking inside her.

Ethan pulled onto a small, gravel area off the side of the road. He got out and met me at my door. "Come on." Reaching for my hand, he led me to a wooden fence. On the other side of it was a huge drop-off. We were on top of a mountain, looking out across the river.

"It's beautiful."

"I thought you'd like it." Ethan gently turned my face toward his and brushed his lips across mine. It was a sweet kiss, but there was something behind it. Desire.

I pulled back. "We're out in the open."

"It's dark."

"Until a car drives by."

Ethan sighed. "Sorry. It was a stupid idea. I just thought that, after the other night…"

"We could go home." I really wasn't ready to, and not because of what Ethan was suggesting. I didn't want to leave this view yet. "Or we can stay here for a while first."

"You like it?"

"Yeah. It reminds me of when I was six, and I used to go visit my aunt in Maryland. There weren't any mountains like this, but her house was on the water, and her backyard sloped down toward a dock. When I stood in her sun room and looked out over the water, I felt like I was flying. Like I was a bird and nothing could touch me."

"Then we'll stay, and you'll fly." He took my hand, kissing my fingertips.

Yes, Ethan was a typical guy who thought about sex, but he never let his own urges stand in the way of whatever I wanted. I leaned my head against his chest as I stared out over the water.

We stayed for two hours. I hadn't intended to be there that long, but between the view and being with Ethan, I was in heaven. I kept going back and forth between breathing in the fresh mountain air and breathing in Ethan. The boy was an amazing kisser.

Finally, we went home. Ethan moved one of the bigger rocks to the side. He hadn't had time to disassemble the strange rock circle yet, but it was pretty annoying having to step over the same rock every time we went in and out of the cottage. "I'll get the others in the morning," he said.

I got ready to shower while Ethan ate one of the sandwiches he'd brought home from the diner. Making out made him hungry. I turned the water all the way to hot and was pleasantly surprised that it was actually warm. Still not hot, but definitely not lukewarm either.

I got undressed and looked down at the necklace. Ethan was right. It was silly of me to shower and sleep with it on. But still, I didn't want to take it off. While the warm water washed down the drain without me, I debated. I decided I'd take it off to shower but put it back on afterward. Baby steps.

I undid the clasp and left it on the sink. I stepped into the shower and basked in the fact that I wasn't freezing cold. Maybe the pipes were getting used to being used again, or maybe the hot water heater was finding its second wind. Either way, I enjoyed my shower for the first time since I'd come back to life.

I heard movement in the bathroom, and I tensed up. Was Ethan in here? Was he planning on surprising me in the shower? I suddenly felt cold. I shut the water off and reached my arm out from behind the curtain, groping for my towel. I grabbed it and wrapped myself up before I pulled the curtain back.

The door was still closed. Maybe I'd imagined it. Or maybe I'd heard Ethan in the kitchen. I stepped out of the shower, and a cool breeze hit my right side. I turned to see the window open. I hadn't opened it. I'd never opened it, not once since we moved in. It didn't have a lock on it, so it opened all the way up.

My eyes flew to the sink. My necklace was gone.

CHAPTER TWELVE

"**E**THAN!" I burst out of the bathroom.

He jumped up. "What? Are you okay?"

"No. My necklace is gone. I left it on the sink. Then I heard something. I thought it was you, but I guess it wasn't. The window is wide open, and I didn't open it. And now my necklace is missing."

"Slow down." He wrapped me in a hug. "The window's open?"

"Yes, and I didn't open it. I think someone came into the bathroom while I was in the shower. I heard a noise."

"Why didn't you see what it was when you heard it?"

How did I answer that? I'd thought it was Ethan, and I freaked out and grabbed my towel to cover up. I couldn't tell him that. "I don't know. I panicked, I guess. I grabbed my towel and got out, but it was too late. Whoever it was had already gone and taken my necklace with them."

"Stay here." Ethan went into the bathroom and looked around. "I don't see anyone out there."

"I doubt they would've stuck around after they stole from me."

"I don't get it." He shut the window and came back into the kitchen. "Why would someone crawl through the bathroom window to steal a necklace? It's not even like it was an expensive necklace."

I had to tell him about the note. It might give us some clue about who broke into our bathroom.

"Ethan, there's something I need to tell you, but you have to promise to stay calm."

His jaw clenched, and his nostrils flared. The longer I waited, the worse he was going to get.

"I found a note in my locker today. I went to get my lunch, and there was a note on it."

"From who?" he asked through gritted teeth.

"I don't know."

"What did it say?"

I closed my eyes, unable to look at him as I said it. "'The necklace suits you. Wear it always.' That was it."

He didn't say a word, so I slowly opened my eyes.

"Ethan?"

"Why didn't you tell me? You saw me right after that, right?"

"Yeah, but—"

"You should've told me."

"Why are you getting so worked up over this?"

"Why? Because it obviously wasn't a mistake. Someone gave you that necklace."

"I know."

"So, do you expect me to be happy that some guy is leaving gifts and secret notes in my girlfriend's locker?"

"Of course not, but it doesn't matter anyway. The necklace is gone. Whoever gave it to me probably saw you and me together and figured it out. So they broke in and took the necklace back."

"Good. I'm glad that thing is gone."

"Ethan, don't be like that." I reached for his arm, but he jerked it away.

"I'm going for a walk."

"It's pitch black outside."

"I don't care."

"Someone broke into our house, and you're going to leave me here alone?" I didn't want to play the helpless girl card because I've never considered myself helpless against anything other than cancer—and now this thing that was happening to me, making me feed off others—but I didn't know what else to say to keep him here.

He stared at me, and, for a moment, he didn't look like my Ethan.

"I'm sorry." Tears welled up in my eyes. Not because I'd kept this from him or because he was upset with me for it. But because I had an even bigger secret, one I knew he wouldn't forgive me for keeping.

He exhaled loudly and pulled me into his chest. "Don't cry." He rubbed the back of my head. "It's just that I lost you once. I don't want to do it again. Especially to some other guy. I couldn't handle that. Not after everything…"

I still didn't know how he'd brought me back. I tilted my head and stared into his beautiful blue eyes. "What did you go through to bring me back? You never told me."

"You don't need to know." He let go of me and walked into the living room as if the conversation was over.

"I didn't think you needed to know about the note in my locker, but that's not how you feel." Maybe it was a low blow, but I needed him to see this from my point of view.

He sat down on the couch. "It's nowhere near the same."

"You're right. It's not. I kept something that didn't even concern you a secret. You're keeping something that has everything to do with me secret." I knew he was going to get mad, so I sat down on his lap, keeping him in his seat. I took his face in my hands and kissed him. I held the kiss long enough for him to think about what I'd said. Think, but not react. When I let go, I leaned forward, resting my forehead against his. "I need to know, Ethan. I need to know what you did to give me a second chance."

"Why does it matter? Isn't being here with me enough?"

"You know it is. I love you, but I need to understand what happened. People don't get do-overs in life. So, why did I?"

"Because I love you." He pulled me toward him, kissing me hard.

I didn't know if it was losing my necklace or fighting with Ethan, but I was charged up. I kissed him back, running my fingers through the hair on the back of his head. His lips worked their way down my neck, sending shivers down my spine. I forgot about our fight. I forgot about my necklace. I forgot about the people I'd killed. It was just Ethan and me.

The next thing I knew, we were in the bedroom, and, this time, I didn't stop him. I didn't run away.

I woke up at 2:38, shivering and gasping for air. Ethan was sound asleep, looking peaceful. I had to get away from him before it was too late, but the feeling hit me hard. The feeling of death. I fell to the floor in a heap. The sound probably could've woken a corpse, but Ethan slept through it. I crawled out of the bedroom and to the front door. The carpeting burned my knees as I dragged my legs across it. I wasn't sure I could even make it to the car this time, and part of me didn't care. I only had to get far enough away from Ethan so that he wouldn't get hurt. If I died…well, I was already supposed to be dead.

I used the doorknob to pull myself up. I had to unlatch the dead-bolt. I held on to the doorknob and reached my other hand up, swatting at the chain. I managed to loop my finger through it. I tugged, which was more like letting my arm fall back down, and the bolt slid out. I turned the lock on the doorknob and twisted it open. Every movement felt like it took all my strength, but I got the door open.

I tumbled down the front steps and landed half on one of the big rocks. A jagged edge dug into my back, and I winced. My vision blurred. At first, I'd thought I knocked myself out, but then I realized I was having another vision. I braced myself for images of Trevor. He was my last victim, so it would be his face I saw. His future I glimpsed. Only it wasn't his future anymore.

Everything went black, and then it was like a curtain lifting. It was the old man again—the one I couldn't identify. I struggled for breath, partly out of surprise and partly because my body was shutting down. This time the man wasn't as old. He sat on a bench, feeding the birds. The woman from the previous vision wasn't with him. He was alone. Just him and the birds.

When he ran out of birdseed, he leaned his head back and stared up at the sun. He sighed, and a single tear dripped down his cheek.

"Not a day has gone by that I haven't thought about you. You should be here with me now."

His shoulders shook and more tears lined his face. "What's that old saying? Time heals all wounds? Something like that. Well, whoever said it was a liar. Some wounds never heal. Losing you never stopped hurting. I'll mourn you until the day I die, and I'll love you even longer." He leaned forward and buried his face in his hands. My heart broke for him—whoever he was.

Everything went dark again. I heard noises around me, and I turned my head from side to side, but my vision hadn't returned yet. *Oh, please don't let it be Ethan.* If he found me, if I touched him…

Slowly shapes came into focus. Trees, grass, rocks. Lots of rocks.

I realized I was moving more easily. I was breathing more easily. What had happened? Did I kill someone without knowing it? *Not Ethan! Please, not Ethan!*

I sat up and looked around. The only things around me were the rocks, all perfectly lined up in a circle again. Someone or something had fixed the rocks, put them back in their pattern while I lay on the ground.

My head felt woozy, like I was hung over, but I hadn't had anything to drink. I slowly got to my feet, still scanning the yard, looking for whoever had done this. Maybe it was the same person who had stolen my necklace. I thought back to the guy who was peeking in the window. The one who'd broken into the house. He knew my name. He knew I could kill with my bare hands. It had to be him.

Suddenly the realization that I was outside alone in the dark with a stranger lurking around set in. I ran back into the cottage and locked both locks behind me. I went around the house checking all the windows, too. He wasn't getting inside again.

I pulled the curtain back into place after checking the lock on the window above the kitchen sink. I was breathing hard. I turned on the faucet and splashed cold water on my face. No way would I be able to go back to sleep after all this, so I grabbed a paper towel and dabbed my face, trying to think of how I'd pass the time until morning without waking Ethan. I reached for a second paper towel when I saw the note on the counter. A yellow Post-it note. I froze.

My eyes zeroed in on the handwriting. Every letter was perfectly straight.

Where's your necklace?

Those three words sent terror coursing through my body. Whoever had given me the necklace had been in my house tonight.

He—or she, now I wasn't so sure—had come into the cottage while I was out in the yard having a vision and trying not to die.

Two break-ins in one night? It was hard to believe, but it had to be two different people. One stole my necklace, and the other wanted to know why I wasn't wearing it anymore. How had so many people discovered where I lived? The whole point of the P.O. box was to keep that a mystery. To make sure people didn't connect Ethan and me any more than thinking we were together. We had even toned down the couple stuff at school, so people would think we had only recently gotten together.

I couldn't help it, but Beth's name came to mind. She always knew so much. She was the queen of gossip, and she was good at figuring things out. Could she have pieced together more about Ethan and me than she was letting on? And which intruder was she? The one who stole my necklace, or the one who gave it to me and wanted to know why I wasn't wearing it anymore?

This was too much to process. By morning, I only had more questions, and one thing was for sure. I had to keep an eye on Beth. I had to find out what she knew.

CHAPTER THIRTEEN

ETHAN slept in, so I watched infomercials on the one TV station that came in. Thankfully Ethan had gotten the TV working again after my peeping Tom collided with it. Really I wasn't even watching, but I figured it would look suspicious if Ethan found me sitting in a dark room staring at the wall. So I put the TV on as a decoy. Meanwhile, my brain went over every possible reason Beth could be messing with me.

"Hey." Ethan was all smiles as he came into the living room.

I hoped he wouldn't make a comment about last night. I'd end up blushing and feeling self-conscious. "Morning."

"I'm going to hit the shower, and then we can drive out to that storage place. It's about two hours from here, so if we leave in the next twenty minutes, we should make it back in time for our shift at the diner."

"Sounds good." I went into the bedroom and got dressed. I was eager to get away from this place. Now that I knew that it was so easy for people to break in, I didn't feel safe here, and it wasn't like I could tell Ethan. *So I was dying again last night, and I hit my head on a rock and blacked out, but I had another vision of some strange old man, and when I woke up from it, I was breathing normally, and the rock circle was back in place. Oh, yeah, and did I mention I found another note, which means someone else broke in?*

Oh crap! The note! I ran out of the bedroom and to the kitchen. The note was still on the counter. I hadn't even been able to bring myself to touch it last night. The bathroom door opened. Speedy

Ethan was ready to go. I grabbed the note and slipped it into my back pocket.

"All set." I faked a smile and pretended I'd been waiting for him.

I locked the door behind us and almost bumped right into Ethan. "What's wrong?"

"Did you move the rocks back?"

Another thing I'd forgotten. "No." There, it wasn't a lie. I stared at the rocks circling the house, like I was as surprised as Ethan. "Do you think it was whoever broke in and stole my necklace?"

"No. It was probably those guys from the diner. They were pretty mad about getting kicked out."

"They didn't get kicked out. Shannon did. She's the one who made them leave."

"Doesn't matter. I bet they're screwing with us."

Us. Crap! "Do you think they know we live together?" If that was true, then more than just two people knew about our living arrangements.

"I don't know. Maybe." He shrugged. "I'm thinking we should leave the rocks, at least for a little while. They'll get tired of messing with us if it looks like we don't even care."

"I guess that makes sense." If only ignoring my problems really *was* the answer, but my Hyde side wouldn't let me ignore them, neither would my conscience.

We took Route 80 most of the way to the storage facility. How Ethan knew which one to go to was a mystery to me. There were tons of them, and they all looked the same. We pulled up to a gated entrance, and Ethan used a passkey to open it. We drove around the building to a set of smaller, climate-controlled garages.

"That's us." Ethan nodded to the row of doors on our right.

"You said this is your cousin's storage unit?" I followed Ethan out of the car and down the lot to a big garage door with the number 1221.

"Yeah, but he moved to California last year. Told you he wouldn't be using the cottage or this place."

That was good to know. At least none of Ethan's family would be breaking into the cottage while we were sleeping. That was reserved for strangers who liked to scare me.

Ethan used his passkey to open the garage door on the storage container. It wasn't very big, but it was packed with things.

"Whoa, look at this stuff." There were chairs, an ottoman, pots and pans, dishes, an old stereo system. It was like the family had packed up all the good stuff and left the junk to rot in the cottage.

"We can take anything you want back to the cottage. It's not like anyone is going to use it."

"Why would your family save all this stuff if they never plan on coming back to the cottage? Why are they even still keeping the cottage? They could sell it."

Ethan sighed. "You're always so curious about everything."

"Sorry." I was prying. I didn't have a right to question what his family did. I should've been grateful we had a place to stay, and now we'd have some decent furniture, too.

"My great-grandfather built the cottage. No one has the nerve to sell it or tear it down, so it just sits." Ethan started picking through a stack of books to avoid looking at me. This must have been a sensitive family issue. One I'd missed thanks to cancer.

"But if we hadn't moved in, it would've fallen apart eventually."

"I know. No one else seemed to figure that out, but I couldn't let that happen. I have great memories here."

I reached for his hands and turned him toward me. "You'll have great memories here again."

He kissed me, and I felt the full weight of his decision to come here. It was about more than just saving me. He was saving a part of himself, too. It was a relief to find out Ethan wasn't basing his new life on me alone. That would have been too much pressure for me to live up to.

"Why don't you look around and pick out some things you'd like to take back with us? I'll go find your ring. I put it in the top drawer of a desk in the back corner."

"Okay."

He disappeared in the back of the container. Even though it wasn't big, it was pretty dark in the back part of it. I stayed toward the front and tried out a wingback chair. Not as comfortable as it looked. I spied an old beanbag chair and cringed. Ethan was definitely going to want that ugly, brown thing.

I walked over to a tall piece of furniture covered with a sheet. It looked like a full-length standing mirror. I'd always wanted one. I grabbed the edge of the sheet and pulled it off. Dust flew everywhere, covering my face and arms. I staggered backward, choking.

"You okay?" Ethan asked.

"Yeah. Just dust." I patted my arms and the front of my shirt, wiping the coating of dust from my clothing. "I'm going to step outside and get this off me."

"All right," Ethan called back.

I stepped into the sunlight and sneezed. The sneeze led to coughing, and my lungs constricted. It wasn't just the dust doing this to me. I was having trouble breathing. I was...

No! Not again. It was too soon. Usually I had a little time between attacks, but last night's attack had been different. I still wasn't sure what had happened last night, why the attack had stopped. Why I was alive. There hadn't been a body lying next to me when the vision ended, so I couldn't have killed anyone. Was I getting better? Could the worst be over?

I tried to remain calm, telling myself this would pass. Like last night, it would pass, and I'd feel okay again.

The coughing intensified. I looked up, squinting to see Ethan. He was still searching the desk. I couldn't put him in danger. Until I knew this would pass, I had to get away from Ethan. I moved as quickly as my body would allow, past the two other storage garages on the end of Ethan's and around the corner. I came to a door that said "Office." I stopped and stared at it. I could see movement on the other side of the cloudy glass window in the door. If I went inside, I could make this feeling stop, but it would make someone's heart stop, too.

I bent forward, putting my hands on my hips and struggling to get air into my lungs. They felt the size of shriveled peas. It wasn't stopping. Last night had been a fluke. If I didn't do something soon, I was going to die.

I took a step toward the door and reached for the doorknob, but before my fingers grasped it, I stopped. I couldn't do this anymore. I couldn't kill to save myself. Just because my life had ended early and I felt like the universe owed me something, I didn't have the right to decide my life was more important than someone else's.

I eased myself to the ground, coughing and choking on the air, which felt as heavy as concrete. My body went cold and rigid. My legs stuck out in front of me, and my back leaned up against the building. I had only minutes left. This was my last chance to change my mind. To save myself.

The will to live took hold of me and battled my brain. I tried to stand, to get to the office, but my conscience worked against me, slowing me, letting death catch up to me.

The office door opened, and a man smoking a cigar stepped out. He was humming as he counted a handful of rubber-banded bills. I stuck my foot out, tripping him. He stumbled forward, and I cursed myself for being weak. He fell a few feet away from me, still too far for me to touch.

"Sorry, I didn't see you there," he said, assuming he'd tripped over me, never suspecting I was trying to take him down. He grabbed the money and quickly pocketed it.

I swallowed, getting a tiny sip of air in my body.

"Do you need help? You don't look so good." He looked up at the sky. "Is it the sun? Heatstroke maybe? It's unusually hot today."

I couldn't answer. His cigar had fallen out of his mouth when I tripped him, and it rolled toward me. I extended my finger toward it.

"Oh, there it is." He picked up the cigar, grazing my finger with his hand.

I swallowed another sip of air. The slightest touches were keeping me from death, but how long would this last? How long could I hold out?

He bent down next to me. "Tell you what, I'm going to call 911 for you. You could probably use an IV or something to rehydrate." He reached into his shirt pocket and pulled out his phone.

My fingers crept toward him, lured by the heat coming from his body.

"Yes, this is George Peterson down at—" He stopped and stared at his phone. "Damn cell reception. I lost the call. They probably didn't hear any of that." My head lolled to the side, and I fell toward him. He dropped his phone and reached for me, supporting my head in his hands.

His touch sent waves of warmth to my freezing cold body. I shivered and then warmed. I breathed in—short, raspy breaths. Not enough. I raised one hand and waved George toward me.

"What is it? Did you want to tell me something?" He leaned toward my face, waiting to hear what it was I had to say.

I raised my hand to his neck, and he thought I was trying to pull him closer. He leaned down farther, allowing me to press my other palm against his chest. Instantly his life began to leave his body and enter mine. Air filled my lungs. I felt the warmth of my blood flow throughout my body.

George made a gurgling sound, and my eyes snapped to his face. He was shriveling at my touch. His body caved into itself, and his eyes pleaded with me as the life drained out of them. He slumped forward on me. My body shook with tears that threatened to spill out. I was so weak. Too weak to let myself die. To put an end to all of this. I hated myself, hated the monster within me.

"Sam?" Ethan called.

Oh, God! He couldn't find me like this. He knew about the body at the gas station and at school. If he found me near George right now, he might start to piece things together, figure out the common factor in all the deaths. Me.

I scrambled to my feet and opened the office door. I dragged George by his feet until he was in the office. I locked the door behind us. It would be difficult to explain later if Ethan found me in here, but at least it would buy me time to hide the body. I dragged George behind the counter and made sure none of his limbs were sticking out. "I'm so sorry," I whispered, as if the words could help him. Satisfied that no one would find George before Ethan and I got out of here, I put my ear to the door and listened for Ethan.

A knock made me jump. The doorknob jiggled.

"Hello?" Ethan called. "Anybody working today?"

I stayed frozen in place, afraid the slightest move would give me away. If I could hear Ethan, then he could hear me, too. I waited for him to leave before peeking out the cloudy window on the door. No sign of him, but I had to be careful. The window didn't allow me to see down the row of storage containers. Ethan could be standing two units down, and I wouldn't know it until I'd stepped out of the office and fully into his view.

My pulse thundered in my ears, limiting my hearing. I wanted to wait him out to make sure he was really gone, but the longer I stayed here, the more Ethan would worry, and my chance of lying my way out of the situation would decrease. I unlocked the door slowly, careful not to let it click back into place. I hesitated a few seconds to make sure Ethan hadn't heard the lock, that he wasn't coming back to look for me.

I turned the knob slowly until it wouldn't turn anymore. Holding it in place, I pulled the door open an inch and peeked out. I didn't see any shadows or movement, so I opened it a little more. Still nothing. I stepped out and pulled the door shut behind me. I glanced in both directions before bolting across the parking lot to the back of the building. Ethan wouldn't come this way. He'd go back to the car thinking that's where I'd gone.

I followed the building around to the front gate. My only chance was to come up on the car and pretend I'd gotten turned around since all the garages looked the same. Once again, I had to play dumb, no matter how much I hated it. But there were a lot of things about my life that I hated these days.

Ethan came out of garage 1221 as I walked up to the car. "What happened? Where were you?"

"I got lost." I turned around and looked at the building, pretending to be confused by the layout. "I went back to the car because I got some dirt or something in my eye, but someone yelled for help."

"Really? I didn't hear anyone." Ethan scrunched up his face.

"I guess it's tough to hear outside noises from the storage garage. You were all the way in the back of it." It scared me how easily the lies spilled from my lips. He nodded, waiting for me to continue. "I thought it was you calling me at first, so I followed the voice. But it turned out to be some guy who lost his passkey and couldn't get in the gate. I didn't know how to get the gate open without a key, so he ended up calling the office for help. After that, I had a little trouble remembering how to get back here. I think the heat is messing with my head." I could thank George for that excuse.

"Well, unfortunately, I have some bad news."

So many things came to mind. He'd found the manager's body.

His family had called and said they were checking the cottage in case Ethan was hiding out there.

"It's your ring. It wasn't in the desk drawer where I left it."

"What? Do you think your family is here? Did they come looking for you?"

He shook his head. "No. I don't think so. Besides, they have no idea I put the ring in the storage garage. My parents probably assumed I kept it with me. I should've kept it with me, but I couldn't."

I didn't want him to have to explain his actions to me again, so I reached for his hand and squeezed it. "Then what happened to my ring? Why isn't it here?"

His face turned cold. "Someone broke in and took it."

CHAPTER FOURTEEN

WHAT was with everyone stealing my stuff? This was getting ridiculous now. It was like someone had it in for me, knew I was a monster and was trying to mess with me.

"Was anything else missing?" I was determined to find some indication that this wasn't all about me. That things like this happened to other people, too.

"Not that I could tell." He ran his fingers through his hair. "There could be other stuff missing, though. I don't really know what my cousin had in here. I didn't look around that much when I put the ring in the desk."

"But still." I shook my head. "Why would someone come to a storage facility, pass up a bunch of stuff they could sell, and only take a ring that was hidden in a desk drawer? How would they even know it was there?"

"Good question."

"Are you sure you put it in here? Is there any way you forgot what you did with it? That you lost it?"

"No!" He sighed, making an effort to calm down. "I'm sorry. I didn't mean to snap at you. I just don't understand this. I put the ring here to keep it safe. I knew you'd want it back."

I stared at him, hating that whoever was screwing with me was screwing with Ethan, too. He hadn't done anything wrong. He didn't deserve this. He wasn't like me.

"What if…" I stopped, afraid that if I said what I was thinking, Ethan would get more upset. But I couldn't help thinking the ring I found in that wooden box really *was* mine. It didn't make sense. Ethan hadn't put it there, but if my ring was missing from the storage facility, and two people had already broken into the cottage, it didn't seem so strange that someone could've planted my ring in that box.

Ethan was staring at me, waiting for me to finish my thought.

"Sorry, this heat is messing with me." I shook my head, pretending to brush off the heat. "I was going to say, what if we pack up some things to take back with us and stop for milkshakes on the way home? I could really use a cold drink." Ethan used to bring me milkshakes all the time when I was sick. It was our thing.

"Sure." He kissed the top of my head, which was easy considering he was 6'2" and I was only 5'6".

I pointed out a few pieces of furniture to bring back to the cottage with us—an end table, an ottoman, and a leather chair. Ethan somehow managed to fit it all in the trunk. The nice thing about his car was it was a hatchback. The trunk was enormous; with the back seats down, it was almost like having a small truck.

"Anything else?" Ethan wiped his brow with the back of his hand.

I eyed the beanbag chair, knowing he was waiting for me to give the okay. "Take it." I elbowed him in the ribs.

"You sure? It doesn't exactly go with anything, and I know you don't really like beanbag chairs."

"I like you, though." I smiled and reached up on my toes to kiss him lightly on the lips.

"Like?" he said, after we pulled apart.

"Sure. You're my best friend, aren't you?"

He cocked his head to the side. "Well, yeah, but I'm your boyfriend, too."

"Duh. I know that." He was fishing for reassurance. "You know I love you. I just wanted you to know I like you, too."

"That's what the beanbag chair is all about?"

"Yup, and don't you forget it." I playfully pushed him toward the storage garage as I got in the car.

Ethan had this amazing way of making me forget the bad things in my life. He'd done it when I had cancer, and he was doing it now, too. But I couldn't forget for too long. Too much was a mystery to me right now, and after our outing this morning, I could add my missing ring to the list. And then there was George… The list I added him to was entirely too long.

After Ethan packed up the car, we hopped back on Route 80. Ethan said he knew an ice-cream shop not far from here. His aunt and uncle used to take him when he was a child. I stayed in the car while he went inside for our milkshakes.

He left the car running so I didn't melt in the heat, and I let the air conditioning blow right on my face. I could see the huge line in the ice-cream shop. It looked like everyone within a twenty-mile radius had come out for ice cream. I couldn't blame them. It was really hot today. It was going to be a while before Ethan got to the front of the line, so I turned on the radio and leaned my head back. Music filled the car, drowning out the thoughts in my head.

At some point, I started to drift off, but then I heard a strange buzzing sound. I sat up, realizing it was coming from the radio. It was one of those emergency alerts. I turned up the volume.

Please be advised that the heat index is unusually high for this time of year. Take extra precaution against heatstroke by staying hydrated and indoors as much as possible. There have been several incidents of heat-related fatalities in the area.

I wondered if the police would think George was one of the heat-related fatalities. I switched the radio off, not wanting to hear any more. Even in the air-conditioned car, I could feel beads of sweat forming on my forehead. I opened the glove compartment to search for a napkin or tissue.

Ethan wasn't exactly neat. The glove compartment was filled with gum wrappers and melted protein bars. Yuck! No napkins. I got out of the car and opened the trunk. Maybe there were some floating around back there under the furniture we'd packed. With Ethan, you never knew where you'd find things. But other than a lone sock, I didn't find anything.

Back in the car, I searched the floor under my seat. Gross, but I was desperate. A piece of paper sliced my finger, and I jerked my hand back. "Stupid paper cut." I squeezed my finger to stop the stinging. Then I reached my other hand under the seat again, wanting to know what had cut me.

I pulled out a yellow Post-it note and froze at the sight of it.

Another one? I could see the black magic marker bleeding through it from the other side. My hand shook as I flipped the note over.

Put your ring back in the box.

My ring? I didn't have my ring. Or did I? Did this mean the ring I had taken from the wooden box really was mine? And why would whoever was sending me these notes want me to put the ring back? If it was really mine, I wanted to wear it, not keep it tucked in a box out of sight.

All these questions clouded my mind, temporarily masking the fear that was creeping up my spine, but I couldn't hold it off forever. The fact of the matter was that someone had been in Ethan's car. Probably while we were at the storage facility. Maybe while I was stealing the life from George.

I wasn't safe at home. Three break-ins had proven that. I wasn't safe at school. Someone had gotten into my locker and left things for me twice. And now I wasn't even safe in Ethan's car. I wasn't safe anywhere. Whoever was messing with me found me everywhere I went.

A tap at my window made me jump. I dropped the note on the floor and quickly covered it with my foot. Ethan was holding two milkshakes in his hands and balancing a large order of fries in the crook of his arm. I lowered the window and reached for the milkshakes, placing them in the cup holders in the middle console.

"Thanks. I was afraid I'd drop your fries if I tried to open the door."

"Why'd you order fries when we're headed to the diner? We can get them there for free. You know we have to conserve our money. We have bills now." Ethan had managed to put the electric bill in a fake name, too, but we still had to pay it, or it would be shut off.

"I know, but Jackson threw me an extra twenty last night for bailing him out in the kitchen. He said cooks should make more than busboys." He shrugged. "Besides, you love to eat fries with your vanilla shakes."

I did. Most people thought it was gross to combine the two—I'd been known to dunk my fries right into my milkshakes—but I loved it.

While Ethan walked around the car and got in the driver's seat, I grabbed the note off the floor and shoved it in my pocket.

"Thank you." I leaned over and kissed him. His lips were cool. He'd obviously had a few sips of his chocolate shake. My lips lingered on his. The coolness was refreshing.

When I pulled away, Ethan smiled. "Note to self—buy Sam more milkshakes."

I ate my fries and downed my milkshake before we made it to the diner. I was full and my insides were blissfully cool. Things were looking up.

"You know, I actually like working at the diner." Ethan slurped the remains of his shake. "Jackson's great, and I like cooking. If we could afford food at the house, I'd cook for you all the time."

"That sounds heavenly." I pictured Ethan cooking in our kitchen. Of course, in my mind he was shirtless while he was doing it.

"How are you liking the job?" He turned to look at me. He was always trying to make sure I was okay with the way our new life was going. He knew school wasn't the greatest for me, so he was hoping I loved the job at the diner as much as he did.

"Gloria's great, and the tips are good. Well, most of the time anyway." I thought of Nora, who hadn't given me a single tip. That reminded me she owed Gloria for her last bill. "I hope Nora doesn't show up tonight."

"Who's Nora?"

"That girl who comes in every day and only orders coffee."

He shrugged, not sure who I was talking about.

"She has jet-black hair and bleached-blonde eyebrows. You must have seen her."

He shook his head.

"She always wears a green dress."

"Sorry, don't know her. Does she go to our school?"

Good question. "I don't know. I haven't seen her there, but that doesn't mean much. It's a big school, and we've only been there for two days."

"Ask her."

"I try not to talk to her. She's…strange. And she never tips me. I got into it with her yesterday because she skipped out on her bill the night before. I got her to pay me, but then she ran out without paying for the bill she'd just rung up. It wasn't much, only coffee, but still."

Ethan smirked. "I'd be surprised if she shows up again. Gloria must be pissed."

"Actually, I think Gloria was more mad at me."

He narrowed his brow. "That doesn't make sense. She took your side against Shannon."

"I know, but I did let a customer walk out without paying. Twice."

"I see your point." Ethan pulled into the diner and parked. He shut the car off and turned to me. "Let me know if Nora shows up tonight. I'll set her straight."

"Are you kidding me? The second I turn my back on her, she'll probably steal the coffee pot and run." I laughed, letting him know I'd be fine. I'd figure out a way to deal with Nora—if she even showed up.

Saturdays at the diner were like Super Bowl Sunday at a sports bar. Beyond crazy. Poor Gloria looked frazzled and about to drop. I stashed my purse behind the counter and grabbed my apron.

"Sit," I told Gloria, as I took the tray of food from her hands. "Which table?"

She pointed to the booth in the corner before slumping onto the only open stool at the counter.

I headed over, trying to look like I had this waitress thing down pat. "Okay, who had the bacon cheeseburger with sweet potato fries?"

The table of people looked up at me, most likely wondering who I was.

"I'm Sam. I'll be taking over for Gloria. Now, about that bacon cheeseburger?"

The guy nearest me raised his hand like he was in a classroom. I stifled a laugh as I placed the plate in front of him.

"Reuben?"

"Here," said a girl across the table.

I delivered the rest of the orders and tucked the tray under my arm. "Anything else I can get for you right now?"

Everyone shook their heads, already digging into the food.

"I'll be back to check on you in a bit."

I did that about thirty more times, introducing myself to tables Gloria had already seated and placed orders for. No one complained about the staff change, probably because I could zip around the diner at four times Gloria's speed.

Once everyone was eating, I got a glass of water and placed it on the counter in front of Gloria. "It's hot today, and it's even hotter when you're running around. Drink this. I don't want you dehydrating on me." I thought of the alert on the radio. I couldn't lose Gloria to heat exhaustion.

"Thanks, Samantha. You are a lifesaver."

I swallowed hard. If she only knew how wrong she was. The only life I saved was my own, and at the cost of others'. And here I was trying to act normal, making myself forget what I really was.

"Um, waitress," someone called.

I snapped my head up. The voice came from the other end of the counter. I saw her green dress before I saw her face. Nora.

"You've got to be kidding me." I stormed over to her, leaving Gloria looking after me and wondering what was wrong.

"I hope you came to pay your bill."

Without a word, she took a small change purse from the pocket of her dress and counted out the exact price of a cup of coffee.

"Thanks for the tip," I said, swiping the change off the counter.

I let her sit there, without coffee, for ten minutes, while I helped everyone else in the place. Finally Gloria gave me a look. I didn't see what the big deal was. Nora never spent more than $1.75. It wouldn't be any big loss if she stopped coming. But I didn't want to upset Gloria, so I picked up the coffee pot and brought it to the end of the counter. I grabbed a cup from the shelf and put it in front of Nora. But I didn't pour the coffee.

"What, am I supposed to serve myself now?" she asked.

"$1.75."

"You haven't even given me my coffee yet. Why should I pay you?"

"Because you have a reputation for drinking and running. $1.75 or no coffee."

She huffed at me, but she took out her purse again and slammed a dollar and three quarters on the counter. I wondered how she always had exact change. She couldn't even *accidentally* tip me.

I took the money and poured the coffee. As I passed Gloria on my way back to the coffee station, she clapped her hands.

"What?"

"Nicely played. I knew you'd figure out a way to handle her."

I smiled. Just like that, I was forgiven. I poured Gloria another glass of water before checking on my tables.

The hours flew by. The crowd never lightened. My feet were screaming as I wiped down the counter after the last customer left. When I got to the spot where Nora had been sitting, I picked up her cup, revealing a yellow Post-it note.

No way! Nora was the one leaving me the notes?

I turned it over.

I know what you are.

CHAPTER FIFTEEN

MAYBE the note wasn't from Nora. It could've been a coincidence that someone left it under her cup. This place had been packed tonight. Anyone could have left it without me seeing. But what if it *was* Nora? That would mean she knew my secret. Did that also mean she was the same person who had left the other notes?

I studied the handwriting, but it was smeared by a ring of coffee from the bottom of the cup. I couldn't be sure if it looked like the other notes or not. I couldn't even be sure Nora was the one who'd left it. Although the threatening nature of the note definitely fit Nora's personality.

"Ready to go?" Ethan asked, coming up behind me.

I dropped the cup, spilling a few drops of coffee on the note.

"Sorry. I didn't mean to scare you." Ethan grabbed a towel off the counter and began mopping up the spill.

"It's okay. I'll get it." I took the towel before Ethan could see the note underneath it.

"I don't mind helping."

"I know, but you've been working just as hard as I have, and this is all I have left to do." I wiped the towel and the note into a plastic washtub under the counter and brought it to the kitchen.

Jackson was out back taking out the trash. I could hear him slamming the metal lid closed on the garbage container. I fished the note out of the washtub and tore it up before burying it under food scraps in the garbage. I stood there for a moment with the message on the note swimming in my head. *I know what you are.*

I thought of the peeping Tom from the cottage. I'd almost forgotten about him with everything else that had happened since then. My life was one big jumble of problems, and that guy had gotten buried under the others. But he knew my secret. Maybe he was the one who'd left the note. It was crowded tonight. I could have missed him somehow. I'd hoped I wouldn't see him again after Ethan threw him out. If the guy had the guts to come here and risk running into Ethan again, he must really want to get to me.

I jumped when a hand touched my shoulder.

"It's me." Ethan turned me around. "Are you sure you're all right?"

"I'm just tired. This place was crazy tonight. Even my fingernails hurt."

Ethan chuckled. "I didn't know fingernails could hurt." He brought my fingers to his lips and kissed each one. Sometimes I wanted to melt right into him. If I wasn't so sweaty and didn't smell like stale coffee and melted cheese, I probably would have.

"I really need a shower." I brushed a stray hair out of my face and turned away.

He took my hand. "I wouldn't care if you were covered in dirt. You'd still be beautiful to me."

I stiffened at the thought, remembering my first night back—after I'd climbed out of my own grave. Ethan and I were both dirty after that. Sure, he'd done all the digging, but I still had to climb out of my casket. A small sound like a whimper escaped my lips.

"Hey." Ethan brushed his hand against my cheek. "No bad thoughts, okay?" He leaned his face to mine and kissed me, making every thought wash away. He had that effect on me.

The back door opened, and Jackson cleared his throat. "Did I somehow stumble into your bedroom? Because I was looking for my kitchen."

I pulled away from Ethan, feeling my cheeks warm from embarrassment. "Sorry, Jackson."

"All my fault," Ethan said, winking at me. "Is there anything else I can do for you before we head out?"

"Nah, go on home. I'll see you tomorrow."

"Goodnight, Jackson," Ethan and I said.

"Oh, isn't that cute." Jackson shook his head and mumbled, "Teenagers in love."

Ethan and I smiled at each other as we walked out of the kitchen. Gloria was sitting at the counter rubbing her foot. She looked up when she saw us. "I'm not sure how many more crowds like that these old feet can take."

"We could come in earlier tomorrow if you'd like," I said. We could definitely use the money, and it was obvious Gloria needed the help.

Gloria waved us off. "That's very nice of you, but I can't ask two teenagers to give up their entire weekend to work in a diner. I don't pay you enough to take away your youth."

Taking away youth. Her words hit me like a slap in the face. That's what I had done to Trevor—stolen his youth, stolen his life so I could have mine.

"Besides, you're not looking too good." Gloria narrowed her eyes at me. "You coming down with something?"

Yeah, a bad case of being sickened by the thought of myself. "I'm just tired. We'll see you tomorrow afternoon. But if you change your mind about us coming in early—"

She got up and herded us to the door before I could finish my sentence.

Ethan laughed as we walked to the car. "I kind of love that woman."

"Don't make me jealous." I playfully jabbed my elbow into his ribs.

"Oh, yes. You should be jealous. I've always had a thing for grandmas."

"Well then, sonny," I said in my best grandma voice, "give us a kiss."

Ethan backed away and put his hands up to keep me from getting too close. "Okay, that was disturbing."

"Over the grandma thing?"

"Definitely." He opened my door for me, and as soon as I was in the car, he bent down and kissed me. "Definitely better than kissing a grandma."

"So, you have something to compare it to?" I laughed as a look of disgust crossed his face.

"That's so evil," he said, but he was stifling a laugh. He shut my door and walked around the car.

My eyes caught a glimpse of a shadow at the side of the diner. I figured it was Jackson or Gloria, so I raised my hand to wave, but the figure stepped into the light. It was *him*. The peeping Tom.

Ethan got in the car, and I reached for his arm. "Look!" I pointed to where the guy was standing, but he was already gone. I'd only looked away for a second to get Ethan's attention, but that was all it took.

"What?"

"It was—at least I think it was that guy, the one who was looking in our bedroom window."

"Where?" Ethan opened his door again.

"No." I reached for him. "Please, don't go after him. I'm not even sure if it was him. It's dark. My eyes could've been playing tricks on me."

Ethan didn't look convinced.

"Even if it was him, he's gone now."

"Tomorrow I'll ask Jackson and Gloria if they've ever seen him. He's pretty hard to forget with the bleach job."

"He doesn't bleach his hair. He's a platinum blond. He's really pale, and his eyes are really light blue. All his features match. He definitely doesn't dye his hair."

Ethan cocked his head at me. "How closely were you looking at him?"

"He was in our bedroom, only about two feet from me. Believe me, I got a good look. When someone tries to attack you, you remember things about them, especially their face."

Ethan sighed. "You sure you don't want me to see if he's there? I don't want you to be afraid to come here."

"I'm fine. Besides, this place is always packed. What could one guy possibly do to me with that many people around?"

"That doesn't exactly make me feel better. I don't want anyone to come after you. Ever. There's no good time to have a stalker."

"I know that." I leaned my head back on the seat. "Can we please drop this? I'm really tired, and I'm dying to get in the shower."

Ethan stared at me for a minute before starting the car. When he pulled out of the parking spot, he drove around the diner.

"Ethan, what are you doing?"

"I want to make sure he's gone. Humor me."

What could I do? I wasn't driving, and I didn't want to get into a fight with Ethan over some creepy guy. We drove around the diner twice, just in case Ethan missed anything the first time around. I tried to keep my eye-rolling to a minimum. I knew he cared and that was why he was being cautious, but I wasn't helpless. Finally satisfied, Ethan pulled out of the diner and headed home.

"Want to watch a movie before bed?" Ethan asked, trying to forget our almost fight.

"A movie? We don't have any."

"I found a DVD player and some DVDs in the storage facility. They're pretty old, but there are a few comedies and even a horror flick."

"No horror flicks for me, thanks." My life was a horror flick these days.

"Comedy it is, then."

We pulled into the driveway and stared at the rock formation.

"I guess I have to move these again in the morning. I still don't see why anyone would bother to do this. Some of the rocks are heavy."

"I thought we were going to leave the rocks for a little while, so whoever did it would lay off the lame pranks."

Ethan held my hand as we wove through the rocks to the front door. "All right, I'll leave them for a little longer. It's just a pain to get around them."

Inside I headed straight for the shower. I needed to wash the events of the day down the drain, and I needed a good cry. My emotions had been a roller coaster lately. I was trying to deal with this strange way I'd come back to life and the terrible things I had to do to stay alive, and I was trying to put on a happy face for Ethan. If he knew how miserable I was most of the time, he'd feel guilty. And who knew how he would feel if he knew my secret. Which was why I couldn't let that peeping Tom near Ethan again. I couldn't chance him telling Ethan what he knew. The question was, how did he even find out?

The water rained down on me as I went through all the possibilities. My peeping Tom had seen me kill Herman, the creepy guy I'd almost collided cars with. He'd been at the gas station when I killed the guy in the cowboy hat. I couldn't remember what the guy working the register at the gas station quickie mart had looked like. It could've been him. But why would he follow me all the way out here?

The water went cold before I came to any real conclusions, and I cursed at myself for using up all the warm water. Ethan hadn't showered yet. I wrapped a towel around me and walked out of the bathroom with my head hung low. "Sorry, I guess I lost track of time in there."

Ethan looked at me in my towel. I usually brought my clothes into the bathroom with me so I could get dressed before I came out.

"Are you mad?" I asked.

He gawked a little more. Boys. I shook my head and walked into the bedroom. I threw on a tank top and pajama pants and combed my hair. A few minutes later, I heard the shower running. Ethan could probably use a cold shower right now. I chuckled to myself, making a mental note that wearing nothing but a towel was a great way to get out of a potential argument with Ethan.

I put my comb down on the dresser and was reaching for the light switch when there was a knock on the window. I whipped around. Someone was standing at the window, looking in. Someone with platinum-blond hair and pale blue eyes. Oh, God! Had he watched me get dressed? I stormed out of the room and out the front door. It was stupid. I knew that. But I was pissed. I had had enough of this guy following me around, leaving notes—if it *was* him. I was putting an end to it tonight.

I left the front door wide open and turned the corner. He was leaning against the house, waiting for me. The smug bastard knew I'd come out here.

"Who the hell do you think you are?" I stormed up to him and smacked him across the face.

His head turned to the side, and he pressed his open palm to his cheek where I'd left a big, red mark. It went well with the black eyes he had from Ethan breaking his nose.

"That's for peeking in my window." I moved closer to him, and he backed up against the cottage. I punched him square in the stomach, and he let out a whoosh of air as he doubled forward. "And that's for watching me get dressed, you pervert."

He moaned and coughed, looking at me like I was the one who'd done something wrong.

"Well, what do you have to say for yourself?" I held my fists up, ready to punch him again if need be.

"I didn't watch you get dressed. All I saw was you brushing your hair."

"Sure. Like I believe that."

"I'm telling you the truth." He straightened and held his hands up in defense. "I'm not going to hurt you, and I'm not trying to catch glimpses of you naked, if that's what you think."

"Then what are you doing following me around? And what's with the notes?"

"Look, I need to tell you something, and you have to trust me."

"Trust you? You bashed my boyfriend's head into the side of our house!" My arms flailed, and he ducked, afraid I was going to hit him again.

"He came at me with a hammer. What did you expect me to do?" I stopped swinging my arms, and he shook his head. "I had to get the hammer away from him. I tossed it in the woods when he dropped it. Doesn't that prove I'm not this monster you're trying to make me out to be?"

"Not wanting to go to jail for murder doesn't make you a good guy. You didn't have to hurt Ethan. If you weren't a creep, you wouldn't have." My mind lingered on the image of Ethan threatening this guy with a hammer. He'd never been a violent person. What was happening to him?

"I needed to talk to you. He got in the way."

"Yeah, well, I don't want to talk to you. All you've done is threaten me with things you supposedly know about me. I've had it. Stay away from me, or Ethan coming at you with a hammer will be the least of your concerns."

"Because you'll kill me yourself? It doesn't work that way. You don't get to choose when you get the urge to steal life from others."

Oh, my God. Up until then, I'd tried to tell myself there was a chance this guy only *thought* he knew my secret. But he really did. Right down to the last detail.

"Get out of here!" I screamed.

"Sam!" Ethan came running outside in his pajama bottoms. "What the hell?" he yelled when he saw me with the peeping Tom.

The guy stared at me and shoved a piece of paper into my hand before taking off toward the woods. Ethan ran after him, leaving me to look at the yellow Post-it note in my hand.

Dylan 555-0851

His name was Dylan. He knew my secret, and he wasn't about to let me get away with what I was doing.

I had to keep him quiet. Somehow.

Ethan came back out of the woods and jogged toward me. He was going to be really upset and demand to see the note. I was sure he'd destroy it. So, I did the only thing I could think of. I memorized Dylan's number.

CHAPTER SIXTEEN

"**W**HO is he? What did he say to you? And why the hell did you go outside with him?" Ethan's face was bright red. Dylan wasn't the only one he was angry with.

I handed Ethan the note.

"Dylan? Is this his phone number? You've got to be kidding me. What, does he want to date you? Is he the one who put the necklace in your locker?"

"Ethan, calm down." I reached for his arms, but he shook me off.

"Don't tell me to calm down. You're my girlfriend, Sam. Do you have any idea what I've been through? Do you know what I went through to bring you back?"

"No, I don't. You won't tell me!" I lashed out at him, unlocking the anger building up inside me.

He tore the note into pieces and let them fall to the ground. He stared at me for a second before grunting and running his fingers through his hair.

"Ethan, please tell me." I tried to calm down, knowing he wouldn't give me an answer if I was acting like a raving lunatic.

"Why did you come out here?" he asked, ignoring my plea.

"Answer my question first."

He punched the side of the cottage. "Damn it, Sam. Obviously, it took some pretty heavy stuff to bring you back. It's nothing I want to relive, and, believe me, you don't want the details."

I sighed. At least I was making some progress. I decided to answer his question. "Dylan tapped on the bedroom window, and when I saw him, I freaked out. I had just gotten dressed. I figured he saw the whole thing, and it really set me off. I ran out here, and I slapped him in the face and punched him in the gut."

"Groin," Ethan said. "Always knee to the groin. The scumbag deserved it."

"He said he didn't see me get dressed."

"Don't be naïve, Sam. Of course he saw you, but he wouldn't admit it."

"Listen, I know it was stupid, but I just reacted."

"You're being reckless. This isn't like you. You were always so levelheaded."

"That's because I was sick." Tears welled up in my eyes. "When you're dying at seventeen, you tell yourself whatever you can to not be pissed off at the world. I'm done with that now. All this stuff that's been happening, I don't deserve this. I shouldn't get crap like this to deal with after everything I've been through."

His face fell. The anger left completely. He looked hurt, heartbroken. "You're unhappy here."

"No, that's not what I mean."

"Yes, it is. I brought you back and tried to give you the life you wanted, the life you should've had in the first place, but you're miserable."

"No, Ethan, listen to me."

"You hate school. You hate the cottage. Your ring is missing, and the only thing that's made you happy was a stupid necklace I didn't even give you. *He* did."

"That's not true, and we don't know if he gave me the necklace."

"He's a freaking peeping Tom, Sam. Open your eyes. He's been following you around at school, at work, and here." Ethan was yelling, but I knew I wasn't the one he was mad at. He was angry with himself. He thought he'd failed in his attempt to make things better for me. He blamed himself for my unhappiness.

I launched myself at him, pressing my lips against his. He stumbled backward at first, not sure why I was kissing him when he was yelling at me. I opened my eyes and looked at him, not taking my mouth from his. His features softened, and he kissed me back. I didn't let up. I wanted to stop thinking about everything. I wanted him to realize I was happy with him. He was everything to me.

I wrapped my arms around his neck, and he picked me up by the waist. My legs wound around his waist as we walked back into the cottage. Ethan locked the door, but we didn't pull apart for a second. We went straight to the bedroom, and he laid me down on the bed. I had more questions I needed answered, but they were going to have to wait. Right now all I wanted was Ethan.

I woke up with the first rays of sun shining in the window. I used to sleep in on Sundays. Mom would go to the deli and get fresh bagels for breakfast. Ethan always got a cinnamon-toast bagel, but I didn't care for the sweet flavors. I liked salt bagels. They made my mouth pucker, but it was nothing a little coffee couldn't cure. Mom preferred sesame, and Dad liked poppy seed. We each had our own tastes. I lay in bed wondering what Mom and Dad were doing this morning. Had they carried on the Sunday bagel tradition after I died, or had the tradition died with me?

Ethan rolled over and propped his head up in his hand. "Morning."

"Good morning."

"Did you sleep okay?"

"Great, actually." I snuggled into him, feeling his bare chest against my cheek. I wasn't sure what I'd been so scared of when it came to being with Ethan. I mean, he was Ethan. I should've known it would be amazing.

"We have plenty of time before work today," he said. "It's not even seven yet. What do you want to do?"

"I don't know. What's there to do around here?"

Ethan smiled, and I could tell an idea was forming in his head. "It's supposed to be hot again today, and I know the perfect way to spend the morning."

"How?"

He sprang out of bed. "Can't tell you. It's a surprise, but you'll need your bathing suit, sunblock, and sunglasses."

"We're going swimming?"

"Only if you fall in." He wagged his eyebrows at me as he disappeared from the room. I heard him singing in the bathroom. Ethan wasn't exactly a great singer, but the bands he listened to were more into yelling than singing anyway. I laughed to myself as I got ready, layering shorts and a tank top over my bikini.

Ethan was ready two minutes later. I was never going to figure out how that boy could get dressed so quickly. I was tempted to see if there was a world record for it, because he'd probably be a shoo-in. I took a few minutes longer to brush my teeth and pull my hair into a ponytail. When I was finished, Ethan handed me a granola bar while he scarfed down a protein bar.

"Come on. It's going to get crowded quickly. I want to be one of the first ones there."

"And where exactly is *there*?"

"You'll have to wait and be surprised."

We drove about twenty minutes down the road and pulled into a canoe rental place.

"We're going canoeing?" I'd never done it, but I'd always wanted to.

"Yup. Nothing beats canoeing down the Delaware River."

"You've done it before?"

"Sort of. My uncle took me. He did most of the rowing, but I think I can handle it."

Ethan paid the woman at the counter, telling her we'd be out for about three hours. That meant we'd be going to the diner all nice and sweaty. Oh well. I didn't care. Canoeing sounded great.

As we brought the canoe down to the boat launch, an awful thought struck me. I was going to be trapped on a canoe with Ethan for hours. Normally, that would have been heaven, but what if I had an attack? I didn't think I'd have the strength to dive overboard and swim away from Ethan. I'd tried to stay away from the storage facility manager, and that hadn't worked. The urge to live was too strong, and no matter how much I didn't want to kill, my survival instincts took over, forcing me to do what was necessary for me to survive.

"What's wrong?" Ethan asked.

I realized I'd stopped walking. I had to get out of this. "Um, I'm not feeling so good all of a sudden."

"You're kidding, right?" He put the canoe down and felt my forehead. "You don't have a fever."

"My stomach is doing flips." That was true. I was nervous and sick to my stomach with the thought of possibly hurting Ethan. "I'm not sure being out on the water, rocking in a canoe, is the best thing for it right now."

He looked crushed.

"I'm so sorry."

"It's not your fault," he said, but I could hear the disappointment in his voice. "Wait here. I'll go return the canoe and get our money back. Sit and relax until I'm done."

I sat down on the sand, feeling awful about all of this. I couldn't even have a nice morning on the water with my boyfriend. This sickness was ruining everything.

"Good call," came a voice behind me.

I turned around. Dylan.

I sprang to my feet. "I told you to leave me alone."

"Do you really want me to do that? You didn't go out on the water with your boyfriend, so obviously you don't trust yourself."

"Stop it! Stop pretending you know everything about me, and stop following me. If Ethan comes out here and sees you…"

"Are you worried for me? Don't want your boyfriend to beat me up again?"

"I don't care about you at all. I don't want Ethan to be upset."

"He never asked you what you wanted, did he? I mean, before he brought you back."

My lungs stopped working. Dylan didn't just know about me killing people. He knew Ethan had brought me back from the dead.

"It's okay. I'm not going to tell anyone."

I swallowed, forcing myself to find my voice, not to show fear. "Not as long as I pay up, right? Well, I don't have any money. I work at the diner. You know, that place where I saw you last night. You were watching me there."

"I don't want your money."

"Then what do you want?"

"Where's your necklace?"

Before I could answer I saw Ethan walk out of the rental place.

He was putting his money back into his wallet, so luckily he didn't see Dylan.

"Go!" I said in a loud whisper.

Dylan turned toward Ethan and then looked back at me. "The necklace," he said as he took off running down the beach.

So, he *had* given me the necklace. Maybe Ethan was right. Maybe Dylan did have a thing for me. That would make him even more sick and twisted than I'd thought. Who would willingly want to be with a killer? Or was he asking about the necklace because he wanted it back? Maybe he wanted to get it back and forget about me. If only I had it to give back to him. Maybe he'd go away for good.

"You want to go home? Lie down until work?" Ethan asked, walking up to me.

"Yeah. Sorry again for ruining your idea. I really wanted to go canoeing with you."

"Some other time." He kissed my forehead before draping his arm around my shoulders and walking me back to the car.

Since we'd never gotten to watch that movie last night, Ethan put it on, and we passed the morning laughing at the bad acting. When the movie ended, we still had some time before our shift, but we both decided to go to work anyway. We knew Gloria and Jackson needed the help, even if they were too nice to ask for it. I was feeling fine, good actually. No attacks brewing at all.

Gloria yelled at us the second we walked through the doors. "I told you not to come in early. We're doing just fine without you." But I could see the relief on her face. She wasn't fooling anyone. She was happy we were there.

Ethan squeezed my elbow before heading into the kitchen, where I heard Jackson give a joyful yell. He didn't hide the fact that he liked having Ethan around as much as possible.

I put on my apron and grabbed the coffee pot, but it slipped from my hands as big, black spots filled my sight. Damn it! Another vision. Scorching hot coffee spilled all over the floor and my feet. Luckily my sneakers took the brunt of it, but a few drops burned my ankles. I cried out in pain, and I slumped to the floor as I lost my sight completely.

A few customers screamed, and I felt Gloria's hands propping up my head. Ethan was at my side, too.

"Sam!" His voice was full of panic. "Sam, can you hear me?" He held my hand and gently patted my face. My eyes were open, but I couldn't see a thing. Then the curtain lifted, and there was George, the storage facility manager. He was sitting in front of a fire, and a Christmas tree was all lit up to his left. He handed a gift to a woman sitting on the couch next to him.

"Here you go, sweetie. I know you're going to love this one."

She tore open the wrapping paper and opened the small box. "The Bahamas?" She threw her arms around George. "I didn't think you knew I wanted to go."

"Are you kidding? I saw all those magazines you left lying around the house. I may work a lot, but I'm not oblivious to everything. And thanks to me working so much, we can afford to stay for two weeks."

Her smile widened. "George Peterson, you are the best man I know."

The scene darkened, like someone dimming the lights. Everything went black again, and Ethan's voice filled my ears. I was sure he'd been talking this whole time, but I couldn't hear him over the vision playing in my mind.

"Yes, she collapsed. She has some burns on her legs from coffee she spilled, and she might have hit her head on the floor. She's not responding."

"Ethan," I said, beginning to see his outline. "Hang up the phone. I'm fine."

He dropped the phone and held my face in his hands, looking me over. "What happened?"

"I fainted, I think. I'm okay now, though." Physically, I *was* fine, other than the few burns. Emotionally, I was a wreck. George Peterson had been a good man, and now he'd never get to take his wife on that trip to the Bahamas. Disgust and pain tore through my insides. How much longer could I handle fooling everyone? How much longer could I allow myself to live at the expense of others?

Ethan helped me sit up. "Take it easy. The paramedics are on their way."

"I don't need the paramedics." There wasn't anything they could do for me.

He shook his head, not believing me. "People don't faint for no reason."

Gloria's eyes widened, and she leaned down and whispered in my ear, "You're not pregnant, are you?"

I pulled back. "What? No!"

"What?" Ethan asked.

I wasn't about to tell him what she'd said. If I did, *he'd* faint. "Nothing. Now can you guys give me some room? I'd like to get off the floor. The coffee is soaking into my shorts."

Ethan insisted on holding my arm while I stood up, but Gloria backed away. Jackson was watching from the door of the kitchen.

"Seriously, guys, I'm fine. A little clumsy and maybe dehydrated from this heat, but I'll be okay."

Gloria insisted I sit down at the counter and drink some water before I even attempted to start working. Ethan made me promise to let the paramedics look at me before I sent them away.

The whole process took an hour. One long, humiliating hour. I knew what was wrong with me, and it wasn't anything modern medicine could fix. I was relieved when the paramedics left and I was cleared to work. At least waiting on tables would take my mind off things for a little while.

"Samantha, your *friend* was here." By the way Gloria said friend, I knew she was talking about Nora.

"Ugh, please tell me I missed her. That would be the only good thing to come out of this very embarrassing afternoon."

"Yes, you missed her, but she asked me to give you this." Gloria handed me a white envelope.

I wrinkled my brow, wondering if Nora had actually paid me all the tips she'd stiffed me on.

I took the envelope. "Thanks."

"Finish that water before you start taking orders, got it?"

"Yes, Gloria." I took another sip to satisfy her, and then I opened the envelope. Inside was a yellow Post-it note.

Meet me out back.

CHAPTER SEVENTEEN

I LOOKED around, making sure Nora wasn't lurking by the bathroom or by the door. I didn't see her anywhere. I stared at the note some more, not even sure why I was considering meeting her. She'd been nothing but a pain in my ass since I met her. She owed me tip money, and she'd gotten me in trouble with Gloria.

So why did I want to see what she had to say?

I know what you are.

If she really had left me that note, I had a reason to go meet her. I couldn't risk having another person tell my secret. Nora was at the diner every day. She could easily tell Ethan about me. She could ruin my life. I couldn't let her do that. I had to at least talk to her and see what she knew or what she thought she knew.

"Gloria?" I stuffed the envelope in my purse and put it back behind the counter.

"You feeling all right?" she asked.

"Yeah, much better, but I was wondering if you could cover for me for another minute or two. I'd like to get some fresh air before I get to my tables."

She eyed me, trying to figure out if I was really okay or if I was faking.

"Seriously, I'm good. I just want to get some fresh air. It's a little stuffy in here from the crowd."

"Okay. Ten minutes. And if you're a second late, I'm coming out after you."

"Thanks." I squeezed her forearm. "Oh, and could you not tell Ethan? He'll just worry, and I'm really fine."

She nodded. "Ten minutes."

"Ten minutes." I looked toward the kitchen to make sure Ethan wasn't coming out. Satisfied I was clear to go, I made my way to the back door. No one ever went back there. It led to Gloria's office, and customers weren't allowed back there, even though the office was always locked tight.

I slipped outside, relieved to feel a slight breeze on my cheeks. I needed that after the heat in the diner. Gloria had the air conditioning running, but with the heat coming from the kitchen, the heat of the coffee pot, and the body heat from all the customers, it felt like a sauna.

I looked around for Nora, but I didn't see her. Was this a joke? She could've been messing with me, seeing what she could get me to do. I still wasn't convinced the previous note—the one under her coffee cup—had been from her. After Dylan gave me his name and number on a yellow Post-it, I kind of thought he was the one leaving me all the notes.

"Hey." Nora stepped out from the shadows. "I'm surprised you actually came."

"That makes two of us." I crossed my arms, letting her know I wasn't in the mood to socialize or play nice. "Well, I'm here, so what do you want? I have to get back to work."

"I want to know where your necklace is." She motioned to my bare neck.

"You're kidding, right?"

"Are you not wearing it because I said I wanted it? You don't trust me or something?"

I scoffed. "No, I don't trust you, but that's not why I'm not wearing it." While she stared at me, plotting her next move, I thought back to the night my necklace was stolen. It was just hours after Nora tried to buy the necklace. Why hadn't I put it together before? *She* was the one who took it. *She* broke into the cottage that night.

I had to go on the offensive. Let her know I wasn't afraid of her. "I know you took it. I don't know how you managed to break in while I was showering, but I'm sure it was you."

She shook her head and looked at me like I was a complete moron. "Why would I be asking you about it now if I had it?"

Normally that would've been a good question. It made sense. But I didn't trust her at all. It could've been a trick. Something to throw me off.

She stepped closer. "Look, maybe I should've mentioned this before, but *I* gave you that necklace."

"What? How can you expect me to believe that?"

"I was trying to protect you from yourself. I know what's going on with you. What you're doing to stay alive."

I froze. She knew. Really knew. Now that made two people. Nora and Dylan. "You left the necklace in my locker? But then why did you ask for it back that day at the diner?"

"I thought I'd gotten it wrong. That you weren't the girl the spirits were telling me to protect."

"Spirits?" My first thought was that she was crazy. Spirits communicated with her? Then again, I could drain the life from people just by touching them. If that was possible, then why not this?

"I'm a witch." She said it like it was the most normal thing. Like she was telling me she was a cheerleader—except *that* I would've had a more difficult time believing.

"So, you do spells?"

"Yes, like the one on your necklace. It's a protection spell."

"What was it protecting me from?"

"Yourself. Like I said."

I had to find out exactly how much she knew, so I knew what I was up against. "What do you mean?"

"You came back from the dead, right?"

"How—"

She held up her hand. "Witch, remember? The spirits communicate with me. They told me what happened to you and what you've been doing to people. Did you really think you were that good at covering your tracks? The police would've pinned all those deaths on you if I hadn't used magic to erase your fingerprints from all the victims and crime scenes. The spirits have been letting me know when you take a life and where to find the body."

"So, you gave me the necklace to stop me from hurting people."

A wave of nausea swept over me. This whole time I'd been snippy with Nora, trying to get her to go away, and she was trying to help me. She was the reason I wasn't in jail for murder. Could I really have been that wrong about her?

"Yes."

"But why? It's not like I was nice to you."

"I wasn't very nice to you either, but I had to make sure you were *her*. The one I'm supposed to help."

"I still don't understand." My whole world had been flipped upside down. Nora wasn't the enemy, or even a nasty girl too cheap to leave a tip or pay her bill. She was a witch, and she wanted to help me. "Why would you do this for me?"

She shrugged. "I felt sorry for you. You didn't ask for this to happen, and since I have the ability to help you, I thought I should."

She'd put a protection spell on the necklace for me. That was why I'd felt so good when I was wearing it. Why I didn't have any attacks when it was on me. "It was strange, but I felt really possessive of the necklace when I got it. Like I knew it was supposed to be with me."

"Because it was. I bet you even felt compelled to put it on as soon as you saw it."

"I did. Then I didn't want to take it off. It was always so warm against my skin."

She nodded. "A side effect of the spell."

"I guess I should thank you."

She waved me off.

"And I should apologize for letting the necklace get stolen. Someone broke into my house and took it while I was in the shower."

"Yeah, you said that already." She narrowed her eyes at me. "Have you noticed anyone hanging around you, following you maybe?"

I knew she was trying to help me, but this was still weird for me. I had gone from really disliking this girl to wanting to spill my guts to her. I hesitated, not sure if I should mention Dylan.

She sighed, getting impatient. "Look, do you want my help or not?"

"Yes. It's just that I don't know you. This is a lot to take in all at once."

"You think it was easy for me to decide to help someone who," she lowered her voice even though we were the only two people out here, "is killing people to keep herself alive?"

My breath caught in my throat. When she put it that way, I felt like an idiot. She was a witch, and she was willing to help me. I should've been kissing her feet.

"I'm sorry. You're right. And there *is* someone who's been following me."

"Have you talked to him?"

"Yes, but not much. He broke into my house, more than once, and he keeps showing up wherever I am. The diner, the river."

"What did he say to you?" Her tone was completely serious. She wasn't happy I had talked to Dylan.

"Um, he said he needed to talk to me, but every time I saw him, we were interrupted. He got into a fight with my boyfriend, too. Ethan won't let Dylan anywhere near me. In fact, when we saw him at the diner, Ethan drove all around the place to make sure Dylan had left and wasn't going to jump out at me or anything."

She was clenching her fists now.

"What?"

"You know his name? I thought you didn't really get to talk to him."

"I didn't. He gave me a note. A yellow Post-it note, like the ones you left for me." I purposely used the plural to see if she'd own up to the note under her coffee cup.

"What did the note say?"

Damn, she'd avoided my trap. "It had his name and phone number."

"Do you still have it?"

"No. Ethan tore it up."

She nodded. "Good. Don't call him. Don't talk to him."

"Wait. Why are you so sure Dylan is a threat to me?"

"He's got platinum-blond hair, right? Skinny guy?"

"Do you know him?" Nora didn't seem like the social type. How would she know Dylan?

"He's like me. Only he doesn't use his magic for good."

"He's a witch?" My knees felt weak, like they were going to give under the weight of all this information being thrown at me.

"Yes, and not one you want to mess with. We need to protect you." She paced as she talked.

"Can you make a new necklace?" If I had another one, I could live a normal life, be like everyone else—except for the coming back from the dead thing.

"I can…" She paused, and I knew there was a "but" coming. "But it will take time."

"How much time?"

"More than you have. You'll need to feed again before then, maybe even a few times."

Feed. That was an awful way to look at it, but it proved she knew all about my secret. "I don't want to hurt any more innocent people."

"I might have a solution." She leaned in close. "What if I told you I knew some bad people? Bad witches who need to be stopped before a lot of people get hurt?"

"Bad witches like Dylan?"

"Yes."

I narrowed my eyes. "You want me to kill them?" She couldn't be serious.

"Better them than an innocent child, right?"

"But if they're witches, couldn't they overpower me? Use a spell or something?"

"Leave that to me. I'll make sure they can't use magic on you."

I shook my head, having a really hard time accepting all of this. Nora seemed to have everything planned out for me, but I was still full of questions. "I can't control when the urge comes over me. How will we work this out?"

"Take this." She reached into the pocket of her dress and pulled out a cell phone.

"Your phone?"

"*Your* phone. It's a prepaid one. I have my number programmed on speed dial. It's the only number in there. When you start to feel an attack coming on, call me. Immediately. Don't hesitate, or we may be too late."

I held the phone in my hand and stared at it like it was a bomb. How had she done all this?

"Don't tell anyone you have the phone. Not even your boyfriend. He'll ask questions, and he shouldn't know we're working together. He wouldn't understand. Not yet at least."

Another thing to keep from Ethan. Just great.

"Can't I tell him we're friends? I'm already keeping secrets from him. I don't want to add another to the list."

Nora sighed. "Sure. Go ahead, but don't tell him I gave you a phone. He'd never understand that. No one gives someone they just met a cell phone."

"Okay." That made sense, and I wouldn't really be lying. I'd be withholding information he really didn't need to know.

Nora looked at her watch. "You better get back in there. We don't want someone coming to look for you and finding us together like this. It looks too suspicious."

"Right."

"Keep the phone on you at all times, and use it when you need to." She turned and walked away before I could say thank you or goodbye.

I put the phone in my pocket, covering the bulge with my apron. I replayed the plan in my head. Kill witches who'd gone bad? I didn't have any other choice. Until Nora made me a new necklace, I was going to be a witch killer.

CHAPTER EIGHTEEN

GLORIA was coming toward the back door when I stepped inside. She tapped her watch. "Cutting it close."

"Sorry. The breeze tonight felt amazing. It's been so hot. I think that's why I fainted. I'm not used to this heat." Gloria had no idea I'd spent the last two months of my life in bed in my air-conditioned house. My body had forgotten what heat felt like.

"Well, if you start feeling faint again, you sit that little butt of yours down. You hear me? I don't care if the place is packed. I'll manage on my own if I have to."

"But if it's packed, where will I sit?" I smiled so she'd know I was kidding. "I'm fine. Really."

She kept a close eye on me all night, and every so often, she'd hand me a glass of ice water. The first time she did it, I thought it was for a customer, but she said, "Drink up." I obeyed to keep her off my back. I liked having someone to care about me the way my mom used to, but it was hard, too. I wasn't a cancer victim anymore. I was...I still had no clue what to call myself.

At about seven-thirty, a crowd of kids from school walked in. Luckily, Shannon wasn't with them. But as they took a seat in the back, one guy separated from them and sat at the counter. A guy with platinum-blond hair.

My night was about to get a whole lot weirder.

I carried the coffee pot back to the counter. I didn't make eye contact with him, but I mumbled, "What are you doing here? If Ethan sees you, he'll kill you."

Dylan looked around. "I don't see him anywhere."

"He works in the kitchen now."

"Good. Then we don't have a problem."

No, we still had a problem. A big problem. "I know who you are," I said, feeling the irony of being able to use those words on someone else.

"Yeah, I know. I gave you my name."

"That's not what I'm talking about." I pretended to refill the sugar, keeping my head down so it didn't look like I was talking to him.

"Oh?" He sounded amused, and it bothered me more than I cared to admit.

"Yeah, and if I were you, I'd stop following me around."

"Or what?" He leaned across the counter and whispered, "You'll kill me?"

I slammed the lid back on the sugar and faced him for the first time. "Whatever you're ordering, we're out. Don't come again."

I turned and walked away, giving the table by the bathroom their check. I busied myself with other customers, not even glancing in Dylan's direction. He didn't know who he was messing with. I was dangerous. He might be a witch, but now that I had Nora helping me, there wasn't much he could do to me. He had no idea Nora had come up with a plan to focus my attacks on people like him. People who hurt others. Witches gone bad. I knew I was putting a lot of faith in Nora with no real proof that what she'd said was true, but the alternative was too horrible. Without her, I was still on my own and hurting innocent people. I had to believe she was telling the truth—for my own sanity.

Gloria walked up to me and handed me a napkin with writing on it. "The guy at the counter left this for you."

I looked at the counter and saw Dylan was gone. "Thanks." I took the folded napkin. My name was written on the front. What, no more yellow Post-it notes left? He was losing his touch. I debated throwing the napkin away without reading it, but my curiosity got the better of me. I unfolded it.

Don't trust her.

He had to be talking about Nora. She knew Dylan. She said he used to be like her, but then he started using evil magic. Something like that. Of course he'd try to turn me against Nora. Dylan was the bad guy. He wanted to hurt me, and I didn't know why. All I knew was I had to stay away from him.

Or did I? Maybe he was one of the witches Nora was going to have me… My throat constricted. I didn't want to kill anyone. Not even bad people. But since I didn't have a choice in the matter, I was going to have to get over this. In the long run, I'd be helping people. Keeping them safe from harmful spells, right?

Gloria handed me a tray of food. "Table nine."

"Thanks." I stuffed the napkin into my apron and took the tray. I tried to forget about Dylan and my problems for a while and focused on being polite, making good money in tips. Most of the customers were here on vacation, so they were in good moods. Unless they were on the last leg of their trip and were heading home soon. Those customers were pretty grouchy. I was surprised so many people were still vacationing this late in the season, but I guess if you don't have kids starting school or you're retired, you can vacation whenever you want.

By the end of the night, Gloria had managed to make me drink six glasses of water. I must have needed it, because I didn't take a single bathroom break all night. Apparently I really *was* dehydrated. With all my other issues, I hadn't even noticed.

Nine o'clock rolled around, and I started cleaning up. The diner stayed open till 11:00, but Gloria said it was always dead this time of night. There was no need for Ethan and me to work late on a school night when she and Jackson could easily handle things on their own. I wiped down the counter and all the tabletops.

Gloria untied her apron and took the cash drawer out of the register. She only kept a limited amount of money in the register after nine. "Ethan?" She yelled into the kitchen. I waited to see what she wanted.

Ethan came out of the kitchen. His shirt was covered in brown gravy.

"What happened to you?" I asked him.

"Oh, little spill. Nothing major. It's all cleaned up now." He turned to Gloria. "What's up?"

"I know I said you and Sam could leave, but do you think you could stay a little later tonight and help Jackson? He needs to clean the grill and wash the floors. I had to fire the dishwasher and the cleaning guy. They smoked more than they worked. Jackson could use the help, and I figure you can use the cash. I know it's late and all, so if you don't want to that's fine."

"Um, yeah. I can do it." He turned to me. "Mind hanging around while I make some extra money?"

What choice did I have? He was the one with the car. "No problem. I'll do some homework or something."

"Great." Gloria carried the drawer into the office to count it. She always counted the money in private. I knew it wasn't a trust issue or anything. She had counted the money in her office since they opened the diner, and she was a creature of habit. My being here didn't disrupt her system.

I took a seat at a corner booth with my copy of *Dr. Jekyll and Mr. Hyde*, which had been in Ethan's car all weekend. Unfortunately, I didn't remember the story well enough to pass Mr. Ryan's class without rereading it. I opened up to the page we left off on in class on Friday and read.

"...a qualm came over me, a horrid nausea and the most deadly shuddering... I began to be aware of a change in the temper of my thoughts, a greater boldness, a contempt of danger, a solution of the bonds of obligation. I looked down; my clothes hung formlessly on my shrunken limbs; the hand that lay on my knee was corded and hairy. I was once more Edward Hyde."

I couldn't help wondering if Robert Louis Stevenson had been brought back from the dead, too. The way he wrote about the monster and how it overtook Dr. Jekyll hit home with me.

My hand shook as I held the book. My fingernails turned blue with cold. It was happening. I hadn't started choking yet, but I knew it was coming. Another attack. I reached for the cell phone in my pocket and found Nora's number. I texted her. *Help. Now!*

I'd barely put the phone down when it vibrated with a message. *Out back.*

I got up, using the table to help me in case my legs were wobbly. I looked toward the kitchen, making sure Ethan and Jackson weren't coming out. Gloria was still in the office counting money, which meant I'd have to walk past her. I placed my hands on the wall in the hallway to guide myself. My knees were weak, and the cold was taking over my body. I heard Gloria talking on the phone, and I sank to my knees. I crawled past her door, well below the window and out of her view.

I reached the back door and struggled to get up off the floor. I used the door handle to pull myself up. My fingers could barely turn the lock, and a cough was threatening to burst from my mouth. I did my best to suppress it. Gloria would hear me if I let it escape my lips. I pushed the door open and fell out onto the parking lot. The door swung back and hit me. I whimpered and coughed at the same time. I tilted my head, checking to see if Gloria had heard me.

I had to get out of the doorway. I had to crawl. I grabbed the edge of the curb, using it to pull my weight forward. If only Nora were here. She could help me. But there wasn't a car in sight. Would she come in a car? Or would she be bringing the witch to me? I had no idea.

I finally cleared the door and cringed when it clicked back into place. *Please, let Gloria still be on the phone. Please, don't let her have heard that.*

A green Ford Focus pulled around the back of the diner, stopping right next to me. The passenger door opened, and Nora leaned over the seat toward me. "Get in."

"I don't think I can. I'm too weak." I coughed again as the air escaped my lungs.

"I can't touch you. You know that. You have to get in on your own."

How? I could barely breathe, and my body didn't have the strength to crawl anymore. How would I pull myself into the seat?

"Look, do you want to live or not?" Nora's voice was harsh, but I understood she was trying to shock me into reacting. I was giving up, lying on the ground like this. I pulled myself closer to the car, using anything I could grab onto to make this a little easier.

"Please, give me your hand. I won't kill you. It doesn't work that way."

Nora eyed me, not sure if she believed me.

"I won't kill you," I said again, coughing as my lungs continued to tighten.

She reached her hand over and pulled me up into the seat. Her hand felt so warm against mine. My breathing relaxed a little at her touch, but she quickly pulled her hand from mine.

"Close your door. I'm not leaning across you. It would be too tempting in your weakened state."

She was right. Even if she was trying to help me, my body would attack whoever was closest, just to survive. My brain was powerless against it. It didn't matter what I wanted. It didn't matter that I didn't want to kill. My body would do what it had to. I couldn't help wondering if the cancer victim inside me had anything to do with how much I wanted to live despite what I'd become.

I used the little bit of strength from the breath of air I got while holding Nora's hand to pull the car door shut. Nora immediately threw the car into gear and tore out of there. I caught a glimpse of Gloria coming out of her office as we pulled away. Just great. She'd figure out I was missing. She'd tell Ethan, and I'd have a whole lot to explain when I got back. If I made it back.

Nora was doing well over the speed limit, but I had no idea how far we had to drive to get to the witch Nora had picked out. It was crazy to think I was driving to someone's house to kill them. Even crazier that they had no idea I was coming.

"Nora," I croaked, "I can't hold on much longer."

"We're almost there." She floored the gas, and we whipped around the corner. The tires screeched as she pulled up a driveway. She was out of the car and mumbling a spell before I could get my door open. I watched her wave her hands and wondered what kind of spell she was doing. She'd said she'd make sure the witches couldn't hurt me while I…

She opened my door, still mumbling and holding one hand up toward the house. She waved me toward her. I moved one leg out, not sure if I had the strength to get up.

"I can't." I choked again, but she waved more frantically as she continued her spell. She couldn't talk to me because the spell was requiring her attention. She kept repeating a phrase. It sounded like Latin or some other language I didn't know. I reached for the door and used it to help me out of the car. I'd hoped Nora was going to bring the witch to me. Getting to the house was going to be nearly impossible.

She walked behind me, taking her free hand and placing it on my back. My lungs opened up slightly, and I gasped for air. She was giving me the energy I needed to make it inside the house. We moved up to the front door, while Nora continued with her spell. She reached around me, careful not to get too close, and opened the front door. A staircase stood in front of me, and I prayed we didn't have to climb it. Nora turned me to the right into a living room.

A girl stood in front of the fireplace, glaring at Nora. She was frozen in place, and the air around her swirled, keeping her imprisoned in a whirlpool of invisible force. "What do you want, Nora?" the girl said through clenched teeth. It was hard to understand her because she couldn't move her lips. "What is this all about? Who is she?" Then the girl's eyes widened. "That's her, isn't it?"

She knew about me, too? Did Dylan know this witch? Had he told her about me?

Nora continued with her spell, ignoring the girl's questions. She pushed me forward slightly, and I staggered when her hand left my back. The weakness returned quickly, and my body hungered for life. I swallowed hard as I stepped closer to the witch.

"No!" she yelled. "Please, don't. I don't know what she told you, but I don't deserve to die. Please."

Another step closer, and my hand reached for her throat. I pressed my cold, lifeless fingers against her carotid artery, feeling the life surging through her.

She gurgled. "Don't. You don't have to kill."

My other hand found her heart, pressing against it. Nora mumbled behind me as I drank in the witch's life. It was different than the other times. I felt something mixed in with the life force as it filled me. She screamed in pain, and I watched her face shrivel and age. Her long, blonde hair turned gray and straggly. She gave one final gasp as her eyes closed.

I dropped my hands, feeling energized. No, it was more than that. I felt charged up. The witch was still being held up by Nora's spell. I turned to face her, and she finally stopped chanting. The witch slumped to the ground, hitting my leg on the way down.

"That was—"

"Horrifying to watch?" Even though it wasn't the first time I'd killed, it wasn't easy for me to stomach what happened to my victims. The way their bodies shriveled into themselves was truly scary.

"Don't blame yourself," Nora said.

"How can I not? I killed her." I turned to look at the body on the floor. Old, withered.

"She deserved to die."

"How can you say that? Who are we to determine who should live and who should die? Who says my life is worth more than hers?" I was practically yelling, and tears streamed down my face.

"You didn't ask to be like this." Nora nodded toward the body. "*She* was evil by choice."

"She didn't sound evil when she was begging for her life."

"Not many people do."

"What was her name?" Not knowing who I was killing was worse. Seeing a nameless face in my nightmares haunted me more than knowing who I'd killed.

"It doesn't matter."

"It does to me." I might be a monster, but I still had some humanity left.

She sighed. "Rebecca. Her name was Rebecca."

"What do we do with her body?"

"Nothing. We leave it. Someone will find her eventually. Right now we need to get you back to the diner and come up with an excuse for why and how you took off."

She was right. Ethan, Gloria, and Jackson were probably going crazy looking for me. I wasn't sure how I was going to lie my way out of this one.

CHAPTER NINETEEN

ON the drive back to the diner, I didn't have time to think about Rebecca or how she'd begged for her life. I had to figure out what I was going to tell Ethan and Gloria. What reason could I possibly have for running out of the diner by myself, when Ethan knew Dylan had been following me, and everyone knew I'd fainted earlier in the day?

I was screwed.

Nora took her time, doing the speed limit, while we brainstormed ideas. "Tell them you heard a noise outside, like someone was in trouble. So, you went to see what it was. Say it turned out to be a little girl, and she was lost and crying."

"Why would a little girl be at a diner by herself at nine-thirty at night?"

"I don't know. I'm just throwing out ideas. What have you come up with?"

"Nothing. At least nothing believable. Hell, I could tell them the truth, and they wouldn't believe it."

"You can't tell them the truth. And keep me out of it. I was never with you."

"I know, and thanks for helping me. I don't know what I would've done if you hadn't come." Actually I did know. I would've tried to get away from Ethan, Gloria, and Jackson. I would've collapsed in the parking lot. Then one of two things would've happened. All the life would've drained out of me, and I would've died for the second time at age seventeen. Or Ethan or one of the others would've found me, and they would've died trying to help me. As awful as I felt about killing Rebecca, I was glad it was her and not someone I cared about. God, I hated myself for thinking that.

Nora pulled over to the side of the road.

"What are you doing?"

"I can't drop you off at the diner. Your friends would see me. You have to walk from here."

She was right. She'd done enough to help me already. I couldn't risk exposing her. Not everyone would be so open to the fact that she was a witch and she was helping me stay alive by finding me other witches to kill.

"Thanks again," I said, getting out of the car.

"Hey." She leaned over the middle console to see me better. "Go with the finding the little girl story. Say she was riding her bike and got a flat tire. She came to the diner looking for help."

That wasn't bad. I could make it work. "Okay, I will." I shut the door, and before I could even wave goodbye, Nora pulled away.

I walked up to the diner and saw Ethan standing in the doorway on his cell. The outside lights illuminated the panic on his face. When he saw me, he lowered the phone and ran right at me.

"Sam!"

I swallowed hard and took a deep breath, getting ready to lie.

"What happened to you? Where were you?"

"Ethan, relax. I'm fine."

"Where did you go? Gloria said she came out of her office and you were gone. Your book was on the table, and you were nowhere around. We searched everywhere."

"Who were you on the phone with just now?" If he had called the police, we could get in a lot of trouble. If either of us was fingerprinted, they'd figure out we were using stolen identities.

"Jackson. He went driving around, looking for you."

I breathed a sigh of relief. "Let's go inside, and I'll explain everything."

He grabbed my hand and squeezed it tight. I could feel his worry in the strength of his grasp. When we walked inside, Gloria rushed over to me. She held my face in her hands and looked me over.

"Are you hurt?" she asked.

"No, no. I'm fine."

Gloria brought me to the counter and motioned for me to sit down. "Tell us everything. What happened?"

I laced my fingers to keep from fidgeting. "I was reading my book, and I heard someone cry for help. I looked out the window and saw a little girl. She was only about eight. She was crying. I went outside to see what was wrong and why she was alone so late at night."

Gloria poured me a glass of water, and I took a sip before continuing. "She said she was out riding her bike. She went out without asking because she was mad at her mom. They'd had a fight earlier. So, anyway, the girl got a flat tire, and she couldn't get back home. She came to the diner looking for someone to help her."

"So what, you walked her home?" Ethan said.

"Yeah."

"Why didn't you come get me? I would've taken her in my car or you could've driven her."

"She was so freaked out, and I wasn't sure if she'd get scared if I involved more people."

Ethan shook his head, but Gloria put her hand to her chest and said, "Well, you nearly gave me a heart attack. Next time you tell someone before you go running off like that."

I nodded. "I'm sorry I made you worry."

She started for her office. "I'm going to call Jackson and let him know you're okay."

Ethan waited for her to get to the office before he said anything else. "I don't understand why you would do something like this when you've got that guy following you around."

"I'm not afraid of Dylan."

His eyes widened and he stepped back. "What, now you're on a first-name basis with him?"

"No. He wrote his name on that note, remember?"

Ethan put his hands on his hips. "This isn't like you, Sam."

I stood and reached up on my toes, grazing his lips with mine.

"Don't." He stood rigid, not giving in to me. "You can't make everything better by kissing me. I'm pissed at you right now."

"Ethan, I'm sorry. I should've told you what I was doing before I left, but I didn't think it was a big deal. She said she lived close by. She was just afraid to walk home alone in the dark."

"What was her name?"

"What?" Was he quizzing me now?

"Her name. I'm guessing she told you."

"Rebecca." I blurted out the name on my mind. I knew it was stupid to even say her name right now, but I couldn't help it. I wasn't thinking clearly. I just wanted to get Ethan to stop being mad at me.

"Let's go home. I'm finished in the kitchen."

He didn't say another word to me all night.

With Ethan not talking to me and staying on his side of the bed, I had no choice but to sleep. I felt really energized, and I had to wonder if draining a witch's life also gave me her power. It certainly felt like her power had transferred to me. If I kept doing this, would I become a witch? Would I be able to do spells like Nora? The thought lingered in my head as I drifted off to sleep.

I woke up before my alarm, feeling better than I could ever remember feeling. Sure there were the lingering thoughts of what I'd done to feel this energized, but for the most part, I'd accepted what I had to do until Nora could make a new protective necklace for me.

I got ready for school and ate breakfast. Ethan headed to the bathroom without even mumbling a hello. I wasn't sure how long this was going to last, and I hated that he was mad at me when I was feeling so great otherwise.

I finished my cereal and washed the bowl. Ethan was taking longer to get ready this morning, and I couldn't help thinking it was intentional. He was trying to put off the ride to school, where he'd be forced to acknowledge me at least a little. He finally came out, and before I could say a word, he grabbed my face and kissed me.

I was more than surprised, but I kissed him back, happy he was letting this issue go. When he pulled away, he looked me in the eyes. "I know you didn't mean to make me worry, and you were trying to help that little girl. And I know if you had a cell phone, you would've called me."

Um, maybe not. I'd had the phone Nora gave me, and not once did I think to call Ethan last night.

"So on the way to school, we're stopping at the store so I can get you one of those prepaid phones. I need to get one, too."

"What happened to your phone?" He'd had it this entire time.

"I threw it against the bathroom wall last night."

So that's what those little bits of plastic on the floor had been. I'd stepped on one getting out of the shower.

"Oh." I decided against mentioning the cut on my foot from the smashed phone.

"No big deal. I needed to stop using it anyway. I don't want my parents to be able to trace it to me."

"Right."

He grabbed his backpack and keys.

"Hey," I said, picking up my bag. "I really am sorry, and I think getting cell phones is a good idea. Not that we're apart a lot, but I'd feel better if I could get in touch with you easily."

He smiled and put his arm around me as we walked to the car. He opened my door for me, and my eyes fell on the yellow Post-it note on the floor of the car. I threw my bag down on it before Ethan could notice it. I was careful not to let my bag move as he drove us to Walmart.

"You want to come in or wait in the car?" Ethan asked.

"Um, I'll stay if you don't mind. I need to finish my reading for class."

"Okay. Be right back."

I watched him disappear inside the store before I picked up my bag and the note under it.

She's lying

Had Dylan left this for Ethan? Was he trying to tell Ethan my secret? I balled the note in my fist and stuffed it in my school bag. I'd had enough of this guy. He was one of *them*—the evil witches I was going to get rid of. He was trying to ruin my life, but I wouldn't let him. My anger continued to build as I waited for Ethan. I came to the conclusion that I was okay with killing people like Dylan. If I had to kill, he'd be next.

Ethan ran back to the car with a bag in his hands. He tore open the packages and held both phones out to me. "Pick one." One was black, and the other was silver.

I'd always had a thing for silver. "This one." I took the silver phone.

"How did I know?" He smiled and reached for my phone.

"Hey, what are you doing?" I protested.

"Programming my number into your phone and your number into mine. What, did you think I was stealing your silver phone and sticking you with the boring black one?"

"Maybe." I shrugged, feeling silly for even thinking such a thing. Ethan was too thoughtful to do something like that.

"There you go. I'm the first—and only—number in your speed dial."

"Am I in your speed dial?"

"Yup, and that leaves me with nine more spots for the girls of my choosing." He wagged his eyebrows at me.

I laughed. "I wonder who the lucky ladies will be."

He leaned over and kissed me. My head spun, but not from a vision or an attack. From Ethan.

"What was that for?" I asked, breathless.

"For being first on my speed dial."

"Oh, of course. But I think technically voice mail is set to the first speed dial spot. I can't wait to see what you do to that automated voice. If I got a kiss like that—"

"Okay, okay. Very funny."

We drove to school, and things between Ethan and me seemed back to normal. He kissed me goodbye before our first class, and I slipped into Mr. Ryan's room without being noticed by Shannon or the other future stalkers. I took a seat in the back row and texted Ethan.

In lit class. Last row. Just keeping you updated.

Having a cell phone in school might actually keep this place interesting. I could bust on Ethan all I wanted, and it would be almost like having him in class with me.

The phone vibrated in my hand. Good thing it was already set on silent or I'd be having it confiscated the first day I had it.

Very funny. Love you.

I started texting him back when Shannon blurted out, "Mr. Ryan, Samantha is texting in class."

Technically class hadn't started yet, but I glared at her instead of pointing that out.

Mr. Ryan stopped writing on the board and looked at me. "Ms. Smith, is that true?"

"Sorry. It was my mom. I told her class was starting, and I had to put my phone away."

"Thank you," Mr. Ryan said. He turned around and finished writing on the board.

I stuck my tongue out at Shannon. It was stupid and completely immature, but I didn't care. Let her tattle on me for that, too.

Mr. Ryan clapped his hands together. "All right, so *The Strange Case of Dr. Jekyll and Mr. Hyde*—your thoughts from the weekend's reading."

All the girls in the front row shot their hands in the air so quickly I felt a breeze in the back of the room. Suck-ups. I'd never finished the reading, but since I was practically living the story, I figured I could bluff my way through any questions if Mr. Ryan called on me. Luckily, he didn't. He had his hands full with all the questions the annoying slutty girls had prepared.

One of the guys sitting by me pretended to gag. "My sister actually spends time coming up with questions to get Mr. Ryan to say words like 'love' and 'beautiful.'"

"Really? Why?" I asked, finding it a little strange that he'd even tell me this.

"She wrote in her diary that she pretends he's saying those words to her. Ridiculous, right?"

"Totally." I nodded and realized he was talking about one of the girls in this class. He was a twin. "Which one's your sister?"

"Shannon, but don't let that get around. She pretends to be an only child. She tells everyone we have the same last name because we're cousins."

"Wow, she's a bigger bitch than I thought she was." I blurted it out before I realized I was talking to her brother. "Sorry, I mean—"

"No, you got it right. My sister's a bitch."

"What's your name?"

"Tristan. That's another reason why she tells people I'm her cousin. She hates my name."

"I like it. It's different."

Shannon turned around and glared at me. She'd caught us

talking, and even if she didn't admit to being Tristan's sister, she definitely didn't want me talking to her brother.

I was considering what nasty gesture I wanted to give her in return for the glare when my cell phone vibrated in my bag. It was louder than I thought it would be. I discreetly reached for it, pretending to look for a pen. A new text was on the screen.

Attack another witch and you'll wind up back in your grave.

CHAPTER TWENTY

I CHECKED to see who the message was from, but the number was blocked. I'd just gotten this phone. No one had the number except Ethan. Yet I knew who the text was from. Dylan. He'd found Rebecca's body, and he knew I was the one responsible for her death.

I felt sick to my stomach, and I needed some air. I raised my hand, but it was lost in a sea of hands. Damn those girls and their attempts to impress the hot teacher.

"Mr. Ryan," I said, not caring about calling out or speaking out of turn.

"Yes, Ms. Smith." He motioned for the other girls to lower their hands.

"I'm not feeling very good. May I use the restroom, please?"

"Absolutely." He wrote me a pass, and I took my bag with me.

"Thank you," I said, taking the pass.

"I hope you feel better." Mr. Ryan gave me a sympathetic smile, which elicited angry glares from the girls in the front row.

I walked quickly out of the room and headed for the girls' bathroom. I ducked into the first stall and took out my phone.

Should I text him back or ignore it? If I didn't answer, maybe he'd think he had the wrong number.

The phone vibrated again, and I jumped. My heart pounded. *Bathroom break. Meet me by the boys' bathroom in the English wing* Ethan. I sighed, relieved it was him.

Make it the girls' bathroom. Already here. I texted back.

I put the phone away and stepped out of the stall. A head peeked into the bathroom.

"Come in," I whispered. "No one else is in here."

He rushed inside and scooped me into his arms. I giggled, and he put his finger to his lips. "Shh." He pulled me into the handicapped stall and locked us inside.

I reached up on my toes and kissed him. This was what I'd missed out on all those months I couldn't go to school because the cancer had me bedridden. This was what it was supposed to be like in high school, sneaking visits in the bathroom with your boyfriend.

We kissed until I was out of breath. I pulled away, needing some air. "This was a nice surprise."

"Yeah, well, history was boring."

I raised an eyebrow at him. "You love history."

"Okay, I missed you. We went to bed angry last night, and I didn't get to spend any time with you."

"Sam withdrawal." I nodded. "That's a serious condition."

"I know." He gave me a devilish grin and kissed me again.

My cell phone vibrated in my bag, making a metallic rattling sound against the stall door.

"What was that?" Ethan asked.

"Um, I think I hit the volume button on the side of the phone. I must have leaned on it. It happened in class, too. Almost got in trouble for it."

Ethan leaned in to kiss me again, accepting my lie, but then the bell rang.

"Oh, crap!" he said. "How am I going to explain this? The halls are going to be crowded. I'll never get out of here without someone seeing me."

"Go, go, go!" I opened the stall door and pushed him out.

"Well, look at this," Shannon said.

Ethan and I froze. I closed my eyes and took a deep breath to keep from exploding. Why did it have to be her?

"I'm sure Mr. Ryan will be interested to hear your stomachache is gone."

"What do you want, Shannon?" I narrowed my eyes at her.

"I want you out of this school, but since I doubt that will happen, I'll settle for out of Mr. Ryan's class."

"Why?" Ethan asked.

"Because for some reason, he likes her."

He turned toward me. "You said he didn't like you like that."

"He doesn't," I shrieked. "He's a teacher. That's totally disgusting."

"He's hot, and you know it," Shannon said.

"No, I don't." I looped my arm through Ethan's, not even caring that we were in the girls' bathroom together anymore. "Come on. We're going to be late for our next class."

Ethan came with me, but I could tell he wasn't finished with the Mr. Ryan subject.

"We're not done here," Shannon yelled after us.

I didn't even acknowledge her.

"Are you sure there's nothing else to this thing with Mr. Ryan?" Ethan asked as we walked to Sculpture.

"Yes, I'm sure. It's just Shannon's overactive imagination. You should hear what her brother told me about her."

"I didn't know she had a brother."

"A twin actually, but she tells everyone they're cousins."

"Why am I not surprised?"

"She's a peach."

Ethan laughed. "You know your grandmother is the only one who ever used that expression."

My grandmother used to call me a peach all the time. "Actually, Gloria says it, too, and I like it." Of course when I'd called Shannon a peach, I was being sarcastic.

"Why does she hate you so much? Was it the diner incident?"

"No, she decided she hated me the first time she saw me. I think it's just because she's an evil bitch." Too bad she wasn't an evil witch. I immediately cursed myself for even thinking that. I didn't mean it at all.

Sculpture was actually kind of fun. I had no idea what I was doing on the pottery wheel, but Ms. Matthews let Ethan work with me. We spent more time with our fingers interlaced in clay—which is way more romantic than it sounds—than making sculptures.

When our turn was over, we washed up and headed back to our table.

"Hey, you got a text while you were gone," Beth said, motioning toward my bag with her pencil.

"I did?"

Ethan gave me a look, but I shrugged my shoulders. I reached into my bag, keeping the phone well hidden inside and checked the message. There were two. One from when I was in the girls' bathroom with Ethan and one from a few minutes ago.

Attack another witch and you'll wind up back in your grave.

Attack another witch and you'll wind up back in your grave.

Why was he sending me the same text over and over again? Was he trying to scare me?

"Who was it?" Ethan asked.

"Um, some set-up message from the phone company."

"Really?" He took his phone out of his pocket. Ms. Matthews was very laid back, and as long as we got our work done, she didn't care if we had our phones out in class. "I wonder why I didn't get one. Can I see yours?"

"I already erased it." When would the lies end?

A hall monitor showed up with a pass for one of the guys in the class. I knew he was on the football team because he carried a ball everywhere.

"There goes another," Beth said.

"Another what?" I wasn't even a little surprised she knew what the pass was about.

"They're calling down all of Trevor's friends. He's officially a missing person now, and the cops are trying to find a lead on where he ran off to or who might have kidnapped him."

So far I'd managed to avoid almost all talk about my victims. Trevor and Rebecca were the only ones who had actually been from this town. The investigation meant I wouldn't be able to forget what I'd done to Trevor—not that I really could anyway. But now it was going to be in my face until the police ruled the case closed.

At lunchtime, I was starving. I couldn't remember eating dinner last night. Though I'd certainly had enough glasses of water to fill me up, thanks to Gloria's attempts to keep me hydrated. Ethan got on the lunch line, claiming he had a craving for chocolate milk, but I saw they had giant soft pretzels and knew he was going to surprise me with one. I played along.

Beth was chatting away with the girl sitting next to her. I couldn't remember her name. Actually, I didn't remember the names of any of the kids sitting with us. Beth always did all the talking, and everyone else pretty much listened.

I used the distraction to text Dylan back. Not that I wanted to. I just didn't want him sending any more obnoxious texts while Ethan was around. I'd have to figure out how to block a number on my phone, but until then, I hoped this would shut him up.

Wrong number.

It vibrated almost instantly. What, did he sit on his phone, waiting for it to ring?

Sam?

Nope. Wrong number.

Silence. Hallelujah! I tossed the phone back in my bag, satisfied that was the end of that.

Ethan returned with two soft pretzels and a chocolate milk. "Surprise!"

"Aw, thank you." I kissed him lightly on the lips.

"You two are so cute," Beth said. "How did you meet? I mean, you both just moved here, but you get along like you've known each other for a while."

Damn her and her ability to figure things out.

Ethan squeezed my hand under the table. "We met the day we both got here. In the general store. When I saw her, I knew I had to meet her."

It was times like this that I understood what my mom had always said about Ethan. He was romantic beyond his years.

"And of course she couldn't resist my charm," he added. And there was the typical seventeen-year-old boy attitude.

"Actually," I said, "it was his goofiness that attracted me to him. He knocked over an entire display of toilet paper." I was amazed how the lies just rolled off my tongue. Even Ethan look shocked by how quickly I'd come up with that story. "We've been inseparable ever since." I popped a piece of soft pretzel into my mouth before I took the story too far. After all, it wasn't the same story we'd told Mrs. Melrose in the guidance office. Not that I was worried any students would be gossiping with her.

"Totally cute," Beth said. "I'm predicting you two are still together at prom."

Ethan and I smiled. If only she knew that we'd already been to one prom together. My parents hadn't wanted me to go, but since I was running out of time, they couldn't exactly say no to me.

I finished my lunch while Beth went on and on about Shannon and how she had practically thrown herself at Mr. Ryan in the hallway. The girl had no shame. I just hoped she hadn't mentioned finding Ethan and me in the bathroom together. Seeing Mr. Ryan was going to be awkward until I knew for sure. I was kind of surprised he wasn't avoiding me after Shannon's last rumor about me having a crush on him, but apparently he was used to the female student population acting this way and got over these things quickly.

Beth started in on the break-in next. She said the principal had had the camera by that exit replaced since there was no footage of the old man on it. At least one thing had gone in my favor. She also mentioned an elderly man who was reported missing a month back. He didn't have any family but the neighbors discovered he was gone. Reporters were assuming it was the same guy.

I didn't want to hear any more so I stood up. "I'm going to the bathroom. Be right back."

Ethan nodded and took another bite of his pretzel, which he was now dunking in his chocolate milk.

I tossed my trash and headed to the bathroom across the hall from the cafeteria. I went to the sink and checked my teeth in the mirror, making sure I didn't have any food stuck in them.

"I figured you'd come here eventually. You seem to like the bathrooms in this place."

I jumped at the sound of Dylan's voice. I turned to see him standing in the doorway of the last stall.

"You go to this school?"

"No."

"Then why are you here? And why are you in the girls' bathroom of all places?"

"Waiting for you, like I said." He shifted his weight, leaning against the side of the stall. "My turn with the questions. Why did you lie in your text?"

"What text?" I played dumb.

He took out his phone. "Should I call it now?"

"No!" My phone was still in my bag on the bench next to Ethan.

"So, you admit you lied then? I didn't have the wrong number."

"Fine. I lied. But only because I wanted you to stop texting me."

"Why was my texting you a problem? You didn't want me showing up where Ethan would find you talking to me, so I found a way around that."

"You sent me that same threatening message three times!"

"You didn't respond. I thought it didn't go through. I'm not big on texting."

"You prefer yellow Post-it notes, right?"

He ventured out of the stall. "Look, we need to talk. I don't care how. Phone, text, in person, you pick, but we have to clear some things up."

"No, we don't. I already know all I need to know about you."

"From Nora?" He stepped toward me. "She's lying to you."

She's lying to you. That was what the note on the floor of Ethan's car had said. "The note wasn't for Ethan. It was for me."

"Of course it was for you. I have nothing to say to your boyfriend after he beat the crap out of me." His hand rose to his nose, which was still healing from Ethan's punch.

The door opened, and before Dylan could get back to the stall, Beth walked in. "Whoa, dude, I think you got the wrong bathroom."

Dylan glared at me like this was my fault.

"Do you know him?" Beth asked.

"No. He scared me. I wasn't expecting to walk into the girls' bathroom and find a guy in here. Let alone a guy that doesn't even go to school here."

"Who are you?" Beth asked Dylan. "Did you break in here?" She turned to me. "Another break-in. That's two in less than a week."

Dylan stared at me. If he was waiting for me to defend him, it wasn't happening.

"Stay there," Beth said. "And don't try anything." She opened the door and yelled down the hall, "There's a strange guy in the girls' bathroom!"

Two teachers rushed into the bathroom. I recognized them from cafeteria duty, but I didn't know their names.

"Right there." Beth pointed, as if they couldn't figure out which one of us was the intruder on their own.

They asked Dylan a bunch of questions, and he stood there shaking his head at me. Blaming me. One of the teachers radioed the main office, and a moment later, the school cop came bursting into the bathroom.

"You ladies, go back to the cafeteria," he said.

Beth grabbed my arm and led me out of the bathroom. Ethan was waiting at the cafeteria door.

"What's going on? I heard Beth yell, and then the cop ran in there."

Beth patted my arm like I was a dog. "Some guy was in the girls' bathroom. He scared Sam."

"Some guy?" By the tone of Ethan's voice I could tell he knew it was Dylan.

I nodded.

The bathroom door opened, and the school police officer led Dylan out in handcuffs. The kids in the cafeteria went wild, hooting and cheering.

Dylan stared at me. As he passed by he said, "Nothing is what you think." He didn't sound angry. More like hurt.

Ethan rubbed my shoulders as I stared at Dylan's back getting farther and farther down the hall. I couldn't help wondering if I had things all wrong. Was there a reason I'd memorized his number before I gave Ethan the note? Was there a reason I hadn't told Ethan about all Dylan's attempts to talk to me, all his notes?

Had I made a mistake?

CHAPTER TWENTY-ONE

ETHAN and I made plans to meet up in the girls' bathroom again during next period. He suggested we meet in one of the stairwells, but since most of the hall monitors that period were men, I figured the girls' bathroom was safer. Besides, who would think another guy would risk getting caught there so soon after Dylan was taken away in handcuffs?

I waited in the bathroom, checking the hall for any teachers or other students. All clear. Ethan did a walk-by at first, but then he doubled back and slipped into the bathroom. We walked to the last stall again and locked ourselves in.

"Stealthy maneuver back there," I whispered with a hint of a mocking tone.

"I wanted to be extra careful. Now, tell me what happened. What did that creep say to you? And why would he corner you in a bathroom?"

"Probably for the same reason we're talking in the bathroom right now. He wanted privacy." That was the wrong thing to say. Ethan's face turned red. "Not like that!" I smacked his arm. "He wants to talk to me."

"Why? How do you even know this guy?" Ethan was so worked up he couldn't keep his hands still. He knocked the toilet-paper dispenser right off the wall. It fell with a loud crash.

"Hurry! Get in the next stall over and stand on the toilet so no one sees you."

"Are you kidding me?"

"No." I pushed him under the stall and into the next one as a voice called, "Who's in here?"

I stepped out of the stall, trying to look embarrassed. "Um, I am." I bit my lip and pointed to the toilet-paper dispenser on the floor. "It fell off the wall when I went to get some toilet paper. I swear I didn't do it on purpose."

The woman was a science teacher. Not mine, but I recognized her. She nodded. "I'll call a custodian to fix it. For now, use another stall."

"I will."

"What class are you in? I'll let your teacher know you'll be another minute because there was a mishap in the bathroom."

I could only imagine what the other students would think the mishap was, but I nodded and gave her the room number. I had to get her out of here before she noticed Ethan. His stall door was locked, but since you couldn't see any feet under the door, that was suspicious.

She nodded toward the next stall. Ethan's stall.

"Um, that one is jammed shut or something." I walked past it to the next one.

"Hmm, I'll let the custodian know about that, too."

I smiled and disappeared into the open stall. I waited for her to leave before I came out.

"It's safe," I whispered to Ethan.

He came out, looking nervous. "That was close."

"Yeah, too close. You need to get out of here. I'll check the hallway." I peeked my head out and saw the teacher turn down the next hallway, toward my class. "Now." I waved Ethan on.

"We have to talk about this guy, Sam."

"Later." That would give me time to figure out what I was going to tell Ethan.

"Later," he repeated, giving me a look to let me know he wasn't going to forget about this.

I sighed and walked back to class. I wasn't sure what to tell Ethan. I didn't have Dylan figured out. What if he was telling the truth? But Nora had said he was evil. He'd gone bad from using too much black magic or something like that. I couldn't trust him. It was too risky. That's what she'd said.

I glanced around, making sure no one was watching. We were taking a test on trigonometry. I wasn't going to pass no matter how hard I tried, so I took out my phone and texted Nora under my desk.

Dylan was here.

I squeezed the phone tightly in my hands, hoping to dull the buzzing when her reply came. The second it shook, I opened the text to shut it up.

How? What did he say to you?

Trapped me in the bathroom. He knows what we're doing.

Two seconds later, *Go to the nurse's office.*

Why? He didn't hurt me. I'm fine.

Just go!

It didn't make sense. Did Nora think Dylan had done something to me? Was it possible he'd used a spell on me? Some dark magic that could make me sick?

I shoved my phone in my bag and raised my hand. "Mr. Malinowsky?"

He looked up from his desk. "Yes, Sam."

"May I go see the nurse? I'm not feeling well."

"Are you finished with your test?" He gestured toward my paper with his pen.

I stared at the half-blank page. It didn't matter if I filled in the answers or not. They wouldn't be right anyway.

"Yes."

He waved me forward. I took my bag and my test paper. I kept my head down as I handed him the test.

"Sam, you barely answered any questions."

"I know. I didn't have enough time to get caught up on the chapter this weekend." Okay, so I was playing the new girl card.

"If you needed more time, you should have told me before you took the exam."

"I know. I'm still a little shaken up from what happened earlier. I wasn't thinking straight. I'm sorry."

He shook his head. "I heard about that. Are you okay?"

"Yeah, a little scared is all."

"Understandable." He sighed as he looked over my test paper. "Friday."

"Excuse me?"

"You can take a makeup test on Friday. That's plenty of time to get caught up."

I nodded. "Thank you, Mr. Malinowsky. I really appreciate it."

"No problem. Given your special circumstances, I'll allow it, but keep in mind I don't normally allow extensions. I expect you to get caught up and stay caught up from now on." He scribbled on a pass.

"Yes, sir, and thank you again."

He nodded toward the door as he handed me my pass.

I headed to the nurse's office, wondering what I was supposed to tell Mrs. Wentworth. *That guy who cornered me in the bathroom was a really a witch who has been following me around and threatening to tell people that I kill innocent human beings in order to stay alive.* Yeah, that wasn't going to work.

I stopped in front of the office and took a deep breath before knocking. I heard footsteps, and the door opened. But it wasn't Mrs. Wentworth.

"Nora? What are you doing here?"

"Get inside." She pulled me into the office and peeked down the hall before locking us inside.

"What's going on? Where's Mrs. Wentworth?" I looked around the empty nurse's office.

"She's taking a nap." Nora pointed to the cot behind a thin green curtain.

My eyes widened. "Did you...did you use magic on her?"

Nora shrugged. "It's not going to hurt her. I just made her fall asleep. No big deal. When she wakes up, she won't even remember meeting me."

"So, you did some sort of mind control on her, too?"

"Only a little."

I don't know why it had never occurred to me before, but Nora must be a pretty powerful witch. "What else can you do?"

"Forget about that." She waved me off. "Tell me what happened with Dylan. Every detail. Don't leave anything out."

I started pacing, needing to get rid of some extra energy. I still felt all charged up from draining Rebecca's magic. It was like little bugs crawling under my skin, trying to get out. I wondered if that was what magic felt like, or if I was imagining it. Mom always said I had an overactive imagination.

"Well?"

"Sorry. Um, I was at lunch, and I went to the bathroom. I was standing at the mirror, making sure I didn't have any food stuck in my teeth, when he started talking to me from the last stall."

"What did he say?"

I gave her a look for interrupting me.

She rolled her eyes.

"Like I was saying, he told me he knew he'd find me in the bathroom. It was weird." I'd totally forgotten how strange his first comment had been. Why did he know he'd find me in the bathroom of all places? And then it hit me. "He must have known Shannon caught Ethan and me in the bathroom together! But how? He doesn't know Shannon."

"Shannon?" Nora's eyes widened.

"Yeah, she's this really annoying girl who has it in for me for some strange reason. I never even did anything to her."

"Let me guess," Nora said. "She has long, almost black hair, right? Dresses like she's auditioning for a spot in a music video?"

"How did you know? Have you met her?"

"Oh, we've met."

"I feel sorry for you then. She's a real bitch. And what I don't get is that the entire school does whatever she says. How can someone so evil be so popular?"

"Because she's a witch."

"Exactly my point. Why—" I stopped, and the true meaning of Nora's words sank in. "You mean a *real* witch, don't you?"

"As opposed to a fake witch?"

"So people follow her around because—"

"They're under a spell. One you somehow managed to avoid."

"Is that even possible?"

"Which part? Her putting a spell on that many people or you avoiding it?"

"Both." My mind was spinning. Shannon was a witch?

"It takes a lot of power to create and maintain a spell of that size.

My guess is it's taking all her efforts to keep it up. As for you avoiding it, maybe she doesn't have enough magic to include you in the spell. She might be maxed out already."

"Is she...evil? Like Rebecca? Will I have to..." I didn't like Shannon. Not at all, but that didn't mean I wanted to kill her.

"She's worse than Rebecca. I brought you to Rebecca first because she was the weakest one of them. I wouldn't have you go after the most powerful witch right off the bat. I'm not trying to get you killed."

I needed to sit down. I pulled the green curtain aside and sat next to Mrs. Wentworth's sleeping figure. My lunch was threatening to make another appearance. At least I was in the right place for getting sick. I put my head between my legs and took several deep breaths.

"Shannon was as socially challenged as her brother before the spell. She hated it. Half the school ignored her, and the other half treated her like the stuff you'd find on the bottom of your shoe. It drove her mad, so she tapped into some wickedly strong magic to put a spell on them all."

If Shannon wasn't a witch, I'd actually feel bad for her. Having no friends in high school was torture, but it didn't give her the right to control everyone with magic.

"We'll deal with Shannon later," Nora said. "Tell me more about Dylan."

"He said we needed to talk, which is what he always says. Oh!" I lifted my head to look at her again. "I almost forgot. Ethan got me a prepaid cell phone. A lot like the one you got me, actually. And somehow, only hours later, Dylan was texting me on it. He got the number, and I don't have a clue how."

"You aren't quite getting this witch concept, are you?" She shook her head. "We can pretty much get our hands on anything if we really want it, and if we aren't afraid to use black magic. Now, what did the text say?"

"There were three. All the same. 'Attack another witch and you'll wind up back in your grave.'"

"So, he knows." Nora started pacing. "That means he found Rebecca."

"That's what I thought, too. There's one more thing."

She stopped pacing and looked at me.

"He told me you were lying to me. That nothing was what it seemed."

She smirked. "I'm not surprised. He's desperate. He knows you're targeting evil witches like him, and he's trying to freak you out. Trying to make you turn on me. He doesn't want me helping you. I'll bet you anything *he's* the one who stole your necklace."

"The funny thing is I actually thought he was the one who had given it to me. Before you told me the truth."

"I'm sure that's what he wanted you to think." She took my hands in hers, and my fingers tingled. Was that magic I was feeling in her touch? "Listen to me. You can't believe a word he says. He'll say or do anything to save himself. I'm going to help you get through this, okay? You just have to trust me."

"I do." I had to. She was the only one I could turn to right now.

"Good. One last thing. How did you leave things with Dylan?"

A twinge of guilt stung my insides. "This girl I know came into the bathroom and called the teachers when she saw Dylan. The school cop took him away in handcuffs."

"Unfortunately, that won't hold him for long." She bit her lip as she thought. "Don't go anywhere by yourself. Not even the bathroom. Especially not the bathroom. If Ethan can't go somewhere with you, call me."

I nodded. "Thank you, Nora. I don't know what I'd do if you weren't helping me."

She shifted uncomfortably, making me wonder if she wasn't used to people thanking her. "How are you feeling? Any signs of an attack coming on?"

"No. I feel great. Really energized. And my arms have been tingling. It may sound dumb, but I feel like some of Rebecca's magic is lingering inside me."

"It will probably wear off."

"When the next attack hits?"

"Most likely."

I wondered when that would be.

"You probably won't need to feed as often, though. A witch's life force combined with the energy in their powers should sustain you longer."

"So, I am stealing their powers, too."

"I wouldn't go trying to do spells or anything, but in a way, yes, you are."

That seemed surreal. Their magic was healing me. Too bad I couldn't drain their magic alone. It would've been nice if that were enough to sustain me without having to kill the witches, too. Still, Nora had been right. This was better than attacking innocent people. At least these witches were doing bad things. Evil things. Of course, so was I.

"Don't feel guilty," Nora said, making me think she really could read my mind with her witchy powers. "You're saving people from them. In the end, you're doing a good thing."

I hoped she was right. I tried to tell myself she was.

I left the nurse's office and went through the motions for the rest of the day, not paying attention and only half-caring if my teachers noticed. In last period, I started seeing spots. Luckily, I was sitting down. I didn't want a repeat of my fainting in the diner. We were supposed to be reading from our science textbooks and figuring out this experiment that seemed completely impossible. I was glad we weren't actually performing the experiment, only mentally going through the steps so we'd know what to do in lab tomorrow. I could just see me falling onto a Bunsen burner and singeing all my hair off.

I gripped the edges of my desk to steady myself in case I started to get woozy from the head rush the visions could cause. My sight disappeared, and I waited for whatever was about to show itself to me. It had to be Rebecca. Unless…

The curtain rose. There were flowers everywhere and a long red carpet. It was a garden. Someone was getting married. The wedding party was assembled in front of the audience. Their backs were to me, so I wasn't sure who I was looking at. Was this Rebecca's wedding—or at least the one she would've had?

The couple was exchanging vows now. I could see the girl's face. It wasn't Rebecca. That meant this had to be the mystery guy. The one I kept seeing. The guy who seemed familiar in some way. I begged the vision to zero in on him. If only he'd turn his head.

The couple kissed, and her head blocked my view of his face. It was torture not knowing whose life I was stealing. And why was I seeing so much of this one person's future? All my other visions had been different. One glimpse at each victim's future. But this guy—I was seeing different parts of his life, and he got younger in each vision.

The couple separated and turned toward the audience. My heart clenched in my chest. Oh, God no! I felt more than faint. I felt like I would collapse into myself. Fold up until there was nothing left of me. The mystery guy...

It was Ethan.

CHAPTER TWENTY-TWO

MY heart raced as my vision ended. I blinked back tears, thankful for the darkness. I couldn't look at Ethan's face anymore. If I was having visions of him, of his future, it meant I was somehow draining the life from him, too. But how? In my sleep? When I touched him? Oh God, I couldn't stay away from Ethan. I couldn't. He was everything to me. The only part of my old life I still had. The best part, too.

My cheeks burned with hot tears. I was sure I could see again, but I kept my eyes closed, not ready to face the world. I knew people were probably staring, but I didn't care. Nothing mattered right now. Nothing but Ethan and how to stop him from dying.

Nora. I had to tell Nora. She could use her powers to help me. To help Ethan.

I opened my eyes and grabbed my things. To hell with asking permission and getting a hall pass. I didn't have time to play by the rules. Ethan was running out of time. I stood up and stormed out of the room. Mrs. Stevens called after me, but I ignored her.

I was halfway down the hall when I remembered Nora had told me not to go anywhere by myself. I whipped out my phone and dialed her number.

"Sam?"

"Yeah," I sobbed into the phone. "I need to talk to you."

"What happened? Did you see Dylan again?"

"No. It's something else. Something worse."

The dismissal bell sounded above my head.

"Go to work. I'll meet you there." She hung up before I could say another word.

Students poured into the hallways. I quickly wiped my eyes with the backs of my hands. I couldn't let Ethan see me like this. I wasn't ready to confess everything and tell him he was dying. I just couldn't.

"Hey," Ethan said, coming up behind me.

I whirled around and kissed him, right in the middle of the hallway. I ran my fingers through his hair and pulled him to me. Kids cheered and yelled comments all around us, but I ignored them. I wasn't letting go of Ethan. I wasn't wasting a single moment with him.

"All right. That's enough," Mr. Ryan said.

Ethan gently pulled away from me. I was breathing heavily and fighting back tears.

"Ms. Smith, this is a school, not your bedroom. Please, take this somewhere else." Mr. Ryan stared at me until I moved.

I didn't respond. I grabbed Ethan's hand and pulled him down the hall.

"What's gotten into you? Not that I'm complaining. That kiss was amazing, but what was it for?"

I stopped at the end of the hall, and it took all my might not to kiss him again. "I just—"

"Whose phone is that?" He pointed to my hand.

"Huh?" I looked down. I was still holding the phone Nora had given me.

"That's not the phone I gave you."

"Oh. Um, I found this at the diner when I was cleaning up the other night. I forgot all about it. I guess I thought it was my phone when I grabbed it from my bag." I put the phone away before Ethan asked to see it.

"So, are you going to tell me why you felt the need to maul me in the hallway?"

"I guess after what happened earlier with Dylan I realized how lucky I am to have you. I mean, I already knew I was lucky, but seeing someone totally creepy like Dylan makes me appreciate how wonderful you are."

He leaned in and kissed me. Not a traffic-stopping kiss like I'd given him earlier. A sweet kiss.

"And that thing with Dylan, it was nothing. Only some creep trying to scare the new girl."

"Well, I don't like anyone trying to scare my girl."

"I don't think I'll be hearing from him anymore. I got him taken away in handcuffs."

Ethan smiled. "Yeah, that's something I'll be picturing for a while. He got what he deserved."

"If it makes you feel any better, he told me he didn't want to come anywhere near you after you kicked his ass at the cottage."

Ethan put his arm around me and walked me to the car. "Guess I knocked some sense into him."

I didn't want to point out that beating on Dylan hadn't stopped him from coming after me. I was going to let Ethan have his moment.

Nora was already at the diner when I got there. She was sitting at the end of the counter, drinking coffee. Ethan kissed me before he headed to the kitchen. I put my purse behind the counter and put on my apron, trying to act natural and not go running to Nora.

She waved her hands in the air and mumbled into her coffee. I narrowed my eyes at her, and she smiled. "We can talk now. No one will hear us."

"How?"

"Are you going to make me go through this again?"

"Witch. Got it." I looked around, making sure no one was glancing our way.

"I cast a spell so people won't even notice us. We're in sort of a bubble, shielded from view."

I nodded and leaned my elbows on the counter. The tears came on before I got a single word out.

"There's something I haven't told you. I'm not just having attacks. I'm having visions, too."

"I know." She sipped her coffee.

"You know?"

"Yeah. The day we met, in the bathroom, you'd just had one. And then when you fainted, that was another."

"How come you never mentioned them before?"

"I didn't think I needed to. You're seeing glimpses of the people you killed, right?"

Why did all of this seem so normal to her? Shouldn't she be at least a little surprised?

"Usually, but I've been seeing someone I haven't killed, too."

She put her coffee down. Now I had her attention. "Go on."

"At first I didn't know who he was. He was old, but then I had another vision and he was a little younger. He's the only person I've had more than one vision about, and it didn't stop there. I saw him again today while I was in class. He was getting married. He…" I choked on the words. My throat was closing up.

"Did you find out who he is?" Nora asked.

I nodded, not sure if I could say his name out loud. A whimper escaped my lips.

"It's Ethan." Even though it was Nora who said his name, I burst into tears. My stomach cramped. I felt like someone was squeezing my insides in a vise.

"Don't fall apart on me." Nora came around the counter and held me up by my arms. "Let me look into it. I'll see what I can find out."

"How? How am I hurting him?" My eyes pleaded with her for answers.

"I need time."

"He doesn't have much time left. It was his wedding day. He was in his twenties. He's seventeen, Nora. That's only a few years."

She nodded in understanding. "And you can't give back the time you take."

I hadn't even thought of that. "Do you mean, even if you can stop this, he'll still die before his wedding day?"

She didn't answer, but she didn't need to. Ethan had watched me die of cancer. Wither away to nothing. And now I was going to have to watch the same thing happen to him. Only I was the one doing it to him.

"What do I do?"

"Act normally, and whatever you do, don't tell Ethan what's going on."

Of course I couldn't tell Ethan, but how was I supposed to act normally? I'd gotten a second chance at life. Sure, it wasn't at all what I would've wanted, but I was here. Ethan wasn't going to get that. Unless…

"Ethan is the one who figured out how to bring me back," I said. "He won't tell me what he did, but he knows how to bring someone back from the dead. If I can somehow get him to tell me what he did, then I can save him, too."

Nora shook her head. "Think about this, Sam. We haven't gotten a hold on your situation. Do you really want to risk Ethan coming back the way you are now? Or worse?"

What could be worse than being a killer? And it was Ethan. What choice did I have?

"I won't let him die. Even this…" I gestured to myself, "is better than being six feet under."

"Give me a few days before you talk to Ethan. You said he was in his twenties in the vision. We still have some time to figure this out."

"Why do you care if I talk to him? He could help." I was getting louder and a few people around us were glancing in our direction, squinting like they were trying to see something that wasn't really there.

Nora noticed it, too. "The spell is wearing off. We can't talk anymore." She stood up. "Give me two days. That's all I need."

Two days. How much time would Ethan lose in those two days? So far years were flying off his life. "Two days. Unless I have another vision. Then, I'm going straight to Ethan."

She leaned forward and whispered, "Call me before you talk to him. No matter what."

The rest of the diner came crashing back to me. The people, the loud discussions. The spell had worn off.

"Waitress." A guy held his hand up to get my attention.

I nodded at Nora. "Okay."

She left me to help the customers who had no idea I'd been here this entire time.

Somehow Gloria hadn't missed me in my absence. Whatever Nora had done had made Gloria think I'd been doing my job since I'd walked in the door. Only when we closed up for the night did she sit down and question why she was so exhausted.

"I didn't think there were any more people than usual tonight, but I'm wiped out." She kicked her shoes off and rubbed her feet.

"Yeah, I think everyone was overly demanding tonight. I felt like I was on the go nonstop." I wiped the counter down to avoid eye contact. More lies. Did I even know how to tell the truth anymore?

"Go collect that boy of yours and get out of here. It's a school night." She held her hand out. I untied my apron and gave it to her.

"Goodnight, Gloria."

"Goodnight, Samantha. Don't keep that boy up too late, you hear me? I heard about that kiss in the hall today."

"How did you hear about that?"

"A couple of your school friends were in here. Some girl—what was her name? Beth something or other. She said the whole school is talking about that kiss." Gloria winked at me. "I remember when Jackson used to kiss me like that."

I smiled, but it faded quickly when I thought about why I'd kissed Ethan in the hallway. I was losing him.

Ethan came out of the kitchen and looked back and forth between Gloria and me. "Uh oh, looks like I walked into some girl talk."

"Don't worry," Gloria said. "Samantha is a lady. She doesn't kiss and tell. Your other school friends are a different story, though. They had plenty to say about that kiss."

Ethan blushed. If it were his guy friends who'd said it, he'd be laughing and high-fiving. But coming from Gloria, it was totally embarrassing.

I took his hand, and we walked out to the car. "Let's go somewhere where we can look at the stars for a while, okay?"

"You sure? It's getting late. Don't you have homework or something?" He opened my door for me.

"I don't care. I want to be with you." I sounded needy again, but I *did* need him. I needed to savor every moment I had with him because I wasn't sure how many more there would be.

"Okay." He walked around to his side and got in. "Mountain view or open field?"

"Doesn't matter. You pick."

He drove us back to the spot overlooking the river—the spot we'd stopped at the other night. It was perfect. Just big enough for the two of us. We reclined our seats and opened the moon roof.

"It's beautiful," I said, looking up at the stars.

"You're beautiful." He rolled over onto his side so he was facing me. "But there's one problem with this arrangement."

"What's that?" I mimicked his sideways position.

He patted the center console between us. "I can't get to you."

"I have an idea. Follow me." I got out of the car and climbed onto the hood, leaning my head against the windshield. Ethan did the same. My hair got tangled in the windshield wiper. "Ow. Okay, maybe I didn't think this through."

"Here." Ethan untangled my hair and slipped his arm around my shoulders. "Now you can lie on me instead."

I stared into his eyes. His beautiful blue eyes. "I love you."

"I love you, too." He kissed me, and I pulled him closer. I wanted to feel every inch of his body against mine. His warmth, his love. I kissed him more passionately as the seconds passed. I could feel hot tears welling up in my eyes. I wanted to stay with Ethan forever. That had been the plan. My cancer had come between us, and he'd found a way around it. I wasn't sure what was killing him now, but I owed it to him to find a way to bring him back.

Ethan pulled away and stared at me. "You're crying." He kissed my tear-stained cheeks. "Talk to me, Sam. What's upsetting you?"

"I wish we could be together like this all the time. Now, tomorrow, thirty years from now."

He pulled me closer, wrapping me tightly in his arms. "We can be." He kissed the top of my head, and I breathed in his scent. "We will be."

My insides ached at his words. He didn't even know he was dying. Maybe that was a good thing, because knowing was killing me.

CHAPTER TWENTY-THREE

THE next morning, I sat in Mr. Ryan's class, staring out the window, thinking about Ethan. I'd tried to convince him to ditch school with me. I wanted to go for a long drive, like we used to. I wanted to spend the day soaking him up. But Ethan was Mr. Rational. He said we'd already missed the beginning of the school year, and there was no reason to get even further behind. I tried everything to get him to change his mind, but in the end, we just wound up being late for school.

Now here I was, unable to even pretend I was paying attention to Mr. Ryan or *Dr. Jekyll and Mr. Hyde*. I thought about texting Ethan to meet me in the bathroom, but every time I reached for my bag, Shannon would turn around and watch me like a hawk. I knew she wouldn't hesitate to get me in trouble with Mr. Ryan. I didn't really care if I got in trouble, but I didn't want to make Ethan's last days—however many were left—anything but good.

"Ms. Smith?"

"Huh?" I turned to the front of the room where Mr. Ryan was sitting on the edge of the desk.

"I asked if you could explain the passage I just read."

He'd read something aloud? "Um, sorry, but I'm not sure."

Mr. Ryan sighed. "I'm certain you won't find any answers out that window, Ms. Smith. And I can tell you for a fact that tomorrow's test will count for twenty percent of the semester grade."

The end of the semester was thirteen weeks away. Who worried about final grades this early in the year? I nodded and pretended to show interest in the rest of the class.

By the time I got to Sculpture, I only had one thing on my mind—finding out how Ethan had brought me back. Nora had asked me not to ask him, but maybe if I indirectly dropped a few questions I could get some clue.

Ethan was sitting with Beth when I walked into class. I wanted to talk to him right away, but Ms. Matthews assigned Ethan to first shift on the pottery wheel. He smiled at me and got a blob of clay for his project.

"So," Beth said, sketching her design. "I was at the diner yesterday."

"Yeah, I know." I took out my sketchbook and pencil, pretending to work but really watching Ethan.

"It's funny, but I didn't see you there. You waitress right after school, don't you?"

"Yeah, five days a week. Well, I work on weekends, too, but I go in earlier."

Ethan dropped a large chunk of clay on the floor and was left with a tiny misshapen thing on the wheel. I heard him tell Ms. Matthews that he was working on an abstract piece about minimalism. She totally bought it.

"That's what I thought." Beth turned her sketchbook upside down and continued with the pattern she was drawing. "So I was surprised that I didn't see you. I thought you could be my waitress. I was even prepared to leave you an insanely large tip."

"Oh, well, that was sweet of you. I'm sure Gloria appreciated the tip."

"She's your boss, right?"

I wished I could find a way out of this conversation. Being cornered and questioned by Beth was not good. "Yeah. You know, I just remembered I forgot my—"

"She was running all over the place yesterday. It was like she was waiting on all the tables by herself."

Because she was. "I'll be back in a minute." I got up and walked to the kiln. I fished through the finished projects and found mine. A small vase with uneven lines running around it. It looked hideous, and I was sure it would get me an F, but I loved it. The lines were made with Ethan's and my hands when he laced his fingers through mine.

"You should keep your fingers together if you want a smoother end product," Ms. Matthews said, walking up behind me.

"Actually, it's exactly what I was going for."

"Really?" She eyed me, waiting for an explanation.

I thought of Ethan's minimalism excuse when he dropped his clay. "Yeah, I was going for the skewed perception of beauty in today's society." I wasn't sure where I'd pulled that from, but Ethan walked over and nodded.

"I totally see that. Nice work, Sam."

That was all it took. Ms. Matthews smiled. "Well done, Sam."

When she walked away, I turned to Ethan. "I didn't think I could pull that off."

"There's nothing to it. Pretend everything you do is entirely on purpose."

My mind was swimming with thoughts. How could I turn this conversation into a casual inquiry about my existence? This was so much harder than I thought it would be.

"It's pretty cool how you can bring something to life, isn't it?"

He raised an eyebrow. "You can hardly call making a clay pot bringing something to life."

This wasn't going well. "I don't know. It starts out as a lump of clay. It's nothing. Lifeless. And then you mold it and turn it into something that's full of life."

"Have you been eating the school meatloaf or something? You're acting weird."

I sighed. It looked like Nora was going to get her way. I couldn't figure out how to get information out of Ethan without sounding like a total nutcase. If only Ethan knew Nora was a witch. Then asking about what he'd done to bring me back might not seem so strange. Both were supernatural, right?

"Hey." I put my hand on his forearm for no other reason than I wanted to touch him. I was trying to memorize everything about him. His smell, the feel of his skin, the shape of his face. Every detail. "I wanted to let you know I worked things out with Nora."

"Nora?"

"Yeah, that girl I told you about. The one from the diner."

He wrinkled his forehead. "Is she the one who skipped out on her bill?"

"That's her, but it was a misunderstanding. She paid the bill, and she's been really nice to me ever since. We've even talked about hanging out sometime."

"That's great. I'm glad you're making friends. You should invite Beth along, too. She really likes you."

Too bad Beth was too perceptive for her own good—and *my* own good.

"Nora's kind of weird around people she's never met. She's home-schooled." I didn't know what made me say that, but it seemed like it could be true. She didn't go to our school, so either she attended some fancy private school, which I doubted, or she was home-schooled.

"That's got to get lonely." Ethan squeezed my hand.

"I think that's why she comes to the diner every day. To be around people."

"But you said she's shy around new people."

"She is. That's why I think it's good that she's trying to be more social. She talks to me every time she's there."

Ethan gave me a puzzled look. "Did you say she comes to the diner every day?"

"Uh-huh."

"How have I never seen her?"

"You work in the kitchen now. You're not on the floor with the customers." I shrugged. "I can introduce you today if you'd like."

"Sure. Call me out from the kitchen when she gets there. I'd like to meet her."

I debated telling him right then that she was a witch, but when I looked up, Beth was staring at us. It probably wasn't a good idea to mention the witch thing with her trying to listen in.

Beth didn't say anything to me for the rest of the class, but near the end of lunch, she finally said, "I was thinking of stopping by the diner tonight."

"Oh, yeah?" I tried to act casual, but I didn't want Beth around when I was talking to Nora.

"Do you mind?" She eyed me over her chocolate milk.

"Not at all. I'll buy you a piece of Gloria's famous peach pie."

"I don't eat peaches, but thanks for the offer."

I nodded, trying to be polite. I was probably being paranoid, but Beth made me jumpy. "Well, then you can choose the dessert."

"Sounds good." She got up to throw her lunch away, and I was relieved to be rid of her.

In my afternoon classes, I realized I hadn't had an attack in over a day, and I hadn't had a vision about Rebecca either. Draining the life and power from a witch was sustaining me so much better than I could've hoped. But I also noticed the feeling of bugs crawling under my skin had completely faded. Was that a sign? Was Rebecca's magic wearing off?

I made sure no one was watching, and I texted Nora.

Magic is gone. Think I might have another attack later today.

I waited for what seemed like an eternity. Where was Nora? I watched the clock on the wall tick the seconds away. How could time seem so slow and so fast at the same time? Waiting for Nora to respond was taking an eternity, but knowing Ethan was dying made each passing second fly by.

Finally my phone vibrated in my hand.

I'm on it.

I breathed easier knowing Nora was taking care of things. I wondered who the next witch would be, and I couldn't help wondering if Shannon was on Nora's list.

We got to the diner a few minutes late thanks to a bus breaking down in front of us. Gloria was making a fresh pot of coffee when I stuffed my purse behind the counter and reached for my apron.

"You'd think a school that operated on bells would let the students out on time," she said. As nice as Gloria was to Ethan and me, she could really attack people she didn't know. She'd even fired the new dishwasher after one morning.

"They did. There was an accident, and we got stuck behind it. What do you need me to do? Take over your tables? Finish the coffee? You name it, I'll do it."

She turned around and stared at me. "Are you feeling okay? You're all fired up."

I realized my pulse was racing. What was that about? "I'm fine. I guess I had too much soda at lunch."

"Caffeine. It's wonderful in an exhausting, exhilarating way. You know what I mean?"

I gave a nervous laugh. "Yeah."

I hoped Nora would come in soon. My body was behaving strangely, and I couldn't help thinking it was some sort of withdrawal, maybe from the magic.

I zipped around the diner, handling my tables and Gloria's. After a while, she sat down and let me have at it. I didn't mind. I couldn't stand still. Nora didn't show up until seven.

"What took you so long?" I asked, the second she sat down.

"I had a little trouble with your next…" She paused as the door opened behind her. "Coffee, please," she said, turning over an empty cup on the counter.

Beth walked in and came right up to the counter. "Hey, Sam."

"Hi." I poured Nora a cup of coffee and held the pot up to Beth. "Want some?"

"No, thanks. I'll take a ginger ale."

"Sure."

Nora kept her eyes on her coffee, but Beth turned to her and stuck out her hand. "Hi, I'm Beth. You must be Sam's friend Nora, right?"

Nora's eyes widened. I knew Beth had been eavesdropping in Sculpture. Why did she have to be so nosy? I opened my mouth to say something, but Nora smiled at Beth.

"That's right, and you are?"

"Beth. I go to school with Sam and Ethan. You must be home-schooled. I haven't seen you around."

I saw Nora smirk, but Beth didn't seem to notice. Was it possible she had actually missed something for once? She might lose her reputation as Little Miss Observant.

"I do study at home, so yes, I guess you could say I'm home-schooled."

I smiled. If only Beth knew what Nora studied. Witchcraft wasn't exactly on the curriculum at our school.

"How long have you known Sam?" Beth continued with her line of questioning.

I wondered how long Nora would let her go on before she put a silencing spell on her. Was there even such a thing?

I gave Nora an apologetic look before returning to my other tables. Beth yammered on for an hour while Nora drank her coffee. I was so wrapped up in the two of them sitting there together looking like the odd couple that I forgot Ethan had said he wanted to meet Nora.

"Nora." I walked up to the end of the counter so Nora could turn to face me with her back to Beth. It wasn't exactly privacy, but it was the best I could hope for right now. "Ethan said he wanted to meet you. I'm going to get him from the kitchen, okay?"

A strange look flitted across her face so quickly I couldn't figure out what it was. Most likely she'd had enough meeting people for one night after having to listen to Beth for the past hour.

I reached for her arm, touching it briefly. "Sorry, I know it's getting late, and you probably have to get going. This will only take a second, though. I promise. And you'll love Ethan."

"I'm going to run to the bathroom really quick while you get him," she said.

"Okay." I headed to the kitchen and found Jackson at the grill alone. "Where's Ethan? There's someone I want him to meet." I motioned to the dining room.

"He's in the walk-in, looking for more frozen patties."

"Oh, well, can you ask him to come out when he's done?"

Jackson nodded. "Sure thing, sweetheart."

I went back to the counter and refilled Nora's coffee. I debated asking Beth if she wanted another ginger ale. I was kind of hoping she'd ask for the check.

"Ethan's never met Nora? That's strange."

"Not really. He doesn't come into the dining room much since he switched from busboy to assistant chef."

"He used to bus tables?"

"Yeah, when we first got hired, but Jackson said he could use an extra hand in the kitchen."

"Huh, seems like he would've known that when he was hiring."

"Maybe he did. The sign in the window just said 'Help Wanted.' It didn't list positions, and Ethan never mentioned any cooking skills. He helped Jackson out one night in a jam. We were packed. He's been there since."

Nora came back from the bathroom. "Sam, I really need to get going. I have to check on something." I knew she was talking about the witch she had lined up for me.

"Oh, okay. I guess Ethan is still looking for those patties in the walk-in. Sorry you didn't get to meet him tonight. Maybe tomorrow."

"Yeah. Call me." She left off the "if you need me," but I understood.

"Bye." I watched her go, wishing it was Beth walking out of the diner instead.

"She's interesting," Beth said.

"What do you mean?"

"I mean she's not exactly normal."

Who was she to judge? "I like her." I took Nora's coffee cup and dumped it into a bin of dirty dishes.

"Well, yeah she seems to like you, too, but she's a witch. Like a real live witch."

CHAPTER TWENTY-FOUR

HOW could she possibly know that? I was starting to wonder if Beth was a witch herself. It was uncanny how she seemed to know everything about everyone.

"Why do you think she's a witch?" I tried to play it cool, to not give away that Beth was right.

"I followed her when she went to the bathroom." She played with her empty glass and avoided my eyes.

I flung the dishcloth down on the counter. "Why would you do that?" At first I'd thought Beth was really intuitive, but she wasn't. She knew everything because she spied on everyone. Stuck her nose in everyone's business. She wasn't a witch or clairvoyant. She was nosy.

She shrugged. "I got a weird vibe from her. But anyway, she was mumbling something in the bathroom. Some sort of prayer to some god or maybe even Satan. Who knows?"

"The only god Nora prays to is the coffee god." I laughed, trying to shrug off Beth's accusation. "And how do you know she was praying? Maybe she was singing. Sometimes Jackson plays music in the kitchen."

"You were just in there. You don't remember if he had music on?" She looked at me now, trying to read my expression.

"I wasn't really paying attention." I picked up the dishcloth again and wiped the counter. "I'm kind of busy working, if you hadn't noticed."

"Right." She sat back on her stool. "What do I owe you?"

Finally. I took her bill from the pad in my back pocket and tossed it on the counter in front of her. Okay, so I wasn't exactly being nice, but Beth was getting into things she didn't have a right to.

"See you in school tomorrow." She placed a five-dollar bill on the counter.

"Yeah," I mumbled, baffled why she'd leave me a tip that was bigger than the actual check. Especially since I'd forgotten to buy her dessert.

Whatever. I was glad to be rid of her, and since Nora had managed to skip out on her bill again, I used Beth's tip to cover it. As the night grew on, I started to feel weird. My energy level hit a low, and even though I wasn't gasping for air, I felt like breathing was getting harder and harder. As soon as the last customer left, I texted Nora.

Something weird is happening to me. Might be time.

Gloria took the cash drawer and headed to the office. "Yell good-night before you leave," she said.

"Sure." My cell vibrated in my hand.

On my way.

Great. Now I had to let Ethan know I wasn't going home with him.

I walked into the kitchen. Ethan was washing dishes, which made me nearly fall over. "Whoa! Jackson, how did you pull this off? I didn't think Ethan even knew what a sponge was for."

"Ha ha," Ethan said. "Cleanup is part of cooking. Or so Jackson tells me. Although I haven't seen him do any dishes yet."

"Why would I? That's what I have my junior chef for." He smiled and waggled his eyebrows at me. I assumed Jackson wasn't even going to attempt hiring a new dishwasher since Gloria had fired the last two.

I walked over to Ethan and placed my hand on his back, but then I remembered I was feeling funny lately. I didn't want to accidentally drain any more life from Ethan. I wasn't sure how much time he really had left. I lowered my hand. "You going to be much longer?"

"Um…" He looked around at the stack of dishes. "Looks like a least half an hour. I still have a few other things to do after I finish with these."

"Okay. Then do you mind if I go to Nora's for a little while?"

He nearly dropped the dish he was washing. "You guys are hanging out?"

I shrugged. "What's the big deal?"

"I'm just surprised. I know you said you worked things out, but I didn't realize you were that close already."

"She's nice."

"Was she here tonight?"

"Yeah. I tried to introduce you, but Jackson said you were in the walk-in refrigerator looking for something. Nora had to be somewhere so she couldn't stick around and wait."

"How are you two hanging out if she already has plans?" He looked at me skeptically.

"I guess it wasn't anything big or time-consuming. So are you cool with it?"

"Yeah. Call me when you need a ride home."

"I'm pretty sure she'll drive me home, but I'll call if I need you." I kissed his cheek, just a light peck because my throat was starting to close up. "Bye."

I practically ran out of there, yelling goodnight to Gloria. Nora was already waiting for me in the parking lot.

She gave me the once-over. "You don't look anything like you did last time."

"It feels different, but I can tell it's happening. The air is almost too heavy to breathe."

She backed out of her parking spot and turned onto the main road. After about ten minutes, we turned onto a dirt road.

"Where are we going?" I held onto the door for support as the car bounced on the uneven road.

"My house."

"You brought the witch to your house?"

"I had a visitor earlier. This guy I know broke in and tried to use black magic on me. Luckily, I was too quick for him. I bound him in his own magic. He's waiting for you."

Waiting for me. That's not really how I would've described it. "Does he know? About me?"

"Yes. Dylan must have told him."

I felt queasy, and I wasn't sure if I'd make it much farther.

"Don't get all weak on me," Nora said. "We both agreed this was the best option for now. The spell I need to put on a new necklace for you takes time. I can't rush it or it won't work right."

"I know." I gripped the seat as the tightness in my chest increased. I would've given just about anything for a little of that witch magic right about now.

"We're here." Nora pulled up to a house that was almost as broken-down as the cottage had been when we'd moved in. "As you can see, the witch you're about to meet did a number on this place."

"I'm sorry." I wanted to say more, but I was too weak. I hated that Nora was put in the middle of all this. She was nice enough to try to help me, and all it had done was get her house pummeled by an evil witch.

She came around to my side of the car and took me by the arm. "Hands where I can see them." She knew her touch was helping me, but if I got too close, got into position, I would kill her to save myself. I couldn't stop the monster inside me when it took over.

She brought me up the front steps, which were a crumbled mess of cement pieces. I held onto the side of the house while she opened the door. She took my arm again and led me down a flight of steps to the basement. A guy was gagged and tied to a chair. But not with rope. Like Rebecca, he was held in place by magic, a swirling wind all around him.

He glared at me and shifted in his restraints. His muffled screams echoed in my ears. Nora brought me inches from him and placed my hand on his neck. I felt his warmth, and I inhaled deeply, filling my lungs with air. My other hand found his chest. His heart beat beneath my fingers, quickly at first, fueled by fear. Fear of me. I basked in the life that was filling me, along with the tingling of magic that accompanied it.

As his face twisted in pain, wrinkling with age, I felt my hair float up behind me like a sudden gust of wind was blowing it back. It was the magic. I was sure of it. He was more powerful than Rebecca had been. Every inch of me tingled with life, with power. Finally, he slumped forward, and I lost my hold on him. He was dead, and I could actually see a faint glow on my skin.

"Oh, my God," Nora whispered. "His magic is inside you. All of it. I can sense it."

"I can see it." I held my arms out and watched the silver glow dance across my skin. "I'm not going to stay like this, am I? Ethan will notice this for sure."

"He won't notice a thing. He's human." She walked over and touched my arm. "I don't see a thing, and I'm a witch. I can only feel the power because I recognize it from Ben."

"Ben?" I looked at the witch slumped over on the floor. When I took his magic, I took the power that was swirling around him, too. "How did you know him? How do you know all these witches? They're all evil, right?"

"Unfortunately." She turned away from me like she was ashamed of what she was about to say. "We used to all be in the same coven."

I knew she was a witch, but the fact that she practiced magic with other witches was surreal to me. "What happened?"

"We used to get along. We were friends. No." She shook her head. "We were more than that. We were family. We got together every night and worked on group spells. We bound ourselves to one another."

She paused, and I wondered if she'd be able to finish her story. It was obviously hard for her to talk about.

"Everything was great. Until one day Shannon suggested we try a new spell. One that would make humans bend to our will. I didn't like the idea. Messing with free will was against all the rules we followed. It's not what good witches do."

I nodded, remembering how Nora had said Shannon was treated badly by the kids at school. That was what had made her turn into such a bitch.

"I told them I didn't want to be part of it, but they got angry. They said since we'd bound our powers to one another, the spell wouldn't be at it strongest without me. I told them I didn't care. I wouldn't do it." She sat down on a couch that was covered with a sheet. She lowered her head, and I knew she was holding back tears.

"Nora, I'm so sorry. You don't have to tell me about it if you don't want to."

"No. I need to tell someone. It's been killing me to keep it in."

I sat next to her, placing my hand on her shoulder. "I'm guessing they did the spell anyway."

"Shannon did. On her own. She said if the entire coven wasn't going to take part, then she'd do it alone."

"So, you guys can still do magic by yourselves?"

"Of course, but for the really big spells, we need to combine our magic. Unless we break the magical tie between us."

"How do you do that?"

"The only way to break the tie is by dying."

"Is that why you want me to kill them? So you won't be bound to them anymore?" I couldn't believe it. She had a personal interest in this. It wasn't only about finding victims who weren't innocent. It was about saving herself from the rest of the coven.

"I'm sorry. I should've told you sooner, but I thought this arrangement would help both of us. They're evil, Sam. You don't know what it's been like being bound to them. They're powerful enough to gang up on me. If you don't kill them, they *will* kill me."

I didn't want that. I didn't like that Nora had kept this from me, but she was trying to help me, too. I needed her.

"You still should've told me."

"I know. I'm sorry." She looked up at me with swollen red eyes. "Can you forgive me?"

I nodded. She hadn't told me about all this because she was scared. She was trying to save herself the same way I was. We were a lot alike.

"What about Ben? Why did he come after you like that?"

"He said he was tired of me fighting them. Tired of me playing the good witch. That I was part of the coven, and if I didn't go along with them, he'd break my tie to them for good."

"He tried to kill you?"

"Yes." She looked away again.

"What made him so angry? Was it finding out about Rebecca?" I looked over at Ben again, old, wrinkled, unrecognizable Ben.

"He was with Dylan when he found her."

"So Ben and Dylan were still working together?"

"Yeah. Ben was Dylan's brother."

"What?" I whipped my head toward her. "You didn't tell me that!"

She stood up, finding the strength to put away her tears. "What's the big deal? He was an evil witch. Look what he did to my house. Look what he tried to do to me." She stared at me. "And why do you care if he was related to Dylan? Dylan's evil, too. He's been coming after you, trying to poison you with lies. Trying to hurt you, Sam. You should hate him. You should *want* to kill him."

I didn't *want* to kill anyone. I knew everything else she'd said was true. Dylan wasn't a good witch like Nora, but I felt like I knew him. And that made killing his brother unbearable. "He's going to come after me now for sure."

Nora nodded. "That's why we're going to go after him first."

CHAPTER TWENTY-FIVE

Go after Dylan. Kill Dylan. My brain wouldn't process those words. I couldn't do it. Ever since I'd met Dylan, there was something about him. Something I couldn't put my finger on. But it was the reason I had memorized his phone number. *555-0851*. It was the reason I hadn't told Ethan about all the times Dylan texted me, or when he cornered me at the river. The reason I felt guilty when the school cop took him away in handcuffs. I couldn't tell all this to Nora. She hated him. I understood why she felt that way, but for whatever reason, I didn't share her feelings toward Dylan.

"I want to go after Shannon next," I blurted out. "You said she was the one who started this. Who wanted to do that spell to mess with people's free will. She should be next." I tried to sound assertive. To sound like I was suggesting Shannon because she had been the first one to hurt Nora.

"If we attack Shannon next, Dylan will have time to attack you."

"How many are in your coven? I need to know what I'm up against."

"Five, including me."

"So you, Rebecca, Ben, Shannon, and Dylan." I nodded. "Shannon needs to be next." I had no other options. No other way to delay going after Dylan. And I had to delay it. I had to call Dylan and finally hear him out. Even if all he wanted to tell me was more lies, I wanted to hear it. I had to decide for myself if he deserved to die.

"Do you have any idea how angry he is going to be when he finds out what you've done?"

"You mean what *we've* done."

"Yes. It's not just you he's going to come after. This decision isn't yours alone to make."

I started pacing. "All right. Then let's talk this through."

"There isn't anything to discuss. Dylan is going to come for both of us. He'll stop at nothing until we're dead." She grabbed my arm, forcing me to stop pacing and look at her. "I'm serious, Sam. You don't know him like I do."

She was right about that. I didn't know him. I needed to get to know him, but would that even be possible when he discovered what I'd done? "I'm not ready. Shannon is the easier target. She's so wrapped up in herself and her popularity that she probably won't even notice Ben is gone."

"She knows about you, Sam. Don't fool yourself into thinking she doesn't want you dead, too. You killed her boyfriend."

My eyes widened. "You know about Trevor?"

"Of course I do. I'm trying to save your life. I had to find out everything I possibly could about you. I covered up Trevor's murder the same way I covered up all the others. I wiped your fingerprints off everything and repaired the fire extinguisher. I even tampered with the security camera. You have no idea the lengths I've been going to for you."

She was right. She'd been saving me over and over again, but I still wasn't ready to kill Dylan. "Then if you know me so well, you know I'm not ready to face Dylan. I'm sorry, but I don't want to put us both in a situation where we could get killed. I need time to sort this out. To come to terms with killing him."

"What is there to come to terms with?" Nora shouted.

I couldn't argue with her anymore. She had no idea that all this killing was destroying me. "Look, I'm the one doing the killing. Either we do this my way, or we don't do it at all."

She stepped back, glaring at me. "I'm not some powerless human you can order around, Sam."

"Yeah, well, you're not an evil witch either, so don't pretend you'll resort to using magic on me." I sighed. "We're not going to get anywhere on this tonight, and all of this is pointless right now anyway. I can't kill anyone until another attack comes on."

"Maybe so, but I need to know which witch I'm going to trap for you."

"Shannon. It needs to be Shannon."

She shook her head.

"I'm calling Ethan to come get me." I started up the stairs toward the car where I'd left my purse.

"Wait." Nora followed me. "I don't want him knowing where I live. If he sees this place, he'll start asking questions neither one of us can answer. I'll drive you home."

We didn't talk until we pulled into my driveway. "Please, Nora, I'm begging you. Let it be Shannon."

"When you're moments from death, you won't care who it is."

That was true, but I still didn't want it to be Dylan.

Ethan opened the front door.

"Fine," Nora said. "Now go."

I was barely out of the car when Nora peeled out of the driveway. She was mad, but I'd gotten my way, so I was okay with it.

"Have a good time?" Ethan asked.

Not exactly. "Yeah, but I'm glad I'm home with you now." I wrapped my arms around him, nuzzling my face in his neck.

"I'm glad you're home, too. I missed you." He turned his head and kissed me.

We stumbled back into the cottage, not breaking apart. His hands were on the sides of my face, and I tossed my purse onto the couch. I missed and hit the lamp, which fell over onto the floor.

"Oops."

"Leave it." Ethan brought me into the bedroom. He pulled his shirt up over his head as I sat down on the bed. He leaned back down to kiss me again, and everything went black. No spots this time. Just solid black.

I continued to kiss him, hoping he wouldn't notice I was having a vision. I'd never seen any of Rebecca's future, so I didn't really think this would be Ben's. That only left one option. Ethan's.

His face flooded my sight, and for a moment, I thought the vision had ended. The Ethan in my vision looked the same as the one I was kissing. I pulled back and slammed my palms against my eyes.

"Sam, what's wrong? Are you hurt?"

"No!" I shrieked. "It can't be time."

"What are you talking about?" Ethan reached for my hands and pulled them away from my face. "Sam?"

I saw Ethan lying in bed with me, smiling. He pushed a stray hair off my cheek. "So, what do you think? Should I tell Beth we'll go?"

I screamed, pounded the mattress with my fists. This couldn't happen.

"Sam?" It was Ethan's voice, his real voice, not in the vision. My sight went black, and I cried, big, heaping sobs. Ethan wrapped his arms around me and pulled me to his chest. I cried into his bare chest until I exhausted myself.

It was going to happen soon. I knew it. I didn't know what Ethan had been asking me about. Beth hadn't invited us anywhere, so it couldn't have been today.

"Sweetie, talk to me. What happened?" Ethan whispered in my ear.

I tilted my head back and kissed him, not saying a word. There wasn't time for words. In the morning, I'd have to talk to Nora. I'd skip school if I had to. I needed her to find a way to save Ethan. I knew that meant bringing him back to life. That was it. I pulled away from Ethan. I couldn't beat around the bush anymore. I needed an answer.

"Ethan, how did you bring me back? You have to tell me, and you have to tell me now."

He shook his head. "I told you it doesn't matter."

I took a deep breath. I couldn't worry about what Ethan would think of me when I told him the truth. I had to say whatever I needed to get him to talk.

"I didn't come back normal. Something went wrong."

"Sam—"

I put my finger to his lips. "Let me finish. I need to know what you did, so I can fix this." I was trying to avoid telling him he was dying.

"Fix what? Sam, you're the same person you've always been. Except you aren't sick anymore."

"Yes, I am."

He sighed. "Is it because the cancer is gone? I thought you'd be happy to be healthy, to not have to worry about dying."

"I do have to worry about it. I worry every day. I am dying, Ethan. Right now."

He grabbed my face in his hands. "Listen to me. You only think you're dying. I promise you, you're fine."

"No, I'm not. Think about it. Figure it out. That day at the gas station. The dead guy in the back of the car."

"I know that freaked you out. I'm sure that was the last thing you needed to see after what happened to you, but—"

"No!" I stood up. "You're not listening to me. That guy died because I killed him."

"Sam, you're talking crazy now. What, do you think the universe had to balance out you coming back to life, so it took that guy's life?"

"*I* took that guy's life." I held my hands out to him. "With my bare hands. I killed him. That's why I wasn't in the car when you came out of the store."

"You went to the bathroom, remember?" He reached for my forehead. "Are you coming down with something? Do you have a fever?"

"I don't have a fever, and I didn't go to the bathroom that night. I started to feel like I was suffocating in the car, so I got out. I fell onto the ground. I was dying. Again. I panicked, and that guy came out of the store. He tried to help me, to take me to the hospital. But I did something. With my hands. I stole the life right out of him. He aged from my touch, and I was saved."

"Okay." Ethan scratched his head. "Maybe there were some side effects from bringing you back. You're hallucinating."

"Yes and no. I see things. Glimpses of the lives of the people I killed. Or at least the lives they would've led if I hadn't killed them."

"People you killed? Sam, you didn't kill anyone."

"Yes, I did. It wasn't just that guy. Herman. Do you remember Gloria telling us about him?"

"The guy who crashed into the telephone pole?"

"Yes. That's not really how he died. I killed him. I was having an attack, and I needed to get away from you before I hurt you. I took your car, and I almost crashed into Herman. He got out to yell at me, and I killed him. I drove his car to the top of that hill and staged the accident."

"Okay, that's enough." He got up and crossed his arms. "Either you are really messing with me because you don't want to sleep with me again, or we need to take you to the hospital to get checked out."

I stared at him in disbelief. He thought I was making this up because I didn't want to have sex with him? "I killed Trevor, too. I made it look like he tried to break into the school."

"Trevor?" Ethan kicked the bed. "Damn it, Sam. Trevor is missing. And that guy who broke into the school was in his seventies."

"No, he wasn't. He was Trevor. I drained the life out of him. That's what I do. It's how I kill people to keep myself alive. I take their life force, drain it out of them."

"Stop it!" Ethan's face was bright red. "That's enough."

"You don't believe me." My bottom lip trembled. Ethan had never not believed me.

"I believe you're sick. I believe I screwed something up when I brought you back."

I stepped toward him. "Then tell me how you did it."

"You've become obsessed with this, and it's messing with your head." He reached for my hands. "Please, let this go. Let me help you."

"You can help me by telling me the truth about what you did. I have to know. It's a matter of life and death."

"No, it's not. No one is dying because of you. You're confused."

I tore my hands from his. "Why won't you tell me? How bad is it that you aren't even willing to say it out loud?"

He ran his fingers through his hair and tilted his head back. I waited for what felt like an eternity for him to speak. I couldn't take it anymore. "Ethan!"

He looked at me, his eyes red and puffy. "I would've done anything. Anything."

"I know. I'm not going to be mad at you. I don't blame you for any of this. I just need to know."

"What will knowing change?"

It might change losing him forever, but I couldn't say that. I hated having to keep so much from him, but after how he'd reacted to me telling the truth about what I'd become, I couldn't tell him he was dying. He'd think I was crazy. He probably already thought I was crazy.

"Can't you tell me simply because I want to know?"

"It's not that easy."

"Yes, it is. It's words. Say them."

He shook his head. "If I tell you, it will only make you worse. Those things you said about you killing people, that scared the shit out of me. I can only imagine what you'd say if you knew the truth."

He *did* think I was crazy. My confession hadn't done anything but ruin my chances of finding out the truth. Ethan was a dead end.

But he wasn't the only one who knew I'd come back from the dead. Nora knew. Except if she knew how I'd come back, she would've told me. We'd shared a lot. It would've come out eventually. That left me with one option. Dylan. I had to call him. I had to set up a meeting to get this all out in the open.

I had no idea if he'd found out about Ben yet. If he had, then I was dead. He'd kill me. But I had to try. He might have the answer I needed. And if he did kill me, well, Ethan and I would end up together after all. Six feet under.

CHAPTER TWENTY-SIX

"I HAVE to go," I said, looking around for my purse.

"Go where? It's nighttime." Ethan reached for me. "Sam, please. Don't do this. Stay here and talk to me."

"Are you going to tell me how you brought me back?" My eyes bored into his.

He sighed. "No."

"Then I can't stay." I broke free from him, remembering my purse was on the living room floor. I scooped it up and walked out the front door. I grabbed the hidden key from the wheel well and got in the car. I had to get out of here before I called Dylan. If I didn't, Ethan would try to stop me. Or worse, he'd get in the car. I couldn't go see Dylan with Ethan tagging along.

I backed out of the driveway and pulled onto the main road. I drove until I came to a red traffic light. It seemed like a good time to call Dylan, so I dialed his number.

He picked up on the third ring. "Ben?"

The name shot through me, tore my insides to shreds. "No," I choked out. "It's Sam."

"Sam?" It was clear he never expected me to call.

"I want to talk." He obviously didn't know about Ben, or he wouldn't have thought I was him. But the frantic tone in his voice meant he knew Ben was in trouble.

"I can't now. It's not a good time. Tomorrow. After school."

"It can't wait."

He sighed. "Look, my brother is—never mind. I can't talk now."

"Don't hang up! You've been cornering me since I moved here. Now I'm telling you I'm ready to talk, and you're blowing me off?"

"I want to talk. I just can't right now."

"Well, it's now or never." He had no idea why I finally wanted to talk, so I was hoping I could appeal to his own desperation.

"Ugh! Fine. Where?"

"Your place?" I hated the idea of being alone with him at his house, but what we had to discuss required privacy, and I couldn't exactly take him to the cottage.

"No. Not here."

"Why not?"

"The diner."

"It's closed."

"Exactly. That's what makes it perfect. No one will bother us. I'll be there in ten minutes." He hung up the phone before I could protest.

When the light changed, I pulled a U-turn in the middle of the road. No one was around, and I didn't want to waste time. I drove to the diner, wondering how all this would play out. Wondering what Dylan had to say to me and if he really knew how I'd gotten to be what I was.

I pulled into the diner and parked around back. I cut the lights, hoping no one saw me. Gloria and Jackson didn't strike me as the type to set up security cameras in the parking lot. If they did, they would've seen me get in the car with Nora the other day. Gloria wouldn't have let that slide, not after I had collapsed in the parking lot. Not after I returned with that lame story about the girl with the flat bike tire.

I took out my phone and texted Dylan. *Out back. No headlights.*

Two minutes later, he pulled up next to me. He got out of his car and into mine.

"Why is it so important that we talk now?" he asked.

"You know about me, right? That's why you've been trying to talk to me."

He shrugged. "Yeah."

"I need to know how much you know. Starting with how I got here."

He eyed me suspiciously. "You moved here with Ethan, even though you two like to pretend you just met."

"That's not what I meant and you know it."

He didn't flinch. "Maybe I do. It would help if you were more specific."

He was going to make me say it. Confirm what he already knew.

"I died of cancer."

"I didn't know it was cancer."

"But you know I died, and you know Ethan did something to bring me back."

"Yes." He wasn't offering any extra information. He was being annoyingly close-lipped.

"Do you know how I was brought back?"

"Yes."

"Ugh." I smacked the steering wheel. "Then tell me!"

"She didn't tell you?"

"She? Who's she?"

Dylan laughed. "Figures. It's just like her."

"Who?" I was losing my patience. I needed answers.

"Nora."

The wheels started turning in my head. Nora. The coven. The others using black magic. It would take black magic to bring someone back from the dead, right?

"You. You did it! All of you. Your coven. That's how you knew about me. It's the only explanation."

"Not quite. What has she told you about us?" He turned in his seat, leaning his back against the door.

"That you were all friends, but Shannon convinced the rest of you to start doing spells Nora didn't want to do."

Dylan laughed. "Why am I not surprised? She *would* blame this on Shannon."

"I've seen the way the entire school does whatever Shannon says. It's clear they're under a spell, so don't try to defend her."

"I'm not. She did the spell all right, but she did it alone."

"I know. Nora told me."

"Right. So why do you think Shannon is the one who corrupted the rest of us?"

"She wasn't?" Could it have been Ben or Rebecca, or was I sitting in the same car with the one who'd convinced the other members of the coven to turn to black magic? I leaned away from him, putting my hand on the door in case I had to make a run for it.

"No. The rest of us laughed at Shannon. It was a stupid spell. Who uses magic for popularity? I mean, I felt bad for her. The kids at her school tortured her, but still."

"Then who? Rebecca?" I raised my eyes to meet his. "You?"

"You met Rebecca. Did she seem like the cutthroat type to you? Before you killed her, that is?" It was clear he hated me for that.

I swallowed hard. "Better to kill an evil witch than an innocent human, right?"

"Except you didn't kill the evil witch. You killed Rebecca."

I thought about the way Rebecca had begged for her life. She hadn't sounded evil, but she wouldn't have. She'd been trying to plead with me. I shook the thought from my mind. "Nora told me you all started using black magic. Rebecca included."

Dylan scoffed. "Rebecca wouldn't go near black magic."

"Fine. Then was it Ben?"

Dylan's face contorted, turning bright red. He clenched his jaw. "How do you know Ben? Did Nora take you to see him?" His hands worked themselves into fists.

If I didn't lie, I wasn't going to make it out of this car alive. "Nora told me about all of you."

He eyed me suspiciously. "Ben wouldn't hurt anyone unless they were trying to hurt him."

That wasn't what Nora had said, and I'd seen what Ben had done to her house. He might have been Dylan's brother, but the guy was pure evil. I remembered what Nora said about recognizing Ben's magic inside me. Could Dylan feel it, too? No. He would've killed me by now. Still, I pushed myself farther up against the door and away from him.

"Fine, then tell me a story. Fill in the blanks for me."

"Go ask Nora to tell you what happened. I don't have time for this." He reached for the door handle.

"I know where Ben is," I blurted out.

Dylan froze. "Where. Is. He?"

"I'll tell you *after* you tell me what I want to know."

He spun in his seat and grabbed me by my shoulders. Yeah, he was evil. I had no doubt now. I was stupid for calling him, for coming here.

"I'm not playing games. Tell me where my brother is."

Playing the Ben card was supposed to give me the upper hand, but Dylan was using it against me.

"If you kill me, you'll never find him." I hoped that leveled the playing field.

He let go of me, but he didn't back away.

"I promise I'll tell you where he is, but you have to tell me what you know first."

He sat there debating it, probably imagining a hundred ways to rip my head off using magic. Or maybe he preferred using his bare hands.

"You've been dying to tell me something, so tell me. I'm right here." I tried to act cool, like I wasn't shaking on the inside.

"You've gone along with everything she's said, haven't you?"

"I'm listening, not answering questions." My heart pounded at my own boldness. It was either a great strategy or the stupidest move I'd ever made.

"Your boyfriend came to us. To our coven. He heard about us through a mutual friend back where you guys are from."

"Ethan approached the coven?"

"Are you going to let me talk? I thought you said you were listening."

I held my hands up, urging him to go on.

"He emailed us and said you were dying. That he needed to know if it was possible to bring someone back from the dead. We told him we didn't do that sort of magic, that we didn't even know if it was possible."

"You're lying." They hadn't turned him away. They helped him. *They* had done this to me. Suddenly I was glad I'd gotten payback. I was a killer because of them. It seemed only fitting that they became my victims.

"Seriously, either you're going to listen or you're not. Pick one, because I have better things to do."

I crossed my arms, not sure if I wanted to hear any more of his lies. But I sat there and let him talk. I'd come this far. I might as well hear him out.

"We said no, and we thought that was the end of it. We figured you'd died, and Ethan had given up. But that wasn't the case. One of us broke the trust of the coven and found a spell to help you."

"Who? Was it you? Is that why you've been torturing me? Are you trying to kill me, to correct your mistake so the coven will take you back?"

"I didn't bring you back. Nora did."

"Liar!" I was so angry I nearly jumped out of my seat. "Nora's done nothing but help me."

"Help you? You think that's what she's doing? She's playing God. She brought you back wrong to get revenge on the rest of us. We kicked her out of the coven the second we found out about you. She'd been using black magic for months, and we tried to be tolerant. We tried to convince her to stop, but after you…well, we couldn't keep her around anymore."

"Nora told me the members of the coven are bound to each other. Kicking her out wouldn't break that tie, so you can stop lying to me. Get out of my car!"

"Not until you tell me where Ben is."

"Get out!" I wasn't just angry at Dylan for lying, I was angry at the world. Ethan was going to die, and the only people who could save him were Dylan and Shannon. Two people I hated. Two people who wouldn't help me in a million years. "Go!"

"Where's Ben?"

"I don't know. I lied." It was the only thing I could think of to make him leave. "I said what I had to in order to get you to talk."

"Bitch!" Dylan yelled. "If I were anything like Nora, you'd be dead right now." He got out of the car and slammed the door.

I peeled out of the spot, taking off down the road. I didn't know where I was going. Only that I wanted to get far away from Dylan.

I was so wired up from what Dylan had said. All the lies. Why had I gone to him in the first place? I should've known he wasn't the answer to saving Ethan. Nora was the only one who could help me. The only one I could trust.

The anger built up inside me. I wanted to get back at Dylan, and I had an idea how. Two ideas, actually. I'd tell Nora I'd changed my mind. That Dylan should be next. Shannon could wait. But first, I had another way to make Dylan pay. To hurt him like he'd hurt me.

I dialed his number and waited for him to answer.

"I can't believe you have the audacity to call me after—"

"You're going to want to shut up and listen to what I have to say."

He stopped talking, but I could hear his labored breathing. He was furious.

"I want to repay you for the hell you've put me through since we met, and I know just how to do it."

"What, kill me like you killed Rebecca?"

"No. Kill you like I killed Ben." I hung up the phone before he could respond.

CHAPTER TWENTY-SEVEN

As soon as I hung up the phone, I called Nora. I had to warn her. She'd been right all along. Dylan was our biggest threat.

"Hello?"

"You need to get out of your house," I said.

"What? Why?"

"I saw Dylan." I wasn't about to tell her I was the one who'd called him. "He knows about Ben."

"How? Ben is still in my basement. I've been trying to find a way to dispose of his body. I hoped we could buy some time before Dylan found out Ben was dead."

"You can't. Dylan knows, and my guess is he's coming for you."

"Why me? Why not you?"

Oh, God! He could be on his way to the cottage.

"You're right. Nora, I'm not home, but Ethan is. He's alone!"

"Okay, calm down." I could hear her moving around, and a few seconds later, I heard the engine of her car. "I'm on my way. For now, call Ethan. Tell him to put the rocks outside your house back into a circle. It will protect him from Dylan."

"What?" I turned down another street, heading for home.

"The rocks—they form a barrier a witch can't cross."

It made sense. All the times Dylan had gotten inside the cottage, the rocks had been out of place. "Did you put them there?"

She hesitated before saying yes. I should've known. She'd been trying to help me before I even knew her.

"The rocks are still in place from the last time you fixed them. We thought it was a prank some kids from school had set up. We left the circle hoping they'd leave us alone if we didn't react to it."

"Okay, good. I'm on my way."

"Nora, wait! How will you get in the cottage if the barrier is up?"

"You'll have to take it down when I get there, but I'll be able to protect us from Dylan with other spells."

I hung up and floored it home. Ethan would have to believe me now. When he saw Nora, and if Dylan showed up…well, there'd be no way Ethan could think I was hallucinating. And maybe he'd be able to tell us how Dylan and the others brought me back. Any hint might be what Nora needed to duplicate the spell and save him.

I pulled into the driveway and burst through the front door. "Ethan!" All the lights were off. Had he gone looking for me? I'd taken the car, but he could've called a cab. "Ethan?" I checked the bedroom. Maybe if he'd been mad enough, he'd have just gone to sleep, let me drive around to blow off steam.

I flicked on the light. The bed was empty. Not even unmade. I grabbed my cell from my purse and dialed Nora again.

"What's wrong? Is Dylan there already?"

"No. Ethan's not here either. The house is empty."

"Are you sure? Did you check every room?"

"Well, no. I checked the living room and bedroom. And sort of the kitchen. The place is small. You know that."

"Look everywhere." She paused and then said, "Were the rocks still in place? Dylan could've used magic to make someone move the rocks so he could get inside."

"Yes. At least I think so. I didn't walk around the house. I came right inside, but the rocks in front of the house were all in place."

"Can you see the back of the house from any of the windows?"

"Yeah, the one in the bathroom." I headed for the bathroom. The door was shut. I hadn't noticed it when I came in. The place was too dark. "Nora," I whispered, afraid that Dylan was waiting for me on the other side of the door. He'd already broken into my bathroom once when he stole my necklace.

"What? Are you okay? Is it Dylan?"

"I don't know. The bathroom door is closed. What if he's in there?"

"Grab a weapon and don't go in there. Stay put. Just be prepared in case he comes out, okay? I'm almost there."

I didn't know what I'd do if I didn't have her. I'd never been so scared. The best weapon I had was myself, but I didn't feel an attack coming on. My breathing was normal. My body temperature was normal. I wished I could tap into the magic I'd drained from Ben.

I kept an eye on the bathroom door as I looked around the kitchen. We had a big carving knife, but it was in a drawer. I wasn't sure I could get it without making noise. Not that I was sure making noise was going to matter. I'd already yelled Ethan's name, and I was talking on the phone. If Dylan was in the bathroom, he was waiting me out.

Terrified, I wrapped my fingers around the handle of the drawer and inched it out. The tracks squeaked, making my breath catch in my throat. What was he waiting for? This was torture. I knew he was in there. I was sure of it. The circle of rocks must have been destroyed in the back, and Dylan had slipped in through the bathroom window, just like before.

I wanted to grab the knife and burst in there, end this agony. But I'd only get myself killed. He was a witch. He used black magic. I didn't stand a chance. I had to wait for Nora and hope she got here before Dylan made his move.

My cell vibrated in my hand, making me jump, and a small gasp escaped my lips. I grabbed the knife before reading the text.

I'm here. Circle is broken in back of the house. Coming to front door.

I backed up, making my way slowly and silently to the front door. Nora was on the porch when I opened the door. I motioned for her to come inside. She put her hand up for me to stay where I was.

She closed her eyes for a moment and mumbled something under her breath. Her eyes shot open and toward the bathroom door. She must have sensed Dylan's presence because I didn't even have to point her in the right direction. She knew where the bathroom was.

She moved closer, and I fell in step behind her. I couldn't stay back. Fear and curiosity were keeping me close to Nora. She continued to mumble her spell as we got closer. Her hands rose in front of her, reaching out for the door. She pulled her hands back to her chest and then pushed forward. A burst of wind blew the bathroom door right open. I cringed, expecting to see Dylan, but instead I saw Ethan lying face down on the floor.

"Ethan!" I pushed past Nora, dropping the knife, and ran to him. His hands were ice cold.

"What did you do to him?"

"Nothing. I was saying a spell to bind any magic behind the door."

"What about that thing you did to break the door down?"

"That's not what hurt him. I'm sure of it."

I gently rolled Ethan onto his side. His eyes were closed, and his face was peaceful. "Oh, God! No, no, no!" I burst into tears. Ethan was dead. He was cold and lifeless and dead. "The vision. I had more time. I had more time!"

"Sam," Nora said.

"He can't be dead. I saw him in my vision. He wasn't supposed to die until after Beth invited us to some party." I shook my head and tears splattered on Ethan's gray T-shirt. "I saw it."

Nora reached for me. "Your visions are of things that *won't* happen. Why did you think he wouldn't die until after you were invited to that party?"

"I don't know." She was right. How could I have been so stupid, so careless? It was Ethan's life, and I'd told myself I had more time to save him. I'd left him to die here alone because I was angry. He'd been with me every step of the way when I had cancer. He'd put up with my mood swings. He'd held my hand as I took my last breath. And this was what I'd done for him. Yelled at him and stormed out. Stole his car and left him to die alone on the bathroom floor.

"Please, do something, Nora." I clutched onto her shirt. "Don't let him stay like this. You must know a spell that will bring him back. Dylan told me you brought me back. I know that's a lie. It was him. Him and the others, but you must have some clue what they did."

Her face hardened. "I do know, Sam, but the spell they used…it's rooted in black magic. Look at how you came back. You have to feed to survive. Ethan would be like you."

"Bring him back. I'll deal with the consequences later. We'll figure something out. Just bring him back."

"He'd need to steal life from someone else. That's how the spell works. You can't give life without taking it from somewhere else. It's about balance."

"Then he can have mine. Take it! I don't want it. I don't want to be here like this, not if it means he's gone."

Nora shook her head. "I can't take borrowed time."

I narrowed my eyes at her. "What does that mean?"

"Your life isn't really your own. You borrowed it from Ethan. That's how the spell works. He can't borrow his own life back from you." She hesitated. "We'd need another life."

I let go of her and placed my hands on Ethan's lifeless body. How had I been draining his life from him without even knowing it? "Then get one."

"I'm talking about killing someone."

"I know. Dylan's probably on his way here. We'll use his life." I looked up at her, hopeful that this would be the answer to our problem.

"No." She walked away, chewing on her nail as she thought. "He's angry right now. That makes him too powerful. I'd never be able to control him and do the spell at the same time. But I have an idea."

"What? We need to hurry. Dylan's going to be here any second."

"I need to do a locator spell to find him and Shannon."

"Why Shannon? Nora, what are you talking about? We have to focus on saving Ethan."

"I am. We need to find Shannon so we can steal her life."

"Oh." I thought about it and nodded. "Yeah, okay." She was one of the ones who had done this to me. It seemed fitting that she'd be the one to sacrifice her life for Ethan.

"She won't be expecting an attack, so I can catch her off-guard and bind her powers. I'll be able to do the spell then. It's not going to kill her right away; you know that."

But it would over time. Just like my being alive had slowly killed Ethan. My God, the coven had taken Ethan's life without telling him. I hated them even more for that. "Ethan and I will run away. Somewhere Shannon and Dylan can't find us."

"They can find you anywhere. The exact same way I'm going to find them now."

"With a locator spell." That left us with only one solution. "We have to kill them, don't we?"

"Yes. I can bind their magic until you and Ethan need to feed again. Once they're dead, you'll both be safe."

But we'd still be monsters. I glanced at Ethan again. Monster or not, I had to do this. "Do the spell."

Nora grabbed some things she needed from the cabinets and got started. She pulled the wooden box from under the sink and gave me a strange look. "What are you doing with a witch box?"

"A what?"

"A witch box. This is supposed to protect your house from witches."

I narrowed my eyes at it. "I found it when we moved in."

"Well whoever did this is definitely an amateur. It's not working. I wouldn't be able to be here if it was. Something must be missing. A personal effect, probably."

"There was a ring inside it. It looked just like the one Ethan had given me for my birthday. It was a ruby, my birthstone."

Nora reached for the ring sitting on the edge of the sink. "This one?"

"Yeah. I forgot about it. It's not my ring. Ethan said he put my ring in a storage facility to keep it safe. He—" I stopped. My ring wasn't in the storage facility. I stood up and joined her in the kitchen.

"What?" she asked.

"We went to get my ring one day, but it wasn't there. Someone had stolen it." I eyed the ring in Nora's hand. "That's my ring. But how did it get in that box? Ethan didn't put it there."

"Another witch did."

"But who? The only witch helping me is you."

Nora shook her head. "I don't know. Maybe it was a trap, something to make you feel safe. It could be a decoy. I'll bet Dylan made it. It was probably how he planned to win you over, pretend he was trying to protect you when really it was him after you all along."

"Speaking of Dylan, shouldn't you get moving with the locator spell? He should be here soon."

She put the ring back on the counter. "I don't think he's coming here. He'd be here already."

"So where did he go?"

"My house, most likely. He was bringing the fight to me. When he doesn't find me, he'll come here next."

"Should we move Ethan? Do this somewhere else?"

"Where?"

"The diner. I know the keypad number to get us in. At least, I think I do. I'm pretty sure Gloria uses the same number for all her passwords and stuff."

She nodded. "I can get past a lock no problem. Let me locate Shannon, and then we'll move Ethan to the car. You can drive him to the diner while I get Shannon."

"Okay."

As she did the locator spell, I stared at the ring on the counter. It *was* my ring. The one Ethan had given me. Now that he was dead, I wanted it back. I slipped it on my finger, and tears welled up in my eyes. "I'll bring you back, Ethan," I whispered. "I'll bring you back."

"Let's go," Nora said. "I found her, but we need to move fast. She may not stay in one spot for long. Not if Dylan calls her."

We each grabbed hold of Ethan and carried him to the car. Nora gave us a magical boost so we could move faster. We laid him across the back so no one would see him while I drove to the diner.

"Where's Shannon?" I asked, strapping my seatbelt.

"She's at a spot in the woods where we used to meet as a coven. I'll surprise her there. With all the trees, I should be able to sneak up on her pretty easily. It's not far from the diner. See if you can get Ethan inside. Bring him to the counter and lay him across it if you can."

I nodded.

"One way or another, this all ends tonight," Nora said.

I pulled out of the driveway behind Nora and drove to the diner. I looked around before getting out, making sure there was no sign of Dylan. This was where I'd left him, so I was pretty sure he didn't expect me to come back. I ran up to the keypad on the back door and punched in Gloria's code. The door buzzed and then opened.

I ran into the dining room and grabbed a chair to prop the door open. I wouldn't be able to work a keypad and carry Ethan at the same time.

His body was stiff and hard to move. I ended up having to wrap my arms under his armpits and drag him. It was easier to move him across the diner floor since Jackson had just buffed it. I sat Ethan down on one of the stools and leaned him back onto the counter. It took every ounce of strength I had to get his entire body on the counter, but I did it. I had to have him ready when Nora got here with Shannon.

"Soon, Ethan. You'll be back with me soon." I kissed his forehead.

The back door opened, and I heard footsteps coming down the hallway.

"I've got him all ready, Nora." I turned to face her.

But it wasn't Nora.

It was Dylan.

CHAPTER TWENTY-EIGHT

HE glared at me. "And what exactly do you plan to do with my brother?"

He thought I had Ben. I stepped back, giving Dylan a view of Ethan's body.

"I told you what happened to Ben. I wasn't lying. Unlike you, I actually told the truth." I kept the counter between us, afraid of what he was going to do to me. "Did you follow me here?"

"Locator spell. I'm sure Nora was doing one to find me."

"Not quite." We hadn't had time to worry about locating Dylan; besides, we knew he'd eventually find us.

"Where is she?" He looked around. "Let me guess, waiting in the kitchen to ambush me?" He moved toward the kitchen, and I backed around the counter so he didn't have to walk right by me. He flung open the door.

I looked around for a weapon. Anything to use against him. I wasn't about to leave Ethan's body, so I needed something to defend myself. At least until Nora showed up. I reached for a glass sugar jar. It was heavy, and if it broke, the jagged glass would be a decent weapon. If not, at least I could hit him over the head with it.

Dylan came back into the dining room and eyed the jar in my hand. "So Nora told you about the salt, huh? Let me guess, you were planning to draw a circle of it around yourself so I couldn't hurt you? Is that what she told you to do?"

Salt? He thought I was holding the salt. My mind flashed back to the time I refilled the salt in front of Nora. She had been adamant that I move away from her. Witches didn't like salt. I made a mental note.

"You came to kill me, is that it? Stop the monster you created?" I turned my body, reaching for the salt behind my back.

"*I* didn't bring you back."

"Your coven did, and you're part of it."

"No, we didn't. *Nora* did."

Before Dylan could say another word, he flew backward into the kitchen door. It swung open, and he disappeared inside. I whirled around to see Nora. She had Shannon with her, wrapped up in a magical swirling mist.

"Lay some salt across the entrance to the kitchen. It will contain him in case he wakes up before we finish this." Nora moved toward Ethan, but I was frozen in place. "Go! If he wakes up, he'll ruin everything. Ethan's life depends on Dylan staying out of the way."

I carried the saltshaker to the kitchen and lined the floor with it. "How did you figure out what spell to use? You weren't there when the coven brought me back, so how do you know what they did?" I kept my eyes glued to Dylan, lying motionless on the kitchen floor. His head was leaning against the metal island he'd collided with.

"Spells leave traces. That, and Rebecca likes to run her mouth. She bragged all about that spell. Bet she doesn't think it was so fantastic now." Nora went behind the counter and grabbed a knife.

"What are you doing?"

"I need some of Shannon's blood. It's the only way to make sure it's her life Ethan is stealing."

I didn't want to watch. Didn't want to know what the spell entailed. After all this time of wondering what Ethan had done, I had a front-row seat to the whole thing. It was hard to watch. I didn't understand a word Nora was saying. She held the knife over Ethan's body, waving her hands above him. Finally, she walked around him to where Shannon was locked in her invisible prison.

Shannon had been unconscious when Nora brought her here, but as Nora continued her spell, Shannon's eyelids fluttered open. She looked at Nora and her eyes widened. Then she turned to me and shrieked, "You killed my boyfriend. Isn't that enough? You have no idea what I went through to make sure the police couldn't ID

Trevor's body. If people suspected anything supernatural... How many people are you going to kill before you realize you shouldn't be here?"

Nora waved her hand in front of Shannon's face, and her mouth slammed shut. She struggled to speak but couldn't. I'd never seen her look this helpless before. She truly hated me. She wanted me dead, just like Dylan did. I couldn't believe she'd helped cover up Trevor's murder. If she hadn't...

Nora took the knife and dragged it across Shannon's cheek. I turned away, unable to watch. Shannon's muffled screams were agonizing. They sent chills down my spine. This was awful. We were torturing her. I knew what I did to people wasn't any better, and all of this was necessary to bring Ethan back, but it was too much to bear.

I watched as Nora carried the knife very steadily, making sure she didn't spill a single drop of Shannon's blood. She brought it to Ethan and held it above his head. With one hand, she parted his lips. Then she tipped the knife forward, spilling Shannon's blood into his mouth.

My stomach lurched. I'd heard of people calling themselves vampires and drinking blood, but seeing someone drink another person's blood—especially when it was your dead boyfriend—was terrifying. Nora finished the spell and bowed her head.

"What now?" I choked out.

"We wait. It takes a little while for the dead to wake."

"Is this the same spell they used on me?"

Shannon let out another muffled scream.

"Can't you stop her from making that noise?" I covered my ears. "I can't take it."

"That's your conscience getting to you." Dylan's weakened voice came from the kitchen. I turned to see him still lying on the floor and looking pretty bad.

"That injury will take a lot of energy to heal," Nora said.

"Energy?" I asked.

"Yes. We can heal ourselves if we harness the energy in our magic. But that's one nasty cut on his head, judging by the amount of blood on the floor."

I cringed, not just at the sight of the blood, but at the thought of

Gloria and Jackson coming to work in a few hours to find this place wrecked.

"I'll manage," Dylan said.

"Good luck with that." Nora walked over to me. "I don't suppose you're feeling the need to feed, are you?"

I shook my head. Ben's life force and magic were keeping my body pretty well maintained.

"Oh well. My guess is that Ethan will need to pretty soon after he wakes. With any luck, you'll be ready by then, too. Then we can end this. One evil witch for each of you."

Dylan laughed. It was the laugh of a crazy person. "That's your big plan, Nora? Feed us to your little creations?"

"Don't call us that!" I snapped. "Besides, Nora wouldn't have had to bring Ethan back if you guys hadn't done this to me in the first place." I didn't want to think it, but Ethan would've been better off if I'd stayed dead.

"You keep telling yourself that, Sam. Whatever you need to do to be able to live with yourself. But why don't you ask Nora why she shut Shannon up?"

"To keep her from screaming," Nora said. "That's obvious. Keep up all this annoying banter, and I'll shut you up, too."

Dylan laughed. "You can't. Not with that salt barrier in the doorway. You can't touch me, Nora. But you didn't think about that, did you?"

"Of course I did." She stepped within five feet of the barrier, not daring to go any closer. "But I won't be the one touching you. Sam will. Or Ethan. Whichever. I'm flexible."

"You sure about that?"

Now Nora laughed. "Dylan, this is pathetic. You've lost. Admit it. At least then you can go down with a shred of dignity. Right now you're just acting like a whiny little bitch."

I walked over to Ethan and touched his hand. It was still ice cold. "Nora, how do you know you did the spell right? He's still so cold."

"Oh, she knows," Dylan said. "Believe me, she knows."

Nora waved him off. She put her hand on my shoulder. "Relax. Everything went exactly right. Ethan will be with you again soon. I promise."

"Waiting is killing me. And listening to *him*," I motioned toward the kitchen, "isn't helping."

"Ignore him. He'll say and do anything right now to make this harder on you. That's what evil people do, Sam."

I nodded. I had to forget about him and focus on Ethan. He'd be waking up soon, and then we'd get out of here. Go somewhere far away and forget all of this. But Nora had said we'd need to kill Dylan and Shannon first. Otherwise they'd keep looking for us. I didn't even want to think about how I'd explain this to Ethan. He'd have to believe Nora was a witch. He obviously knew witches were real. He'd gone to the coven to bring me back.

Ethan's fingers twitched, and I rushed to him. "Ethan!" I took his hand in mine, and tears dripped down my face. It was happening. He was waking up. He was alive. He opened his eyes and looked around for a minute before he found me.

"Sam? What happened?" He tried to sit up, but he was woozy and he fell back down.

"My head."

"I think you might have hit it. You fell on the bathroom floor." I brushed his hair away from his forehead. "What do you remember?"

He swallowed hard. "I was in the bathroom. I was going to take a shower, try to relax after our fight."

"I'm so sorry I left. I never should've run off like that."

"You're here now." He gave me a weak smile. "But what happened to me? I don't remember anything else."

"You…" I couldn't say it. Even though he was back now, I couldn't bring myself to tell him he'd died.

"Come on, Sam. Man up!" Dylan said.

"Who is that?" Ethan tried to sit up again, but I held him down.

"Easy. You hit your head, remember? You might have a concussion."

"Sam, what's going on?"

I sighed. "Okay, we're in the diner."

"I can see that."

"Right. Well, I came home tonight and you were…"

"Dead. The word is dead," Dylan said.

God, I wanted to smack him.

"Dead?" Ethan squinted at me.

"Yes. Ethan, everything I said to you earlier, it was all true. I'm not crazy. I'm not hallucinating. I came back wrong. I hid it from you because I was afraid of how you'd react. And I didn't want you to think I was ungrateful for getting a second chance. I know you went through a lot to bring me back."

"Wait. Are you sure *you* didn't hit your head?"

"Yes, I'm sure. I need you to listen carefully. Dylan is in the kitchen. He's been following me around, right?" I paused. A thought slammed into me. Hard. Ethan didn't know Dylan. He had no clue who Dylan was before Dylan broke into our cottage. If Ethan had gone to the coven to bring me back, Dylan hadn't been part of it.

I rushed to the kitchen, standing just outside the salt. "Ethan doesn't know you."

Dylan nodded, but he grabbed his head and cringed. He was still bleeding. Nora had been right. Healing himself required a lot of energy, and he was too weak to do it right now.

"You're finally catching on," he said.

"Ben, Shannon, and Rebecca, it was them, wasn't it? But you weren't part of it. I knew there was something about you—"

"Try again, Sam," Dylan said.

"What do you mean? Not all of you did the spell? Was it just Shannon? Is that why she hates me so much?" I turned to face her, and she shook her head. I didn't believe her for a second. She knew what I could do to her, and she was scared.

"Ask your boyfriend," Dylan said. "You don't seem to want to listen to me, so go to someone you trust."

That made sense. Ethan had the answers. He'd had them all along. I walked back over to him, still lying on the counter.

"Is that guy seriously in the kitchen? My kitchen? Where I work every day?"

"Forget about him. Ethan, you have to tell me what happened. How did you bring me back? I know you went to the coven. I've met all of them. I know it was witchcraft that brought me back. So there's no reason to try to hide this anymore, to try to protect me from the truth. I can handle it." I squeezed his hand in mine. "Please, tell me which members of the coven helped you."

"I didn't go to a coven, Sam. I went to one person. A witch someone from school knew."

"Who was it?" My fingers tightened around his.

"This girl. I don't know her name because she never told me."

A girl. So it was Rebecca. It had to be. Ethan knew Shannon from school. He would've named her if that was who had helped him.

"Rebecca," I said. "Her name is Rebecca. Or at least it was."

"What do you mean was?" He lifted his head slightly to see me better.

"I killed her, Ethan. Just like I told you. My body can't maintain itself. I get weak, and I need to feed off the life of others. I really did kill that guy from the gas station. And Trevor. They were accidents. I didn't mean to do it. My body takes over, and I can't stop it. I'm a prisoner to this thing that takes over when the life is draining out of me." I started crying. "Please, don't hate me. It's not my fault. I didn't ask to be this way. I don't want to be this way." I buried my head in his leg, sobbing huge tears.

He slowly sat up. "Sam, I—"

"Before you say anything, there's something you need to know." I looked up at him, afraid to see the expression on his face. Afraid he'd never look at me the same again. "Dylan was right. You died tonight, and I had to get a witch to bring you back. Nora helped me. But now you're going to be like me. You'll have to kill people to stay alive. I'm so sorry, but I couldn't lose you. I couldn't let you stay dead."

He stared past me, not saying a word.

"Ethan, please say something. Please, don't hate me."

"You're Nora?"

"What?" I turned to see Nora, now standing behind me.

"Hello, Ethan. Nice to see you again."

"Again?" I looked at Ethan. "You know her?"

"She's the witch who brought you back."

CHAPTER TWENTY-NINE

No. That couldn't be true. Ethan was confused. He'd just come back to life, and he was confused. When I came back everything seemed different, off. That was all this was, Ethan not being able to make sense of things.

But Nora knew him. How would she know him if she wasn't the one who'd helped him bring me back?

Ethan sat up on the counter, and I backed up next to him, facing Nora.

"You dyed your hair," Ethan said. "Was that so I wouldn't recognize you?"

"Is it true?" My voice cracked. "Did you bring me back?"

"Oh, Sam. It was too easy to trick you. To make you believe Dylan and the rest of the coven were the bad guys, the ones who were trying to kill you." She stepped closer, and Ethan slid off the counter, so he was blocking me.

"Don't come near her," he said, sounding more alert.

"Always trying to save her, aren't you, Ethan? You were so desperate when I met you. All serious and heartbroken."

I glanced at Shannon, still imprisoned in the corner. She shook her head at me, and even though she couldn't talk, I knew what she was thinking. I was an idiot. I'd been played by Nora. For once, I agreed with Shannon.

"Why did you do it?" I asked. "Why did you lie? You could've told me you were the one who brought me back."

"Told you *I* was the one who used black magic? *I* was the one the coven threw out? You wouldn't have trusted me."

She was right. I would've been afraid of her at the very least. "What else did you lie about?"

"See, that's the beauty of it. I barely had to lie. You already know most of the story. Just substitute my name for Dylan's—and in a few places Shannon's—and you've got it." She smiled, obviously proud of herself.

"She poisoned you against us, Sam," Dylan said. He was on his feet now and looking a little better, but he was still trapped by the salt. "She told you we were trying to kill you, but we never were. We didn't like that you were alive and killing people. That much was true, but we never tried to kill you. The fact that you came back like this is *her* fault."

"How?" I stared at Nora, my supposed friend. I wanted to hear it from her.

"Dying for love—it's romantic, don't you think?" Nora smirked as she circled around Ethan and me.

"I didn't die for love. I died of cancer."

"*You* did. Yes." Nora stepped in front of Ethan. "But *he* didn't."

That's right. Ethan had exchanged his life for mine.

"Did you know that by helping her bring me back, I was stealing life away from you?" I asked him.

Ethan turned away. He'd known. He'd willingly given his life for mine.

Tears spilled down my cheeks, and my body shook with anger. "How could you do that to me? After everything I've been through. You were the only good thing in my life. The one thing I clung to while I was fighting to stay alive just one more day! I loved you! How could you bring me back, knowing it would kill you? Knowing you'd leave me here alone?" I pounded his chest with my fists. I'd never been this angry with him, but this was unforgiveable. No wonder he'd refused to tell me the truth. He knew part of me would hate him for this, for making me watch him die.

"Sam." He choked back tears and wrapped his arms around me. "I would've died on the spot to bring you back. You're everything to me. You didn't deserve to die so young."

I pulled away from him, feeling the bile in my stomach rising. "I'm nothing without you, Ethan. You know that."

"I can't apologize for what I did. Your life means more to me than my own. I'd do it all over again if I had to."

Nora clapped, like she was enjoying the show. "Do you want to know my favorite part?" Nora asked with a huge smile.

This was going to be bad in an earth-shattering sort of way. I was sure of it.

"You never would've had a taste for human life if I hadn't given you some of your boyfriend's."

Ethan whirled around to face Nora. "That's why you needed my blood? You said it was to transfer my life force to Sam."

Nora laughed. "The spell did that on its own. I needed Sam to do a favor for me. In exchange for giving her back her life."

"A favor?" Of course. "The coven. You wanted revenge on them for kicking you out. So what? You made me into this zombie, witch-killing monster just so you could get back at them for shunning you?"

"They did more than shun me. They took away a power I wasn't willing to live without. Sure, I'm powerful on my own. But as a coven, we had the ability to do much bigger spells. Ones that would've made us invincible." She walked over to Shannon and grabbed her face, squeezing it in her hand. "But these goody-goodies wouldn't hear of messing with black magic like that." She let go of Shannon's face. "I almost had this one convinced. I even showed her that spell to make every student at that pathetic school bend to her will. But she was mad about some teacher not paying enough attention to her, so she refused to go along with my plan to convince the others."

Mr. Ryan. He'd stopped Shannon from turning into what Nora had become. He'd saved her by not giving in to all her obvious come-ons. He really *was* a good teacher.

Nora brought her hand back and slapped Shannon across the face. A big red handprint smeared the blood on her cheek. Nora had slapped the gash she'd cut into Shannon's face earlier.

"Wait!" I yelled. "You dripped Shannon's blood into Ethan's mouth during that spell."

"She did what?" Ethan spit several times as if that would erase the problem.

"You said that would make sure it was Shannon's life Ethan drained by being here, but that blood is what's going to make him feed off others, isn't it?"

"Very good, Sam." Nora looked at Ethan. "Oh, and another thing I forgot to mention when you asked me to save your girlfriend— I don't know how I neglected to tell you earlier—is that she'd see glimpses of the lives she stole. Not only is she killing to stay alive, but she's being tortured by visions of what their lives would've been if she hadn't fed on them."

"You sadistic witch." Ethan lunged at her, but she held her hand up and mumbled something. He slammed into an invisible wall and fell to the floor.

"Ethan!" I bent down to him, making sure he was okay. As angry as I was at him, I still loved him.

"And those visions Sam had," Nora leaned forward so only the magical barrier separated them, "they were of your future, too. She saw you marry another woman. Guess I was wrong about you falling to pieces after she died. Turns out you would've moved on just fine."

Ethan sprang to his feet and lunged again, but the same thing happened.

"He's not the brightest one, Sam. Are you sure he was worth all this trouble?"

"Shut up," I said through clenched teeth. I had to figure out how to get Ethan and me out of here. How to temporarily knock Nora out so we could run for it. But I needed time to think, to form a plan. I had to keep her talking.

Nora laughed. "That's not what you really want, is it?" There was that almost mind-reading thing she did. "You want to hear all about how I deceived you, don't you? It was easy, even with that one over there trying to protect you from me."

"Dylan tried to protect me?" My eyes shot to him.

"The witch box with your ring in it, the necklace, the circle of rocks around your house—those were all me. Every single one of them was supposed to protect you from Nora. To stop her spell from working."

"You said the necklace was from you," I said to Nora.

She shrugged. "What can I say?"

"I didn't have any attacks when I was wearing it, and you couldn't allow that," I said, piecing the puzzle together. "You needed me to start dying so you could get me to kill your coven. *You* stole the necklace from my bathroom that night. *You* used magic to force a human to break the circle of rocks, so it would look like Dylan broke into the cottage tonight."

"Yes, yes, and yes. It was the perfect plan. All I needed was a simple spell to make you trust me, which was easy enough after I stole your necklace; it was the personal possession I needed, and thanks to Dylan being a total spaz and not knowing how to talk to you like a normal human being, it was easy to pin everything on him."

"So you did this to me all so you could kill a few witches who wouldn't go along with your evil plan? What would happen to me after I killed your coven? What then? Were you going to fix me? Make me human again?"

"I wouldn't have any further use for you."

My heart pounded. "You were going to kill me." That's why all my future visions of Ethan didn't include me. I wasn't alive anymore.

"Don't make it out to be such a big deal. You were already dead. You shouldn't be here, and if it weren't for me, you wouldn't be." She stepped closer, lowering the magical barrier she'd created to stop Ethan. "You are nothing more than a pawn in my game. And when I win, I'll dispose of you. Let you finally rest in peace."

Ethan made a move for her, but I grabbed his arms to stop him. She was a witch. He couldn't take her. We were the two weakest people in the diner. Once again I wished I could tap into Ben's power that was still lingering inside me. I didn't know how much longer I'd have it. An attack could come on at any time.

Nora laughed and took a seat. "Sam, be a dear and make me some coffee."

"Are you kidding me?"

"Not at all. If I have to sit around waiting for you two to get all peckish and need to feed, I'm going to need some coffee."

Waiting on her was the last thing I wanted to be doing, but I still hadn't come up with a plan. I started for the coffee pot, but Ethan grabbed my arm, holding me back.

"You don't have to listen to her," he said.

"Oh no?" Nora snapped her fingers. "Sit down, Ethan." His face contorted in pain as he was forced onto the stool next to him. "Good boy," Nora said.

I couldn't watch her make a puppet out of Ethan, so I shot him a pleading look. He shook his head in protest, but he didn't try to get up or make any comments, so I considered it a win. I went to the coffee maker and brewed a fresh pot.

As I waited for the coffee to finish brewing, I glanced down at the salt line on the kitchen floor. If I could break the line, Dylan could get free. He'd be able to attack Nora. Then Ethan and I could run away. But Nora always seemed to know what I was thinking. If she read my mind before I broke the salt line, I'd be finished. She'd bind me in magic just like she had done to Shannon, then wait for me to have an attack. Shannon and Dylan would end up dead, and Ethan and I would be next.

I needed a distraction. Something to draw Nora's attention so I could get to the kitchen.

"How did you pull all this off?" I asked. "You were here at the diner every day. If Ethan could recognize you, why would you chance coming here?"

"Easy. I made sure Ethan never saw me."

"What do you mean? Did you put a spell on him so he couldn't see you? Like you did that day when you came to talk to me and the place was packed? You made it so no one knew we were there."

"Something like that. I made sure he couldn't leave the kitchen. As long as I didn't go into the kitchen, I was fine. We'd never meet. And thanks to my new hair color, he wouldn't recognize me from afar or from any description you gave him."

Beth had been right. "That day I went to get Ethan to introduce you guys, you went to the bathroom and did some sort of spell. Beth heard you."

"Beth?" She cocked her head to the side.

"That girl you didn't like. The one who asked all the questions. She saw right through you. She followed you to the bathroom and heard you doing a spell. You made sure Ethan was too busy to come out into the dining room."

"Ugh, nosy girl. Now I have one more person I have to get rid of."

She sighed. "Well, Sam, the good news is that you'll get to stick around a little longer. I think I'll let you have the honor of killing Beth."

I wished I had Beth around right now. She'd be a good distraction. She'd annoy Nora so I could free Dylan. Of course I wasn't sure Dylan would even help me. I'd killed his brother. I had to hope his will to live would override that fact right now.

I checked on the coffee, noticing a pad and pen next to it. I casually reached for a cup, dragging the pad and pen toward me in the process. I scribbled a note to Dylan. *Will you help me get rid of Nora?* I coughed to cover up the sound of tearing the paper from the pad. I poured the coffee and slipped the note through the window to the kitchen.

I brought Nora her coffee, and she motioned to the stools at the counter. "You can have a seat, too. I'll let you know when I need a refill. If you haven't fed by then."

I walked around the counter and sat down next to Ethan. I glanced into the kitchen. Dylan was standing there, scribbling on the paper. He made sure Nora wasn't watching, and he slipped it back into the window.

"Nora," I said, "can I get some coffee for myself?"

She shrugged. "Why not? The caffeine might speed up your decaying process and make you need to feed. Pour a cup for Ethan, too."

I got up and went to the counter. I took a cup and grabbed the note at the same time.

I'll help, but I haven't forgotten about Ben.

I scribbled back, *Neither have I. I'm sorry.*

I put the note in the window and poured Ethan's coffee. I brought it to him and went back for my own. The note was back in the window.

I blame her more than you.

I wrote one last note. *Get ready. I'm going to break the salt line.* I stuck it in the window and got my own coffee.

This was it. I had to walk around the counter to get back to my stool. I could reach my foot out and drag it across the salt line. All I had to do was break it. Then Dylan could attack Nora. I met Ethan's gaze, and he wrinkled his brow. I looked quickly toward the kitchen and then at Nora. Ethan looked confused for a minute, but then he raised his coffee to his lips and mouthed, "Got it."

I walked around the counter, taking the turn wide. I stuck my foot out and brushed the line. The salt spread, but it was still blocking Dylan's path. I didn't know what else to do, so I let go of the cup, tipping the coffee onto the salt. I pretended to slip.

"I'm okay." I caught the edge of the counter and stood back up.

"Just sit down," Nora said. "Unless you're feeling weak." Her voice perked up. "Could it be nearing feeding time? You tend to get weak and wobbly before an attack comes on."

"Yeah, I'm not feeling a hundred percent right now," I played along.

Nora put down her coffee and clapped her hands. "Oh, good. Time to get to the fun part of the evening."

"That's exactly what I was thinking," Dylan said, stepping out of the kitchen.

CHAPTER THIRTY

DYLAN thrust his arms forward, and a burst of energy knocked Nora backward. She landed next to Shannon. If only Shannon wasn't still trapped in her own magical prison. I grabbed Ethan and pulled him toward the door. I had to get us out of there. This wasn't our fight. This had started long before Nora did the spell to bring me back, and I knew it was going to end with a lot of dead witches.

Ethan and I moved around the counter slowly, trying not to draw attention to ourselves. We were still two powerless humans in a diner full of witches. Nora attacked Dylan with a jolt of energy that sent green sparks through the room. If I didn't know better, I'd have said she was channeling all the electricity in the place and trying to fry Dylan. He dodged to the side, ducking behind the counter.

Nora turned toward Ethan and me. "Stick around!" She raised her hands toward us, and I knocked Ethan onto the floor before she could hit us with her spell.

I was on top of Ethan, and he stared up at me with a pained expression. "Did she hit me?"

I moved off him and checked his chest and limbs for injuries. He was fine. Not a scratch on him, except for the gash on his head from colliding with the bathroom sink when he'd died. "Is it your head?" I asked.

He reached for his chest. "My lungs."

No, not already! His body was giving out on him. He was going to need to feed soon. The urge usually took hold of me pretty quickly.

At least it did before I'd started feeding on witches. Now the magic sustained me longer. If only I could give Ethan some of Ben's magic lingering inside me.

"Stay calm. It's an effect of the spell Nora did to bring you back." Glass shattered and sprayed down on top of us. I shrieked and covered my head. Ethan leaned over me, shielding me with his body. I could feel his skin turning cold again.

Dylan and Nora were throwing spells back and forth at each other, destroying the diner in the process. Ethan and I separated, and I peeked around the counter. If only I could free Shannon. Then she and Dylan could overpower Nora. It was our only chance. With the way things were going, I'd never get Ethan out of here before his symptoms turned into a full-blown attack.

"Stay here," I told him. "I'm going to try to free Shannon."

"How? You're not a witch. You can't break her free from the magic holding her." Ethan was catching up quickly, and he was handling it well. I hoped he'd still be so open-minded when I told him he'd have to kill to stay alive.

"I don't know, but I have to try. We can't sit here and let them battle it out."

"Why not? Dylan's holding his own. We could make a run for it the next time he knocks her down." He stared at me, pleading with his eyes. "I don't want to lose you. If Nora catches you, or if you get in the way of one of the spells…"

I had to tell him. "Ethan, we can't leave. Something is going to happen. To you. The tightness you're feeling in your chest…" A rumble as loud as thunder shook the diner. I didn't know who had cast the spell, but it made everything shake like we were in an earthquake. There wasn't time to explain all this to Ethan. I had to move. "Trust me."

He nodded. The last time he didn't trust me had been right before he died. I knew he didn't want to make the same mistake again. He reached for me, kissing me hard on the lips. "I love you."

It was like he was saying goodbye. The thought rattled my insides. Made me so angry and desperate to save us. "I love you, too." I kissed him again quickly, and then darted under the booth in the back corner.

Nora had Dylan raised about six feet off the ground. She held her hand in the air, looking like she was squeezing something in her fist. Dylan choked. I wasn't sure if he could do any spells. She was strangling him. I couldn't let this happen. I owed him that much. I dove out from my hiding place and charged at Nora. She turned her head slightly, sensing my attack. And before I knew what was happening, Dylan was soaring through the air right at me. He slammed into me, and we toppled to the floor.

"Sam!" Ethan yelled.

"Ethan, stay back!" My entire body hurt, like I'd been run over by a Mack truck.

Ethan was on his feet, but Nora didn't pay attention to him at all. He wasn't a threat as far as she was concerned.

Dylan shifted into a sitting position. He held his hand up and created a shield to block us from Nora's attacks. She pounded spell after spell against Dylan's protective shield.

Nora laughed. "You can't keep that shield up forever." She was right, and Ethan was helpless out there on his own.

"Use the magic inside you," Dylan whispered to me.

What was he talking about? "I don't have any magic left in me. It goes away after a while. I can't feel it tingling under my skin anymore."

Dylan shook his head. "The power never left you. It settled inside you. We don't get that tingling feeling unless we are tapping into the power, actively using it. But it's still there. All of it."

"Nora said I wouldn't be able to do spells." Not that I knew any.

"More lies. You can help me fight her. Channel your energy into that magic. Channel *Ben's* magic."

My heart clenched at the sound of Ben's name. Dylan was helping me, even after I'd killed his brother.

"Ben would want you to take Nora out. He's dead because of her."

"He died because of *me*."

"I'm not saying I don't blame you at all, but Nora used you. It's her fault you came back this way."

How had I been so wrong about all of this? No, I knew the answer to that. Nora had used a spell on me to make me believe her. I had to do what I could to fix it. "Tell me how to use the magic. I want to free Shannon, give us the upper hand."

"Focus on the magic until you feel it tingling under your skin. Then think about what you want to do. Don't let any other thoughts into your head or it won't work. I'll take care of Nora."

"What if I can't do it?"

"Then get Ethan and get out of here."

He was going to save me. After all I'd done.

"Ready?"

Not at all. I nodded. My hands shook, and Dylan ran his fingers on top of my forearm. His touch tingled, and I could see the faint glow of magic inside me.

"See, it's still there. Use it."

I nodded more confidently this time.

"Now!" Dylan threw the shield forward at Nora, and she fell backward. I rushed to Shannon. I didn't have a clue how to break the ring of magic containing her. I reached for it, but Shannon shook her head. I remembered she couldn't talk, so I raised my hand to her mouth and concentrated on breaking the silence spell Nora had cast on her. My hand shook, and I felt the magic tingling through me.

Shannon opened her mouth and inhaled deeply. "Don't touch the magic holding me. It will pull you in here with me, and we'll both be trapped."

"How do I break it?" I stared at the swirling prison.

"Get the salt and pour it on the magic. It will break the spell."

"What if it touches you?"

"It will burn me, but I'll live. Remember, you can't touch it either. You've got magic inside you now."

Ethan was at my side with the salt in his hands. "I can't sit on the sidelines and watch, Sam. I—" He stumbled forward, and his eyes widened.

Crap. It was happening.

Shannon looked at him with fear in her eyes. Ethan could feed off her. It would save him. No. We'd be down a witch, and we needed her to fight Nora. I grabbed the salt and eased Ethan into a booth.

"Hang on, okay?" I told him, knowing it didn't work that way. He had no control over how fast the life drained from him.

I took the salt and poured it on the magic ring around Shannon. She cringed as some of it touched her skin, but the magic disintegrated and she was free.

Nora and Dylan were killing each other. They were both cut up. Their clothes were torn, and their noses were bleeding. They were using all their energy to fight.

"Time to finish this," Shannon said, advancing on Nora. She thrust her arms out, and Nora flew backward, slamming into the coffee maker and falling to the floor. The hot coffee poured down on top of her. I could see her skin bubbling from the scalding hot liquid. Shannon said another spell, and Nora was pinned to the ground by magic.

It was over.

I breathed deeply, thankful that Nora was contained. We'd have to figure out what to do with her, but for right now, she wasn't a threat anymore. Shannon and Dylan stared at each other and then looked at Nora. They nodded in silent agreement.

"What?" I asked.

They both turned to me. For the first time, Shannon wasn't looking at me with hatred in her eyes. We were on the same side, at least for now.

"We have to kill her," Dylan said. "She's too far gone. Consumed by black magic."

Deep down, I knew that was what he'd say, but it still hit me hard.

Dylan walked over to me. "She was never your friend. I know it's hard, but if she doesn't die, she'll come after all of us. She won't leave you or Ethan alone. And if you don't do what she says, she'll kill you both."

Ethan. Oh, God, he was dying. I spun around. He was slumped back in the booth. I ran to him. "Ethan?"

He coughed and grabbed his chest.

"He's dying."

Dylan turned toward Nora again. I rushed to her. She'd put the spell on Ethan. She could remove it.

"Tell me how to break the spell," I said, standing over her.

She laughed. "Sorry, Sam. It doesn't work that way. I can't lift the spell. He needs to feed or he'll die. You should've listened to me. I could've helped you."

"You weren't trying to help me. You were trying to kill Dylan and Shannon."

"What do you care? Shannon hates you. You should've let Ethan kill her. You still could. And if you think Dylan will forgive you for killing Ben, you're a bigger idiot than I thought. He's using you to get rid of me."

I turned to Shannon, hating that I was actually debating it, but it was Ethan. I'd done this to him. I'd told Nora to bring him back. She wouldn't have done it if I hadn't asked.

Shannon shook her head. I saw a glimpse of a silver necklace tucked under her shirt. I stepped toward her.

"What are you doing?" She backed away.

"You have my necklace. You were the one who broke into my house and stole it?"

"No, I wasn't."

"Then how do you have it?" I was yelling now, totally panicked.

"I took it from Nora. I had to ransack her house to find it."

So Ben hadn't come after Nora. He hadn't tried to kill her. Shannon was the one who'd wrecked Nora's house.

"I was going to give it back to you, but she trapped me before I could."

"You expect me to believe you were going to help me?"

"Just because I didn't like you doesn't mean I wanted you dead. And I certainly didn't want you to continue helping Nora kill witches. Rebecca and Ben were my friends."

I held out my hand. "Give it to me."

She removed the necklace and placed it in my hand.

I wrapped my fingers around it. "How are you even able to wear it?"

"The spell I put on it protects you from harmful magic, nothing else," Dylan said. "It's not harmful to witches. That's why Nora was able to steal it."

"Shoddy spellwork, Dylan," Nora said with a laugh. "Your magic is nothing compared to mine. I was even able to keep Sam from rising for four days after I did the spell to bring her back."

"What? Why?" I asked.

"We couldn't have you waking up in the middle of your own funeral, now could we?" She laughed, clearly amused with herself. "I even cast a spell on the mortician so he wouldn't touch your body after I gave you Ethan's blood."

I looked at the necklace. If it protected the wearer from harmful magic, it could help Ethan. I rushed over to him, placing the necklace in his hand. "Hold this. It will help." He was so weak he couldn't even hold the necklace. I had to close his fingers around it.

"That necklace was made to protect *you*," Dylan said, coming up behind me. "It won't help him."

No. That couldn't be true, but Ethan sputtered and coughed again. His fingers were like ice in my hand. I turned to Dylan. "What am I supposed to do? I won't let him die!"

"The only way to break the curse she put on you two is to kill her. She did this. Only she can undo it."

I couldn't believe he was suggesting Ethan kill Nora, but doing that was the only way to make up for killing Ben. I saw that now.

Ethan choked, and the life in his eyes started slipping away.

"You're running out of time." Dylan grabbed my arm. "You don't have a choice. This kind of curse will die with her. As long as she's alive, you're going to be a monster—witchy powers or not. And Ethan's going to die. This time for good."

He was right. If the choice was between Nora and Ethan, I had to choose Ethan. And killing her would mean freeing both of us for good.

"Okay," I said. "Bring her here."

CHAPTER THIRTY-ONE

DYLAN and Shannon used their magic to bring Nora to Ethan. I could barely look at her. Her face was twisted with torment. Her eyes never left me. She didn't even glance at Ethan.

"Don't feel guilty," Shannon said. "She brought this on herself."

Dylan crossed his arms. "Believe me, she didn't feel guilty about you killing Ben and Rebecca."

Still it was hard. I wasn't even the one who was going to be doing the killing this time, yet it was awful. Ethan looked at me, confused.

"It's okay," I told him. "I'll show you what to do, and afterward you'll be you again. I promise." I reached for his hands and placed one of his palms against Nora's neck. Instantly, I saw Ethan's eyes widen at the warmth he felt from Nora's body. The worst part of this curse Nora had placed on us was how good it felt when we were killing someone. We were powerless to resist it.

Nora let out a nervous laugh. "So this is it, Sam? I teach you how to survive and you betray me?"

I knew Ethan was starting to feel better already so I hesitated long enough to say what I needed to. "You used me. You made me a killer, and I'll never forgive you for that. Any 'kindness' you pretended to show me was fake. It was all designed to get me to do exactly what you wanted. To make me a monster. Shannon's right. You're getting what you deserve."

Tears filled my eyes as I took Ethan's other palm and placed it over Nora's heart. She gasped for air, and her skin began to wrinkle with age. She withered and shrank into herself, until the light in her eyes went out, and she slumped forward onto Ethan.

"Get her off," I said, choking on tears.

Dylan pulled Nora off Ethan. "It's over. For good."

Shannon sighed. "I felt the curse release. Ethan isn't using any more of my time."

"What do you mean?" I asked her.

"His existence was taking time off my life, but it stopped when Nora died. I only lost a few years."

I stared at her, and this time I didn't see the girl who bossed everyone around. I saw the insecure witch who just wanted people to like her. "I'm glad you aren't going to die, and I'm sorry Nora hurt you to save Ethan." I couldn't say I was sorry I let Nora do it though. Shannon's life energy had saved Ethan. As awful as it sounded, I would've done it all over if I had to. He was too important for me to lose.

Shannon nodded. She understood how I felt. We might never be friends, but we certainly didn't hate each other anymore, either.

Ethan got out of the booth, looking dazed. "Did I just..."

"Yes," I said, not wanting to make him say it out loud. "But you had to. It's over now. You'll never feel like that again. You'll never have to take another person's life again. Neither of us will."

He wrapped me in a hug and kissed the top of my head. We could finally live normal lives now.

"So," Dylan said, "there's something we have to figure out."

I pulled away from Ethan. "What to do with Nora's body?"

"No. I'll take care of it. There's a spell we can do to burn the body. No one will know what happened to her."

"What about her family?" I asked.

"She didn't have any." He motioned to Shannon and himself. "We were her family before she decided black magic was better than us."

"Oh." She must have been so lonely. Lonely enough to go completely evil. "She should've done the same spell Shannon did to make everyone like her."

Shannon gave me a look, but before I could apologize for insulting her she said, "I'm removing the spell. It was stupid of me to cast it.

Having people do what you say isn't all it's cracked up to be. I know they really hate me."

"I don't hate you," I said. "Not anymore. And maybe they don't *all* hate you."

Shannon smirked. "Trust me, they do." She exchanged a look with Dylan. "What do you think? We could have a new coven. Would be nice to have that power again."

He shook his head. "I know Nora cast a spell on her, but Sam killed Ben and Rebecca."

"I didn't want to." Tears welled up in my eyes. "Please, I'm so sorry. You don't know what it was like. That monster she turned me into was so much stronger than me. I couldn't fight it."

"He was my brother." Dylan's pain was etched in his face.

"I don't know what to say."

"You two could bind your powers with ours so we could be stronger," Shannon said. Everything was about power with her. She was willing to forgive me if she got something out of it in return. She'd probably only hung out with Dylan, Rebecca, and Ben for the same reason. She hadn't really cared about any of them. It was sad, but I guessed her issues at school made her not want to open up to people for real.

"So Rebecca's and Ben's magic, it's mine now? For good? I have twice the magic of a normal witch?"

Shannon smiled. "Pretty awesome, right? Normally you have to be born a witch, but there are some ways to take a witch's power, like you and Ethan did."

I still felt awful about how I'd gotten the magic. Rebecca had begged for her life, and the more I thought about it, the more I realized Ben had only been defending himself and his coven against Nora. I couldn't blame him for that.

I looked down at Nora's shriveled body on the floor. I wanted to hate her more than I hated myself, but I couldn't.

"Sam, believe me, if I thought you were anything like Nora, I wouldn't invite you to join our coven," Shannon said. "The spell she put on you to make you trust her was powerful. You didn't have a choice in the matter."

"Wait a minute." Ethan put his hands up in front of him. "Are you telling me that I have Nora's powers? I can do magic?"

Dylan nodded. "That's exactly how it works. You drained Nora's powers, and now they're inside you. They're yours."

Ethan shrugged. "I can live with that."

A thought struck me. An awful thought. "Nora's magic was evil. Does that mean Ethan will be—?"

Shannon shook her head. "Nora's magic wasn't evil. She *used* it for evil. That was all her doing. She made that choice. As long as Ethan doesn't decide to be evil, he'll be fine. Just like the rest of us."

I looked at Dylan. This decision was his. I wouldn't force him. "I understand if you don't want us to join your coven."

"Ben's power is inside her," Shannon said. "Rebecca's, too. In a way, it would be like having them around."

Dylan hesitated, but finally he said, "All right. But I'm doing it for Ben."

I nodded. I hadn't expected him to do me any favors. "So, do we bind our powers now?"

"No." Shannon spread her arms out, motioning to the broken-down diner. "We clean up."

I looked at the clock, hanging crookedly on the wall. "Gloria and Jackson will be here in an hour. We'll never fix this place up by then."

"Rookie," Shannon said. She waved her hand, and the coffee maker floated from the floor, where it had fallen on Nora, back onto the counter. The broken pieces of glass fixed themselves, and it looked as good as new.

I stared in disbelief. "That was incredible!"

"Glad you think so," Shannon said, "because we have a lot to fix. We'll need your help."

Dylan took Ethan to the kitchen, most likely to avoid me, and Shannon led me to the counter. They showed us how to focus our own minds and our energy on making the broken things return to the way they had been. The tingling sensation was the most amazing thing I'd ever felt. It took us almost the entire hour, but we put the diner back to normal.

Shannon pointed to the clock. "Time to jet."

Five minutes. That was all we had. We'd fought all night long, and I wasn't even tired. I was so high on my new power and the fact that I was me again. Really truly me, only better. More powerful.

I saw headlights pull into the parking lot. "Go, go, go! Gloria and Jackson are here!"

Dylan used his magic to kill the lights, and we took off for the back door. I'd barely slipped outside when I heard the bell over the front door jingle. We jumped in our cars and planned to meet in the woods in the spot where the coven used to get together. Dylan and Shannon took Nora's body and went on ahead to show us the way.

Ethan reached for my hand as he drove. "You brought me back."

"*You* brought *me* back," I said. "We're even." I wanted to jump over the center console and kiss him, but Dylan and Shannon were waiting for us. My reunion with Ethan would have to wait.

We pulled onto a dirt road, one I'd never noticed before. As we drove I heard trees rustling behind us, like a huge gust of wind was making them sway and creak. I looked back and saw the trees bending back into place, covering the dirt road we were on. It wasn't a road at all. Dylan or Shannon must have been creating the path so we could get to the clearing in the woods.

I smiled, imagining all the things I was going to be able to do with my new powers. If I had twice the power of a normal witch, there was no telling what I could do. The possibilities were endless. But I knew one thing for certain. I'd never use my powers for evil. I'd had enough of black magic and death for one lifetime. Instead, I'd use my magic to try to make up for the terrible things I'd done after Nora brought me back. I knew I couldn't undo any of the deaths I'd caused, but I'd find some way to protect the families I'd torn apart. I was determined to make their lives at least a little better from now on.

Dylan stopped his car, and we pulled up behind him.

"This way." Shannon motioned for us to follow.

Dylan was making Nora's body levitate behind him. It was eerie to see her shriveled form floating through the air like that. We came to a clearing with a fire pit in the middle. Dylan levitated the body directly over it.

"Stand in a circle," he instructed.

I wasn't sure how four people were supposed to make a circle, but we did our best. I realized there used to be five witches in their coven.

We were technically one witch short. Although, since I had double the power, the amount of magic we had was still the same. Dylan started chanting in a language I didn't understand, and a golden circle appeared on the ground beneath us.

"It's a protective circle," Shannon said. "We need it before we can bind our powers."

"Okay," Dylan said, addressing us. "Ben used to be in charge, but since he's no longer with us, I guess I'll run the meetings. Is that all right with everyone?"

We all nodded, and I used my eyes to convey a silent apology to Dylan, but he turned away. It was going to take time…lots of time.

Ethan reached for my hand, offering me support. He was lucky that the only person he'd killed was a truly evil witch. I wished I could say the same.

"We need to join hands," Dylan said, "to complete the circle." We stepped closer to the fire pit so we could reach each other's hands. "I'm going to combine the spell to burn Nora's body with the spell to bind our circle, making us a coven, but before I do, I have to make sure this is what you both want. Once we are tied together by magic, we're linked for life."

Ethan looked to me. He didn't know these people at all—not that I was an expert on them either—but Ethan was going to follow my lead.

I nodded. "I'm willing."

"Then so am I," Ethan said.

Dylan looked at Shannon, and she shrugged. "What the hell? Come eight o'clock, I'm going to be out of friends. It will be nice to have a few friendly faces at school."

"Just so you both know, I plan to try to make up for what I've done. Use my magic for good. If you'll help me." My eyes lingered on Dylan.

Dylan took a deep breath, probably trying to come to terms with this himself, and said a bunch of words I didn't understand. Slowly, golden magic floated out from each of us, forming a band and encircling us. Its warmth made me feel at home. Dylan continued with the spell. "Sam and Ethan, do you swear to honor the coven as family, to protect it, and live by the rules we agree upon?"

Ethan and I exchanged glances. "We do."

The golden band intensified, making us glow with a faint burst of yellow. Dylan looked at Ethan and me. "Don't get freaked out at the next part. Nothing can hurt you inside this circle. Trust me."

"We trust you," I said.

He nodded and picked up where he'd left off. With a few more words, the golden magic shot from us to Nora's body, setting it on fire. The flames licked at us, and while I could feel their warmth, I knew they wouldn't burn me. It wasn't really fire after all. It was magic consuming Nora's body.

Within minutes, there was nothing left of her. The magic that had burned her returned to us, and our bodies slowly faded from the brilliant yellow to our normal skin tone.

"It's done," Dylan said, letting go of Shannon and Ethan's hands. "We're bound to each other for life." He turned away, and I couldn't help wondering if he'd ever be okay with this.

"Now what?" I asked.

"We go to school," Shannon said, looking up at the sun rising over the mountains.

Shannon hadn't exactly been right about the entire school hating her. Over the next three weeks, most people just ignored her as if they didn't even know her name, and the few who gave her vague looks of recognition and contempt turned away as Ethan and I glared at them. Shannon had started to give in and act friendly toward us, even when we weren't helping her with spells. In time, I thought we might actually become friends.

Dylan enrolled in our school, too. We used our collective magic to slightly alter everyone's memory of the guy who had cornered me in the girls' bathroom. Everyone thought Dylan was nothing more than another transfer student. And since he was hanging out with Ethan, Shannon, and me, no one thought twice about him at all. In their eyes, Dylan was completely normal.

While Ethan and I could never really replace Rebecca and Ben, we did our best to make up for the parts we'd played in Nora's sick game. Shannon and Dylan helped me put protective spells on the families of my victims. I was even able to help them find peace. I hoped, some day, it would allow me to find some, too. Finally the universe had thrown me a bone. No more cancer. No more feeding on humans to survive. I was a witch now, and with Dylan and Shannon's help, I was getting pretty damn good at using magic. The only thing the magic didn't seem to help with was missing my family, but I needed to let them move on, no matter how much that pained me.

When lunchtime rolled around one day, I suggested we picnic outside on the lawn.

"We aren't allowed to eat in the quad," Dylan said, standing in the doorway, looking out on the quad. He still wasn't over me killing Ben, but I'd expected things to take longer with him. I was just grateful he'd let Ethan and me join the coven.

"Then let's make sure no one sees us out there," I said.

Shannon raised an eyebrow. "Look at the new girl wanting to flaunt her magic." Apparently, she approved.

"Hey, Sam. Hey, Ethan," Beth said, walking up behind us. "Not thinking of ditching lunch, are you?"

How did she always know everything? I leaned over to Shannon and whispered, "How evil would it be to dull her senses a little so she wasn't so observant?"

Dylan shook his head at me. "Don't even think about it." He'd been keeping a close eye on Ethan and me, making sure we didn't screw up. I nodded, not wanting to give him any more reasons not to like me.

"We were admiring the beautiful day," Shannon said.

"Well, if you do decide to ditch, let me know. I don't want to be cooped up in school on a day like this, either." Beth waved and walked away.

Too bad it didn't work that way. We couldn't get too close to anyone outside our coven. It was too dangerous.

"Okay, what if we point Beth in the direction of a different group of friends? That's not evil, right?" I looked back and forth between Dylan and Shannon.

Shannon cracked a smile. "Watch." She waved her hand, and a guy with dirty-blond hair stepped around the corner, bumping right into Beth. They fumbled for a moment and then smiled at each other.

"She's had a crush on him for years," Ethan said. "She told me."

"I know." Shannon raised one shoulder. "I saw her practically drooling over him yesterday, and believe it or not, he likes her, too."

"Did you put a love spell on them?" I asked, wondering if that was against the good-witch code of ethics.

"Nah. They already liked each other. I only made them collide in the hallway. They're doing the rest."

I laughed. "Who knew all it would take to get Beth to stop being so nosy was a boyfriend?"

We all exchanged a glance and stood facing the doors. We waved our hands in a circle in front of us, then turned around and did it again. Anyone who looked out the doors would see nothing but sunshine on the empty quad. We had total privacy.

We stepped outside, and the sun felt amazing. Not too hot, just warm and inviting. Shannon spread her hand out over the grass, and the blades wove into a blanket.

"Nice." I sat down, but Ethan reached for my hand.

"Come with me."

I walked with him while Shannon and Dylan set up our picnic lunch.

"Where are we going?"

"Right over here, out of sight of Dylan and Shannon." Ethan pulled me over to the statue that stood in the middle of the quad. He leaned his back against it and gently tugged on my hand.

I reached for the back of his head, weaving my fingers through his hair. I pulled him to me and kissed him with all the passion that was welling up inside me. It was so incredibly intense sparks could've flown, and thanks to the magic in us they did, in a brilliant display of colors all around us.

Colophon

This book is typeset in Baskerville, a transitional serif typeface designed in 1757 by John Baskerville, Birmingham, England. It is positioned between the old style typefaces of William Caslon and the modern styles of Giambattista Bodoni and Firmin Didot. The Baskerville typeface is the result of John Baskerville's intent to improve upon the types of William Caslon. He increased the contrast between thick and thin strokes, making the serifs sharper and more tapered, and shifted the axes of rounded letters to a more vertical position. The curved strokes are more circular in shape, and the characters are more regular. These changes created a greater consistency in size and form.

Acknowledgements

I can't start a dedication without first thanking Kate Kaynak and the incredible team at Spencer Hill Press. I can't tell you how much I love being part of this family. Trisha Wooldridge, as always thank you for your insight and all you do to make my books better. It was music to my ears when you encouraged me to make this book darker. Thank you to my team of editors, Nanette, Owen, Rich Storrs, Keshia Swaim, and Shira Lipkin, for your attention to details, which as we all know really make a book better. To Jennifer Allis Provost and Kayleigh-Marie Gore, thank you for all your marketing expertise. You two are so much fun to work with. Thank you to Lisa Amowitz for designing the perfect cover for this book. It's pretty and dark, which was exactly what I wanted.

To my daughter, Ayla, who sings "I Feel Like A Monster" better than anyone I know, you are my world. Thank you for letting me talk about my books so much and for continuing to write your own. To my husband, Ryan, thank you for putting up with my crazy hours and stressful days. I appreciate it more than you know. To my mom, Patricia Bradley, I couldn't ask for a better mother, friend, beta reader, or support system. I love you! To my father, Martin Bradley, and my sister, Heather DeRobertis, thank you for listening and for encouraging me. Thank to my friends and family for supporting me and understanding why I'm always on my computer.

As always many thanks and cyber hugs to the book bloggers who have supported this book. Keren Hughes, you are superwoman in my eyes. And finally, thank you to everyone who reads this book. I hope you love Sam and Ethan as much as I do.

About the Author

Kelly Hashway grew up reading R.L. Stein's Fear Street novels and writing stories of her own, so it was no surprise to her family when she majored in English and later obtained a masters degree in English Secondary Education from East Stroudsburg University. After teaching middle school language arts for seven years, Hashway went back to school and focused specifically on writing. She is now the author of three young adult series, one middle grade series, and

several picture books. She also writes contemporary romance under the pen name Ashelyn Drake. Hashway is represented by Sarah Negovetich of Corvisiero Literary Agency. When she isn't writing, Hashway works as a freelance editor for small presses as well as for her own list of clients. In her spare time, she enjoys running, traveling, and volunteering with the PTO. Hashway currently resides in Pennsylvania with her husband, daughter, and two pets.

www.kellyhashway.com